WITHDRAWN

PRAISE FOR SUZANNE BALTSAR

Trouble Brewing

"Witty, sweet, funny, addictive writing. Suzanne Baltsar's debut is the perfect brew for contemporary romance fans."

—Samantha Young, *New York Times* bestselling author of *On Dublin Street* and *Fight or Flight*

"Come for the swoons, but stay for the female empowerment. Disguised as a charming rom-com, *Trouble Brewing* smashes the beer-bottle ceiling with a glimpse into the male-dominated craft brewing world. You'll cheer for Piper as she brews her way to success."

—Amy E. Reichert, author of *The Optimist's Guide to Letting Go* and *The Coincidence of Coconut Cake*

"Funny and full of great characters, Baltsar's debut seems primed to launch a series pairing up other beer-adjacent people in the book."

—*Booklist*

"*Trouble Brewing* is a classic, feel-good love story. It's a quick read and a page turner, thanks to the likable characters and Piper's inspiring determination."

—*Minnesota Monthly*

ALSO BY SUZANNE BALTSAR

Trouble Brewing

SIDELINED

Suzanne Baltsar

G

GALLERY BOOKS

New York   London   Toronto   Sydney   New Delhi

G

Gallery Books
An Imprint of Simon & Schuster, Inc.
1230 Avenue of the Americas
New York, NY 10020

This book is a work of fiction. Any references to historical events, real people, or real places are used fictitiously. Other names, characters, places, and events are products of the author's imagination, and any resemblance to actual events or places or persons, living or dead, is entirely coincidental.

Copyright © 2019 by Suzanne Baltsar

All rights reserved, including the right to reproduce this book or portions thereof in any form whatsoever. For information, address Gallery Books Subsidiary Rights Department, 1230 Avenue of the Americas, New York, NY 10020.

First Gallery Books trade paperback edition August 2019

GALLERY BOOKS and colophon are registered trademarks of Simon & Schuster, Inc.

For information about special discounts for bulk purchases, please contact Simon & Schuster Special Sales at 1-866-506-1949 or business@simonandschuster.com.

The Simon & Schuster Speakers Bureau can bring authors to your live event. For more information or to book an event, contact the Simon & Schuster Speakers Bureau at 1-866-248-3049 or visit our website at www.simonspeakers.com.

Interior design by Michelle Marchese

Manufactured in the United States of America

10 9 8 7 6 5 4 3 2 1

Library of Congress Cataloging-in-Publication Data

Names: Baltsar, Suzanne, author.
Title: Sidelined / Suzanne Baltsar.
Description: First Gallery Books trade paperback edition. | New York : Gallery Books, 2019.
Identifiers: LCCN 2018038305 (print) | LCCN 2018052041 (ebook) | ISBN 9781501188343 (ebook) | ISBN 9781501188336 (trade paper : alk. paper)
Classification: LCC PS3602.A6295 (ebook) | LCC PS3602.A6295 S53 2019 (print) | DDC 813/.6--dc23
LC record available at https://lccn.loc.gov/2018038305

ISBN 978-1-5011-8833-6
ISBN 978-1-5011-8834-3 (ebook)

For Brooke, my first friend in first grade
the second time around. We've come a long way,
and you're still bossing me around,
but you're still my favorite.

And because I can't leave out the other two . . .

For Sarah, my very first editor. It all started with
*NSYNC fan fiction. I owe you this career,
that's why you're my favorite.

And for Steph for always nodding and smiling
at every genesis of myself over all these years.
You laugh at all my jokes, but have never laughed at me,
and for that, you're my favorite.

ACKNOWLEDGMENTS

To write a story about a badass woman, I have to thank all the badass women in my life. First, I'd like to thank my wonderful editor, Marla, for guiding me through this crazy process. Everyone at Gallery, but especially Michelle for being so patient with all of my emails. My agent Sharon always has the best advice.

Eternal gratitude to my favorite authors and friends, the BGW ladies. You're the ultimate.

Thanks to my mom for being the coolest mom of all the moms, and who has a trophy to prove it.

I was in fourth grade when I first saw a girl put on a football helmet, and I thought that was the best thing I'd ever seen in my life. I remember her being tackled and my dad saying, "Look it, she got right back up. Good for her." I didn't know girls could play football or even be on the same field as boys. I didn't know they could get tackled and get back up. Kuri Edwards showed me that we can.

Thank you to all of the women who have inspired this book but are not limited to: Natalie Randolph, Beth Bates, Sami Grisafe, Beth Buglione, Theresa Dion, Holly Neher, Callie Brownson, Liz Heaston, Shelby Osborne, Katie Sowers, Jennifer Welter, Becca Longo, Toni Harris, and Julie Knapp, who is both a football player and homecoming queen.

In a world where girls can supposedly be whatever they want to, we should all strive to be a little more Ice Box and a little less Debbie. Know what I mean?

"That's no cheerleader. That's my niece Becky, and she's pissed."

SIDELINED

CHAPTER

1

Charlie

The sharp smell of bitter coffee permeated the air as the whir of beans in a grinder grated on my nerves. If I actually had a cup of joe in my hand, maybe I wouldn't be so on edge, but the line was taking forever to inch forward. And if I was late to my eight o'clock meeting, I'd lose whatever credibility had been afforded to me.

The man in front of me finally stepped aside, blessedly allowing me to relay my order to the young kid at the register. He seemed to be about sixteen with a good amount of bulk, and the possibility that he could be one of my players passed through my mind. Today was my first official day on the job as the new head coach at Douglass High School in Minneapolis, and I was equal parts elated and terrified. I suspected the media would be all over me as soon as word got out that I was the first female high school football coach in

Minnesota. One of only a handful of women ever to hold the positon in the entire country.

But I had to get through my introduction to the coaches this morning. This was my first test, the first of many, and to succeed I needed my armor: my comfiest Georgia Tech T-shirt, my lucky orange Nikes, and a calorie-filled drink from my new morning spot, Caribou Coffee.

Plus I had to get to school on time—7:34 turned to 7:35 faster than I would've liked.

I stepped up to the counter, reading the kid's name tag. "Hi, Nate, I need a large caramel high rise with extra whipped cream and two dozen assorted bagels, please."

He tapped my order into the register. "Thirty-three ninety-seven."

I handed over my debit card. "And make it quick for me, okay?"

He nodded, offering me a smile. "Sure."

He ran my card and had twenty-four plain, blueberry, and everything bagels packed up in no time. I grabbed my drink from the other end of the counter and headed out into the bright morning sun.

I'd moved to Minneapolis from Atlanta only a few days ago and had yet to find a place to live. All of my stuff was split between a Best Western hotel room and my car, but until school and my job as a physical education teacher began, I had no real income, which made it difficult to line up a more permanent home. I hoped I'd find a place soon—I was low on clean clothes and needed to do laundry, preferably in a place where I didn't have some creepy guy checking out my underwear.

I pressed the unlock button on my key fob, and the lights of my red sedan blinked twice as I made my way across the parking lot. The sun blinded me, and without sunglasses, I had to balance the box of bagels and coffee in one hand to shade my eyes with the other. I broke into an unbalanced jog to close the distance to my car, but a blaring horn and a screech of tires had me jumping backward.

I whipped my head to the right, my heart beating a mile a minute, as a man poked his head out of his window. "What the hell are you doing?"

"What am *I* doin'?" The last thing I needed this morning was to have a near-death experience with some Jeff Gordon wannabe douchebag. "What are *you* doin'?"

"You ran out in front of me," he shouted with a wild wave of his hand.

"And *you're* racin' around a Caribou Coffee drive-thru. This isn't a speedway."

His eyes were hidden by a baseball cap, but I could tell this guy was young. He dropped his arm out of the window, muscles clearly defined. "You make it a habit of running around parking lots like a lost animal?"

I huffed. "You almost killed me, yet this is my fault?"

He pointed and snickered at me. Confused, I glanced down and realized that when I'd jumped back, I'd lost control of my purchases. My bagels lay strewn on the asphalt in a crumbled mess while my iced caramel coffee with extra whipped cream had spilled down the front of my shirt in an uncanny replica of a Picasso painting.

Perfect.

Just perfect.

I growled and threw him double birds. "Enjoy your day, Mario Andretti. Try not to run anybody over."

He readjusted the brim of his hat and I caught the piercing look in his eyes. He licked his lips, the corner kicking up to a cocky smirk. "Don't hurt yourself, sweetheart. One foot in front of the other."

"Fuck off," I grumbled, and bent down to pick up the mess at my feet as he drove off. By the time I had the pebble-covered bagels and my empty cup thrown away, it was too late to go back inside and order more. Plus I needed to change my shirt. There was no way I'd impress anyone looking the way I did, especially coming into the meeting empty-handed now.

I fished through the backseat of my car for another T-shirt. Finding a single wrinkled one, stained with what looked like mustard, I shrugged—it'd have to do. A case of water bottles in my trunk would suffice as my gift to lay at my staff's feet.

I raced over to the school and parked in the back by the gymnasium. The athletic director was there waiting for me.

"Hey, Jim," I greeted him with a nod as I grabbed the water.

He smiled back, tender and empathetic. His dark-brown skin was weathered with sun and time, and if I had to guess,

I'd assume he was in his fifties. But more forward-thinking than I'd give most middle-aged men—or men in general—credit for. "Hey. How're you feeling this morning?"

"A wreck, but it'll pass. I just want to get started."

He gave me a quick once-over. Even with my stained shirt and red face, his confidence in me didn't waver. He gently squeezed my arm. "You okay?"

Shifting uncomfortably, I cringed. "I spilled coffee all over my other shirt and didn't have enough time to—you know what, never mind."

He swiped a hand over his bald head. "Still looking for a place to live?"

"How could you tell?" I laughed in spite of myself.

"Want me to take that?" he asked, referring to the pallet of water I readjusted in my grip.

"No, I'm good."

"Do you need help finding a place? I know a lot of people."

I wasn't normally one for taking charity, not even for accepting help carrying water, but I was desperate. And a door that didn't open with a slide-in key card sounded lovely. "That would be great. Thanks."

Jim nodded and led me through the gym to a long hallway with the girls' locker room to the left and the boys' locker room on the right, but we walked past both. "There's an office in the locker room," he said, his thumb pointing back over his shoulder to the sign that read MEN. "But some people were uncomfortable with you being in there, even though the office isn't anywhere near the changing rooms or showers."

With all my years coaching football, I'd gotten used to entering men's locker rooms without a second thought, but in this new place I understood the apprehension. What I didn't understand was why we'd stopped in front of what looked like a closet.

"I tried to get you a different room but . . ." Jim's face fell, and I gulped back the foreboding feeling stuck in my throat. He opened the door with a key and gestured for me to go in first. It *was* a closet—clean and empty save for a small desk and chair, but still a closet.

"*This* is my office?"

He dropped the key on the desk. "Yeah, it used to be the equipment closet." His obvious sheepishness at the school's not-so-great solution made me feel just a tiny bit better. "You could fit another chair or two, maybe."

I refrained from rolling my eyes and reminded myself to be grateful. I'd long ago gotten used to these types of inconveniences in order for the men who surrounded me to feel comfortable, but there were times when I didn't want to be happy with the crumbs. I wanted the whole pie.

As a head coach deserved.

Shaking off the momentary dissatisfaction, I smiled. I'd get over this. I always did, being the odd *woman* out in the game. After all, it might have previously been a closet, but now this room was my own.

Mine.

"I'll make it work," I said, and he nodded.

"Mrs. LaRue, in the main office, will set you up with a key to let you in the building." He put his hand on my shoulder. "You ready to go upstairs and make history here?"

When he put it like that, my nerves got the best of me, and I blurted out the first thing that came to my mind: "No." When he drew back, confused, I corrected myself. "I'm not here for the accolades, but I'd settle for a winning season."

We walked upstairs to the main hall and took a right to room 113. "This is Coach McGuire's room. Dick used to show film in here," he said; the latter, I knew, was the previous head coach.

He stopped just outside to pat my shoulder. "You'll do great."

"Thanks," I said, steeling my nerves before he opened the door. Five pairs of eyes snapped their attention to me.

I'd played football with boys and coached with men my entire life. When people told me I couldn't, I'd smiled and politely listed my qualifications. This wasn't about proving anything to anyone. I didn't care what people thought of me anyway. I'd been raised in the game. I was good at the game. I just wanted to do what I was best at.

But in this moment, my knees knocked like they were fighting each other.

I kept my head up, brave face on. "Mornin', gentlemen."

Jim stood next to me, the lone friendly presence in the room. "Guys, I'd like to finally introduce you to our new head coach, Charlie Gibb."

"I brought everyone some refreshin' water to start off our meetin'," I said, placing the pallet on the desk in front of me before taking in the faces of my support staff. My focus drifted from one man to the next, each of them regarding me with a mix of curiosity and contempt. All except for the last man. No, the last man's face held only contempt for me. It was Mario Andretti from the pickup truck.

"I'd planned on bagels, but I had a little trouble this morning. Consider it an I.O.U." I smiled.

The guy with the lead foot shook his head deliberately, as if disappointed in me. But he'd created this whole mess to begin with. Son of a bitch.

"Don't worry. I brought some for everyone." He gestured to the open box of bagels in the middle of the table at the front of the room. "Help yourself."

I ground my teeth. No way would I eat his bagels after he almost ran me over. And especially not after he stood up and stretched his hand out to me with a self-satisfied smirk. "I'm Connor McGuire, offensive coordinator."

I met his rough palm with my own, squeezing his knuckles with as much strength as I could muster. Obviously this man was out for my blood. He might have won the battle, but I'd win the war.

I was the general of this squad. And I played to win.

CHAPTER
2

Charlie

I dropped McGuire's hand and turned back to Jim, who smiled. "I'll leave you to it then, all right?"

He stepped out of the room, leaving me alone with these five strangers whose wave of incredulity tried to drown me out. I pulled a desk over to sit in front of them, like a buoy keeping me afloat.

"So, I know all y'all are probably shocked to see me."

"Jim told us who you are, Lloyd Gibb's daughter," the one on the end said. He looked young, like he couldn't even rent a car.

A simple Google search could have told them my dad was Georgia Tech's head coach, but it wouldn't have said much about me besides the couple of seasons I'd played in the Independent Women's Football League and the assistant coaching spot at Tech.

Most people thought I'd gotten to where I was because of my father's reputation, but I resented that. I'd gone through a hell of a lot more in this sport than any of these men could imagine. I had to work harder, break stereotypes, face sexism and harassment, and do it all with a smile on my face. I'd gotten to where I was because of me. Not because my father was Lloyd Gibb.

Next to McGuire, the man with a gray-speckled beard snickered. "Couldn't hack it at a Division One school anymore?"

"What's your name?" I asked him.

"Al Berg. Defensive coordinator. Been here for thirty-two years."

"Thirty-two years is a long time," I said. "Just about as long as I've been alive." Folding my arms across my chest, I tilted my head. "In the last eight years, this team hasn't won more than four games a season. The last time they made it to the playoffs was fifteen years ago, and they've never won a state championship. I know I've got a lot to prove, but as far as I'm concerned, y'all got a lot to prove to me too."

Al looked like I'd slapped his mama.

I went on. "I may not be who you thought you were getting, but if you can't let that go, you're free to leave."

When Al closed his mouth and sat back in his chair, I met each of the coaches' eyes in turn. "I've already heard all the whispered rumors and passive-aggressive insults, so if you have an issue with the fact that I wear a bra instead of a jockstrap, you can come to me directly. I have no tolerance for bullshit."

None of them objected, and I folded my hands on the desk, offering a smile. "Yes, my father is Lloyd Gibb, but I have played football almost my entire life, through college and then on a professional women's team." I side-eyed Al when he mumbled something about girls on the field and cheerleaders. "Where did *you* play professionally, Al?"

His eyes darted away as he wiped the stupid grin off his face.

"Now, since y'all know me, why don't you introduce yourselves?" I looked to my left where McGuire sat, eyes narrowed on me underneath a perfectly worn hat. "Anything else you'd like to tell me about yourself?"

Palm down, he motioned like he didn't want any more cards in a game of poker. The resentment was palpable. But I'd deal with him later.

Al was next, acting less than thrilled to have to speak to me. "I teach biology and earth science here too."

I faced the man directly in front of me. He wore a pleasant smile. "I'm Ken Yang. I'm a transplant from the West Coast. I've been with the team for five years, running receivers and helping out on offense, but I don't work here. I'm a chemical engineer at PVT Resources. Nice to have you with us."

"Thanks."

Next to him, a big, meaty guy ate a bagel "Erik Johnson," he said, wiping cream cheese from his fingers on his shorts. "Line coach, special education teacher at the middle school."

"Nice to meet you."

"You too," he answered, mouth full.

My southern manners had me cringing inwardly. I was no Georgia peach or delicate flower, but my grandma had always taught me that one of the things that separated us from the monkeys was our table manners.

"Last but not least," I said, turning to the youngest coach on the end.

"I'm Ronnie Rosario." He scratched his head where three lines were shaved into his hair by his temple. "I played for Coach Nelson a few years ago and needed some income. He took me on for special teams."

I noticed his solid build and big hands. "Did you play anywhere after?"

He shook his head. "My family owns an HVAC company. I went to work after I graduated."

"Hell of a tailback," McGuire said, his first words to me that weren't laced with wrath.

Ronnie gave me an embarrassed smile. "Didn't help us much then."

"Let's try to get your team some wins then, huh?" I stood up and patted his shoulder before taking another long look at all the coaches. "I'm gonna give this team one hundred and ten percent. I expect the same from you. I appreciate y'all comin' to meet me early. Tomorrow I want to go over the playbook, see what changes we could make. Same time okay?"

"But tomorrow is Saturday," Erik said between bites of his second bagel.

"Correct." I gave him a hard glare so he'd know I wasn't here to mess around. These five men hadn't managed to lead their football team to a winning season in years. I was here to do that. And that meant no sleeping in on Saturdays.

He grunted as he chewed, and I assumed that was his confirmation he'd be there. I eyed the rest of the men before moving my desk back into place. "Bring your ideas and skills development plans. This is a rebuildin' year, fellas, I want to start it off on the right foot. See you in my office tomorrow mornin'."

"*Your* office?" McGuire asked with a raised brow. The silence of the rest of the coaches let me know they were all aware of what his question implied.

I clenched my fists and blinked to the windows. My office didn't have windows.

There was no way we could all meet in my closet like some sad Harry Potter imitation of an office. "Fine. We'll meet here."

McGuire smirked, but I didn't give him the satisfaction of reacting and turned to leave.

"Thanks, Coach," Ronnie said, and I smiled at him over my shoulder. At least I had one of them in my corner.

I made my way straight to the main office, where I met Mrs. LaRue. She had me fill out some papers for a parking pass and key to the building before I headed back to my office. Which was much different from the one I'd had last spring.

When I'd sat my dad down a few months ago, I'd asked

him point-blank, "Do I have a chance here to move up at all? I've been at Tech for five years now, and I'm assistant special teams."

"And recruitin' coordinator," he had reminded me.

"*Assistant* recruitin' coordinator," I'd corrected him. The difference between assistant and head recruiter was quite a bit.

He'd given in with a reluctant nod.

"You know I can do more."

My dad had rubbed his cheek and taken a deep breath. He'd glanced at me, down to his desk, then back at me. "Charlotte, you're swimming upstream."

"What's that supposed to mean?" I'd asked, my voice raising enough that a couple guys outside his office noticed.

He'd gotten up to close the door. "You're an excellent coach, but you've got two things workin' against you: your first and your last name."

I'd huffed, my face heating with anger. He had begrudgingly taught me everything I knew from the time I was a child, and also liked to keep me firmly aware of just how much I had to overcome. "I've had to work twice as hard my entire life because of my first name," I said. "I think I've shown you and everyone else that I can do it."

"And it's still not enough to change the world." He'd sat in his chair with a weary exhale. "Maybe in a few years the world will be different because of what you've accomplished, but for now you're goin' to remain assistant special teams coach."

I'd sat forward, trying not to sound pathetic as I asked, "What am I supposed to do?"

"That's up to you."

I'd left his office in a mood and gone home to open up my computer for a job search.

That's how I'd ended up here, in Minneapolis, Minnesota, in a diverse and forward-thinking city, with an athletic director who wasn't afraid to hire a woman and a principal who didn't care if I was a man, woman, fox, or hound, just as long as he could finally brag about a couple of wins for the lagging school sport. And I could do that for him. For the team. For me.

As I sat down behind my desk, the old leather chair creaked, and I decided I'd make the most of this room. An office did not a coach make.

But in the meantime, I'd grab just a few things: a whiteboard, some markers, magnets, shelves, plastic organizers, a big calendar, and a giant bottle of wine.

CHAPTER
3

Connor

"'This is a rebuilding year,'" Al said in a snickering imitation of Charlie Gibb.

The new head coach.

Charlie Gibb, a woman and the new head coach.

I shook my head. It seemed like I'd been living in the twilight zone since we were informed she was coming on board. To find out I hadn't gotten the job was a gut punch. To find out I'd lost it to a woman was worse. Then to learn she was Lloyd Gibb's daughter, it was like I had been run over by a truck. I was sure the only reason they went with her was for name recognition. There was no way she could be good at this job, she was a *girl*.

I mean, I knew women can do anything men can do. In fact, most of the women I knew were smarter and better people than most men I knew—but football was different.

Football was . . . football. It was rough-and-tumble, vio-
lent and aggressive, helmets smashing and bodies slamming
in an effort to try to rip the heads off of opponents. Something that I couldn't imagine she knew anything about, no
matter who her father was.

"She's not wrong on that account," I said, standing up.
The rest of the coaches did too. I handed the box of bagels
to Erik. "Take 'em home."

"Thanks." He jerked his chin in my direction and lum-
bered out of my classroom, past the United States map
hanging lopsided on the wall next to the door. Ronnie and
Ken followed him, but Al hung back even after I went to sit
at my desk, turning on my computer to send the hint I
didn't want any company.

"What do you think of her?" he asked as I brought up my
e-mail.

I thought she'd stolen this job from me, but before I
even opened my mouth, Al went on.

"I can't believe Jim brought her here. This is all just a
publicity stunt."

I briefly met his eyes before going back to my screen.

"It's not right. It's not right that you got passed over."

I didn't disagree with him, but Al was a gasbag and on
his way out in a few years. I wasn't about to open my mouth
in front of him.

"It's just not right." He accentuated his words with
knuckle raps on the desk.

I deleted an e-mail about a conference and opened up

another message from Ms. Bose, Jaylin's mom. She wrote to let me know that he had a high ankle sprain and would most likely miss the first week of doubles. It was equally irritating and ironic that the players and their guardians had come to know me as the de facto coach. I'd expected—hell, everyone had expected—me to get the job.

Not her.

I sent Ms. Bose a reply wishing Jaylin a speedy recovery—he was our best running back—then shut down the computer. I grabbed my keys. "I'm out of here."

Al shuffled up, struggling a bit to get out of the attached desk and chair. "Yeah. We'll talk later . . . see what we can do about this situation."

"Sure." I shut and locked my classroom door by habit. No one was going to steal my poster of the Declaration of Independence. The only people hanging around the building at this time were some administrative assistants and a handful of teachers trying to get a leg up before the school year started. But Al hung around as if I'd change my mind about talking to him. I wasn't going to. I wanted to go home and nurse my bruised ego with a few beers and ESPN.

I liked to think of myself as a good guy with a strong character, not easily ruffled, but this decision really pissed me off. For so many reasons, not the least of which was that I deserved this. I'd been at Douglass coaching and teaching since I'd graduated college. I'd put my heart into the team, was patient through eight losing seasons, waiting for my time to move up when Nelson retired. And now that the time had arrived, I'd lost out to a woman.

Did that make me sound like a whiny asshole? Probably. But it was honest.

I'D SULKED around the house for the better part of the day before Blake called me. He'd been one of my best friends since high school, and he refused to take no for an answer when I said I wasn't interested in hanging out.

"We're picking you up," he said. "Bear's got the boat ready, and we've got the booze. Be there in twenty."

I grumbled but hung up and grabbed my shoes, hoping to forget about my frustration for a night.

Before long, I was relaxed against the middle seat of Bear's sailboat on Lake Minnetonka. Bear was the third point in this friendship triangle, and his boat was one of the main reasons I loved him. Besides the fact that I'd known him since we were fourteen and he was like a brother to me.

"Aye, McGuire, rig up the jib on the starboard side."

With my sunglasses and hat on, I knew Bear couldn't see my raised eyebrow, but I stared at him nonetheless. I couldn't rig up the jib on the starboard side even if I knew what that meant, and instead tipped my head back to enjoy the breeze coming off the water. Since Bear had retired from professional hockey, he'd taken up a lot of hobbies, but I had to say, sailing was my favorite. With the perfect, cloudless sky above and blue water below, there was no better way to spend a summer evening. Even if I was in a bad mood.

"You lazy piece of shit," Bear called from his spot by the wheel. "You're my second-in-command. How can I be the captain without a first mate?"

"Make Blake your first mate," I said, closing my eyes.

"He's too busy making out with Red."

Red, meaning Piper, beer brewer and Blake's girlfriend. They'd met when he stocked some of her beer in his bar, and she'd become a constant in his life, as well as ours.

I heard a muffled sound from the front of the boat, but I was too content to crane my head up. Blake's voice carried over from where I knew he'd been sitting with Piper. "You know we can hear you, right?"

"Yeah," Bear said. "Get over here, I need a new Gilligan."

Light footsteps trod toward me before Piper said, "If he's Gilligan, does that make me Mary Ann or Ginger?"

"You're Mary Ann, definitely a Mary Ann," Blake said, his voice close to me now too.

Piper laughed. "I don't know if I should be offended by that or not."

I wasn't real keen on old TV shows, and even less keen on doing anything but drowning my sorrows in alcohol.

"I don't like this game," Sonja said as a light kick landed against my calf. I sat up to find her looking at me from under a wide-brimmed fedora. "Talk to me about something."

Sonja was Piper's best friend, a personal trainer and

boxer. And if we didn't make up a ragtag group of friends, I didn't know who did. I, being a teacher and coach, was the only one among us with a nine-to-five job. And apparently the only one with any current stress.

"Not in the mood," I replied after a sip of beer.

Sonja ignored me with a wry grin. "What's up with your football team? What are they again? The Woodchucks?"

I groaned, knowing Sonja was relentless when she wanted something, and gave in. "The mighty, mighty Otters."

I snapped my teeth for good measure, and she tilted her head with a laugh. "You meet the new coach yet?"

This time I turned my face away from her. I didn't want to talk about this. I scrubbed my hand over my jaw. I'd been told in the past that I needed to work on my communication skills, that I wasn't good at expressing emotion. Like I gave a shit.

"Did I hit a nerve?" She sat forward, guessing correctly why I didn't want to chat.

"I'm surprised Bear didn't tell you." Because Bear and Sonja were two peas in a pod, and because Bear couldn't keep a secret.

She briefly looked over her shoulder at the man in question before turning back to me. "We don't tell each other everything."

"Yeah, just like I wasn't looking forward to getting this job at all."

She moved next to me and smacked my shoulder. I wasn't

used to having girls as friends, but Sonja was pretty cool. Piper too. Except they constantly badgered me with questions.

"What happened?"

"They didn't promote me."

She stared at me, waiting for more, and I huffed. "They gave the job to Charlie Gibb."

The words tasted bitter as I said them, and I cringed.

"Well, what do you know about this guy?" she asked.

"Charlie isn't a guy."

A few seconds went by before Sonja picked up her phone and typed. I couldn't believe she could get Wi-Fi out on the lake. "Charlie Gibb is a woman," she affirmed, a smile on her face. "Badass."

As Sonja rejoiced in female empowerment, I seethed in silence. I didn't get emotional over much, but football had been the one constant in my life, and it mollified me when other parts of my life went to shit. It was predictable even in its competitiveness. There were rules, and downs, and an end zone you knew you could work toward. Life wasn't like that. Crap happened, goalposts moved.

The head coach position was my end zone. I was within five yards. I'd thought it was mine.

Until it wasn't, and that was a tough loss to accept.

"Hey." Sonja turned toward Blake and Bear. "Why didn't either of you two say the person who is going to coach the Otters is a woman?"

"A woman?" Piper laughed, clapping. "That's awesome." Then she caught herself. "I mean, not awesome for you, Connor, I'm sorry you didn't get the job. It's just awesome for her, you know?"

"Yeah, awesome." I gulped down the rest of my beer and tossed the bottle into a bucket.

Bear scratched his head, his long hair up in a stupid man-bun that he thought looked good. "Didn't think it was important. That was McGuire's job. She took it from him—"

"Watch your vocabulary, Thomas Behr," Sonja said, pointing a finger at him. "Charlie Gibb is not a villain. She didn't do anything besides accept a job as a football coach."

"I'm just defending my friend," he countered.

"You can defend without being condescending."

"That's true," Blake said as he leaned forward to slap my shoulder. "Could be worse, yeah? Could be—"

"You really want to finish that statement?" Piper asked sweetly, the daggers from her eyes contradicting her tone. "Want to compare a female coach to something worse?"

Blake pasted on a cheesy grin. "I was just going to say it could be worse than being able to learn from a most likely wonderful head coach with plenty of years of experience."

Piper playfully thumped his head. "Yeah, right."

Blake glanced back over to me. He understood that, no matter what way we looked at this, there was no way not to turn my situation into a battle of the sexes. Better to just keep our mouths shut.

Blake grabbed Piper's hand, whispering into her ear, loud enough for us all to hear, "Come on, Sunshine, I'll show you how to raise my jib."

Sonja mumbled, "Oh God," as Bear high-fived Blake. I stared off into the distance. There was no going backward, so I needed to figure out how to move forward. Guess I'd have to take my own advice that I often told the team: one play at a time, one down at a time.

CHAPTER
4

Charlie

We'd spent a solid four hours going over plays and discussing next week's practices in McGuire's classroom. I was met mostly with silence as I told the coaches my plans, but I wasn't going to be intimidated. Ronnie was on my side. Pretty sure I had Ken too. Erik seemed amenable to whoever brought him food. That only left Al and Connor, although I didn't think I'd ever be able to fully win them over. Even with the lunch of subs and chips I'd provided.

I cleared my throat, waiting until all eyes turned to me. "Before we finish up, I wanted to let you know there's gonna be a press conference this afternoon. I'm not a fan of bein' in front of the cameras so it's gonna be short and sweet, but I wanted to ask that you not respond to any requests from the media. I don't want this team turning into a circus act just because I'm here."

Al whispered something under his breath, and Connor breathed out a laugh as he lounged in his chair. Like he couldn't care less about any of this. I was tired of it.

"So, guys, if you'll excuse me, I need to get ready." I stood to leave. "McGuire, I'd like to speak to you in the hall, please."

A secretive expression passed between him and Al as he stood up.

I closed the door and stood directly in front of Connor. He had no choice but to look at me, and to his credit, he did. Most men avoided eye contact when I confronted them. All bark and no bite, this male species.

"I couldn't help but notice you were quiet this mornin'."

"I'm a quiet guy," he said, his eyes narrowing. He didn't have his hat on, and I could see every line and curve of his face—the sharp angle of his jaw, the subtle slope of his cheekbone, the long line of his nose. Not that it mattered. He was a hard one to read with or without a hat on.

"I appreciate that," I started. "But what I don't appreciate is your little snorts and eye rolls and the way you sit."

"The way I *sit*?" He laughed, low and breathy. An annoying sound, a tease of something much bigger, but enough to know it was directed at me. "Jesus, you're a real piece of work."

"Yeah, you sit like you don't have a care in the world. This is the football team you've been a part of for eight years, right? You're just gonna sit there like you have no energy, and nothin' to contribute to our meetin'?"

I didn't wait for him to answer. Whatever he had to say, it wouldn't have been enough.

"I don't care what your reason is for not likin' me. If you want to continue as offensive coordinator here, you need to act like the damn offensive coordinator. So either speak up now or forever hold your peace."

A second passed. And then ten more.

"Jaylin Bose is out for a week at least, with a high ankle sprain. His mom told me yesterday. Jaylin's the best back on the team."

I knew why these were the first words out of his mouth. He wanted me to know *he* was the coach the parents went to. It was a cheap shot to show he was the supposed top dog.

"I'll make sure to call her tonight. You don't need to worry about contacting parents."

He unfolded his arms and shifted his weight between his feet for a moment before rolling his shoulders back. He had a good four inches on me, but I wasn't intimidated by his size. I'd stood up to bigger and tougher-looking dudes before.

"This job was supposed to be mine," he said finally. "I've been here for eight years. I know the players, I know where they need to improve and what they excel at. I know this team inside and out, like the back of my hand."

"Then why didn't they hire you, huh? If you're so good at your job, why aren't you in this position?" I didn't back down from his stare. He was a good-looking, blond, blue-eyed guy from the middle of America. I was sure this was the first time he hadn't gotten what he wanted. And he'd lost it to a woman.

Oh, the *horror*.

Connor seemed to chew on his words before spitting them out at me with a raised voice. "How can you possibly coach a bunch of adolescent high school boys, much less raise our average score per game? What the fuck do you know about football besides your daddy's last name?"

See, I'd done what Connor McGuire hadn't. I'd studied—on everyone and everything. If he thought I was coming into this blind, he was an idiot.

I smiled, making sure my features were set into place before I unleashed the fury.

"What do *I* know about football? Let me tell you. I know you attended Divine Mercy in St. Paul and held the state's record in rushing yards your junior and senior year. I know you were recruited by the University of Indianapolis, where you had a good couple of years as quarterback until you tore your MCL and ACL from a bad tackle. I'm sure you took that pretty hard, but as far as I can tell, you weren't gonna get drafted to the NFL. Far from it. So this thing where you think the world owes you somethin' is bullshit. The world owes you nothing."

I stepped closer to him, close enough to see his nostrils flare, and went on.

"I wore football pads my entire life. I was a receiver at a championship high school until I was fifteen years old. When boys outgrew me, I became the lead placekicker, scoring the most field goal points three years in a row. I was a walk-on at a top D-One school in Florida and played professional football in the women's league for three years before becoming an assistant coach at Georgia Tech. Yes, I worked for my father, but I've recruited and worked with collegiate players for years, and have had a hell of a lot more experience winning than you've *ever* had. But what do I know about football?"

Connor's stiff stance loosened slightly, but he kept up a good front.

I wasn't done yet.

"Just because you and the rest of my male counterparts may be bigger and stronger than I am doesn't mean y'all understand the game any more or better than I do. The job of a coach is to lead. And I plan on leadin' this team to the state championship. You can either buy a ticket for this train or get the hell off. I'll be sure to wave at you in your position on the sideline. Your decision."

Connor's jaw worked as a thick tension lay between us. I had no more words for this guy. It was up to him whether he wanted to stay or go.

He turned his back to me and I noticed his shoulders moving up and down as he breathed. I might've been a bit harsh about his football career, but I didn't care. He needed to be brought down a peg or two. If I could handle the bitter comments and ruthless "honesty" that had been directed toward me my whole life, he could certainly handle a few minutes of blunt truth.

He took a step to the door, and as he touched the handle, I called out to him. "McGuire, if you're going to continue with this team, you'd better have a better attitude come Monday. And don't take the Lord's name in vain in front of me. We're not a bunch of fuckin' heathens."

He turned to me then. "You know the meaning of the word *ironic*?"

"Yeah. A football coach of a losin' team who doesn't know when he's been beat."

He pursed his lips, staring me down for a few seconds before he spun around. The only acknowledgment I got was the resounding sound of the slammed door.

I'd been called a bitch a time or two, sometimes worse than that, and I could only guess what words he had for me. It's not that I enjoyed tearing into someone, but it occasionally had to be done. Women were called names for that. Men were called tough.

It was a backward world we lived in.

I was supposed to meet Jim and Mr. Philander, the principal, at two, and I needed to make myself look more presentable for the cameras. I was no model and wasn't much for fashion, but I enjoyed bath bombs, red lipstick, and a lace bra as much as the next gal.

I changed into a polo shirt with the school's name on it and a new pair of slim khaki pants, imagining Gram rolling over in her grave. I was about to go on TV looking a lot more like a tomboy, which she hated, and a lot less like Miss America, which she loved.

But it was twenty years too late to try to change now.

In an effort to make my gram proud of me from her place in heaven, I took my hair out of the messy bun it was in and ran a brush through it. I had the curse of pin-straight hair, and with its mucky blond-brown color that I hadn't had a chance to fix at a salon, it looked like straw. I swiped on mascara and some ChapStick before heading upstairs to the main office. It'd have to do.

Jim was already there, waiting for me. "Hey, Charlie, how are you today? Settling in okay?"

"I'm gettin' there."

He patted my shoulder once. "Good to hear. I spoke to someone I know about a place you might be interested in living."

"Yeah?"

He handed me a piece of paper with a name and number. "I've known Sonja for about two years now. She works at the gym I go to. She's real sweet. She mentioned in passing yesterday that her friend is moving out of her house soon, and I told her you were looking for a place."

I stuffed the paper in my pocket, about to ask more about this Sonja when Philander walked up.

Mr. Philander was oddly tall and thin, with a long nose that gave him the appearance of a villain from an old-timey movie. "Hello," he said, tugging on the lapel of his sports coat. "Jim, Charlie. Nice to see you both."

Except he couldn't even be bothered to look me in the eyes. A serious flaw, I thought.

"Shall we walk down to the field?"

Jim and I nodded, and the three of us headed out of the school down a slight hill to the football field. I could see the small platform set up with a podium and microphone. A group of reporters was clustered in front of it, along with men and women of all ages. I assumed that a couple of my players were in the mix too, judging from the line of boys at the back. I spotted one who looked familiar. I racked my brain for where I'd seen him before until it came to me: Nate from Caribou.

"Perfect weather for this," Philander said shortly. "This will look good for the school."

"Mm-hmm," I agreed, my stomach twisting into knots with every step closer to the podium.

The very little knowledge I had of the principal was that he liked the spotlight, having the name of the school out there. The more ribbons, championships, and awards, the better. But he wasn't exactly warm and fuzzy.

He nodded at the small crowd as he took his place at the front of the platform. He tested the microphone, then waved for Jim and me to join him, and I took a few steadying breaths. I might have been a football player and coach for most of my life, but I wasn't great in front of crowds. Or cameras.

Instead of listening to Philander talk about Douglass High School, I focused on the kids in the back. I hadn't been around high school kids in a long time, not since I played in the IWFL and actually used my teaching certification for a paycheck. I had become accustomed to working with college players and the attitude that came along with them. By the time players and coaches reached a certain level of notoriety, their outlook changed. It became a little bit more about what the game could do for them, and less about why they played it in the first place. High school football had all the passion without all of the cynicism.

And just as I smiled, remembering my own years as a high school player, I was introduced.

"Please welcome Charlotte Gibb, the new head coach of the Douglass Otters."

I shook hands with Philander, and then placed my palms on the podium to steady my trembling fingers. "Thank you, Mr. Philander, for the introduction, and to Jim Thines for makin' the transition here so easy. I won't take up much of your time. I'd just like to say I'm really excited to be here, and I look forward to this season. Dick Nelson had a long run here, and I hope I can eventually become as loved as he was. In my short time here, I've already learned that this is a tight-knit community and a really great school. I can only promise to do my best for the players and for my students. Thank you very much."

I stepped back from the podium, and, to my relief, Jim took my place, wrapping up the session. Reporters shouted a few questions about my background and my father, but I only smiled and waved quickly before hightailing it off the platform toward the boys in the back of the crowd.

"Hey, Nate, right?" I said, looking to the boy, probably six feet tall, with long arms. "You're on the team?"

He smiled and nodded. "Yeah, Nate Anderson. I'm a junior."

"I remember you from Caribou."

Another player, this one tall and muscular, jostled him. "Caribou king, right here," he said, then stuck his hand out to me. "I'm Marcus Clark. And this is Joel Cooper."

Joel was scrawny and still had some ways of growing yet. Or at least, I hoped so. He seemed like he'd be blown over with a strong wind.

I smiled at them, genuinely pleased that they seemed enthusiastic. "You ready for the new season?"

Marcus clapped his hands together. "So ready, Miss—I mean, Coach."

"Good to hear. I'll see you guys bright and early Monday. Come ready to work."

"We will," Nate said.

I sneaked back into the school while Philander entertained the reporters. Jim saw me and gave me a nod. He knew I wasn't much for this kind of thing.

I quickly packed up my belongings, ready for some much-needed downtime after today, but as I walked to my car, I overheard two men talking with their backs to me. I assumed they'd been there for the press conference.

"You really think she can do it?" one of them asked, proving my assumption correct.

The other man tilted his head side to side. "No. I've never heard of a woman coaching before. I doubt . . ."

I shook my head, eyes to the ground as I tuned them out and got in my car. What people didn't realize was that the more they doubted me, the more I'd work to prove them wrong.

CHAPTER
5

Connor

I always loved the first day of doubles. After a long, hot summer, stepping back on the grass felt like coming home. This year was no different.

Even if everything *was* different.

Charlie Gibb stood in front of the team, an Otters hat on her head. I had to give it to her, she knew how to handle herself. She had every player's attention and made sure to look them all in the eyes as she introduced herself.

She gave a summary of her background, but I didn't need to hear it. She'd given me an earful on Saturday. I'd never had anyone speak to me the way she did, so bluntly. And it took balls.

If she needed anything in this job, it was big balls.

I'd gone home after and looked her up on the Internet. Her career was impressive, and not just for a woman. For anyone. She had a long résumé and, according to YouTube, a really good highlight reel.

There were a few articles written about her but not very many direct interviews because, as she said, she didn't like the limelight. Although there were more than a few comments written under every article and video about her looks or sexual orientation, or another four-letter word that even I didn't dare speak.

I might be pissed she was the head coach, but it had never crossed my mind to call her names or speak about her the way these strangers did.

Although it *was* strange to see a woman lead the team. Even with the plain T-shirt and green mesh shorts, it was hard to ignore the physical difference between her and every other person on this field. She was tall and strong, her arms and legs clear signs that she was an athlete, but her long hair and curves were distinctly female. The shine on her golden skin had me wondering if she'd lotioned up before coming out on the field, but that was exactly the type of comment those anonymous posters wrote about her, and I wanted to be better than them. I shook my head, focusing on her words.

Her voice was much more relaxed as she went over the schedule than when she'd chewed my ass out. Who'd have thought a girl from Georgia with a sweet southern accent would have a mouth like a truck driver?

And would be offended by taking the Lord's name in vain.

"Coach Rosario will start off with stretching, but I want y'all to know that when you come onto this football field, you will be running. We don't walk. We run. Got it?"

The players all nodded, and she clapped her hands together once. "Good. Let's get started. Coach . . ."

Ronnie stepped forward to lead them in stretching, and the players stood up, running to their spots in lines across the field. Gibb grabbed a clipboard and whistle before meeting me by the fifty-yard line. She had already made it known that her goal this first day was to assess each player, but I hadn't expected her to have notes on almost all of them already. She handed me a spreadsheet with the physical stats of every kid, along with any significant notes from last season.

"We gotta get these guys in better shape," she said, staring out over the team.

I nodded in agreement. I'd been trying to do that in the off-season, working them hard in the weight room.

"I spoke to Jaylin last night. Seems like a nice kid."

I nodded again.

"I told him I expected to see him in person tomorrow. He'll need to work to catch up on what he's missed this week," she said, and I slipped my sunglasses on.

With a low, irritated noise, she stepped in front of me, her back to the players as they stood up from their stretching. "I'm glad you took our little chat to heart."

This time I dipped my chin down to look at her. "I'll do what I need to do for this team to win. That doesn't mean you and I have to like each other. We are colleagues, not buddies."

"Good. Then I know it won't hurt your feelings when I say get to work." She slammed the clipboard into my chest along with a timer.

She blew her whistle, nearly in my ear, and yelled, "On the forty!"

The players jogged over to the forty-yard line, facing the goalpost, and I moved to the goal line. Taking sprints times wasn't exactly in my job description as offensive coordinator, but I wasn't about to argue that now. I wasn't going to be the one not being a team player.

Even Al was toeing the line today. Although I didn't expect it to last—he was basically a sloth in human form and had only stayed on staff because he was good friends with Nelson. He had been in my ear again about her this morning. Hard to believe, but he disliked her more than I did. For him, though, it was straight-up sexism. Old dogs, new tricks, and all that.

Gibb wanted the team faster, so we spent a lot of time conditioning. First with sprints, then cone drills and ladders. It wasn't any different from what I would've done. We had a few standout players, but we needed each of these boys to improve to start winning games. By the time ten o'clock rolled around, they were all spent and ready for a break, so we broke into groups to go over the new plays before lunch. The afternoon wasn't much different, more skills work, ending with more running.

Gibb and I avoided each other.

Double sessions were always grueling, long days with little rest, but she kept a tight schedule, leaving no room for the kids to fool around. And by the end of the week, the team was adjusting to the new plays and showing improvement. She set high standards with hard-and-fast rules, punishments set as push-ups, up-downs, or general running around the track until she said to stop, like she had Butcher doing right now.

Scottie Butcher was a slow-as-molasses lineman with a penchant for making jokes on the field. On his third circuit around the track, he looked ready to pass out, and I held my hand up. He stopped running and bent over, taking heaving breaths.

Gibb stalked over to me, her ponytail swinging with every step. She whispered her words to me: "What in the hell are you doin'?"

"The kid is wrecked."

"I don't care if he's pukin', you don't tell him to stop if I told him to keep runnin'."

"That's what you want? To drive these kids into the ground?"

"I wanna show them they're stronger than they think they are. Don't underestimate them because of your own shortcomings." She brushed past me to Butcher and pulled him to stand up straight. She grabbed his helmet and leaned in to say something to him, then hit his shoulder pad. He ran back onto the field.

I didn't want to admit it, but she knew what she was doing. Still didn't like her or the fact that I had to answer to her. But she knew what she was doing.

We had a scrimmage tomorrow and spent the afternoon running every play, making sure they all knew their routes and blocks. But it was pretty clear we had a long way to go.

Gibb gathered the team together at the end of practice, and they took a knee. "This week has been a good start. And I know I'm askin' a lot of y'all, but I want you to ask more of yourselves. I want you to be better. To know that you can do better. Because y'all are capable of more than you know. But if you never try to reach that next level, if you never even attempt it, you're dead in the water." She stepped in toward the middle of the team, gesturing for them to stand. She raised her voice as the players formed a circle around her. "Play hard. Be better. Douglass on three." All hands went in toward the middle of the circle. "One, two, three . . ."

"Douglass!"

The team broke up their huddle, and I clapped a few of them on the helmet as they passed. Jaylin approached me, walking with a barely noticeable limp.

"How do you feel without the crutches?"

"I'm fine."

We started off toward the school. "Don't say you're fine when you're not. It's more important for you to take the time you need to heal."

"Yeah, yeah," he said.

"Don't 'yeah, yeah' me." I lightly knocked his head with my rolled-up playlist.

He laughed. "Damn, Coach. Okay."

We entered the basement of the school and hung a right into the locker room. I held the door open for Jaylin. He wasn't permitted to put on pads or play until next week, but he went toward the lockers to put his playbook away.

Gibb's office door hung open, the sign she was inside, and I was just about to go there myself when I heard a couple of players lagging behind in the hall. I waited to hold the locker room door open for them, but quickly let it close when I caught their conversation.

"Seriously? You think she's hot?"

"Yeah, man, her ass is, like . . ."

They laughed.

"I don't think so," another one said. "She's too manly. She's got huge shoulders. She played ball. Like, who wants to be with a chick who played ball?"

"Dude, I don't even know why you're talking like this. She's our coach. Did you see what she made Butcher do? What a bitch. If she hears you talking about her ass, she'll probably make you run for days with a sandbag on your back."

I knew that voice. It was Brett Spencer, junior quarterback.

"What was that about Coach Gibb?" I asked as the three players came to a halt in front of me, surprise coloring their faces that they'd been caught.

"Nothing," Spencer said, reaching for the door handle next to me. He was a cocky little shit.

I blocked his hand and looked to Brian Krajewski. "What about you? You have anything you'd like to say about Coach Gibb?"

"Nuh-uh." He shook his head, a follower.

Luis Weston snickered, and I glowered at him. Out of these three, Brett was the true troublemaker, but his dad was a well-known businessman who owned a couple of chain stores and was a head booster for the school. Brett took after his father in acting like they ruled the world.

I stepped forward so the three of them couldn't get around me to go into the locker room. "Keep your pads on, we're going on a little field trip." They groaned as I pointed to the doors back outside. "If you want to run your mouths, you better be prepared to run your legs."

"You're kidding me," Weston said under his breath.

"Nope. Go. Now."

They did, mumbling the whole way back. I pointed toward the bleachers. "Helmets on."

All of them rolled their eyes at me, and I was tempted to smack them until they rolled right out of their heads. Instead I said, "You run every bleacher until I say stop."

I was actually impressed that we hadn't had problems with the players being disrespectful until now. But hearing what they'd said made my blood boil. Gibb didn't deserve to be degraded, no matter what went on between us.

I folded my arms over my chest and watched as the trio of boneheads began their trek up.

About fifteen minutes later, Gibb made her way down

the hill toward me. "What are you doin'?" Her eyes toggled between me and the boys running. "You tryin' to run them into the ground?"

I kept my eyes on them as they made their way back down the steps once again. "I'm pushing them to do better."

She stood next to me quietly for a few seconds. I guessed she wanted to know more. "They needed an attitude adjustment," I said, finally turning to her.

She smiled up at me. A real smile, not the one she used when she was about to turn into a dragon. But one where her brown eyes—which I'd never noticed before—softened and her lips tipped up enough to show how one of her teeth slightly overlapped the other on the left side. "Don't we all." She patted my back twice before walking away. "I'll see you tomorrow," she threw over her shoulder.

CHAPTER
6

Charlie

I slid into the booth at the News Room, a cool, upscale restaurant right in the middle of downtown Minneapolis. I hadn't eaten much today, just a protein shake and a couple pieces of fruit. The scrimmage this morning hadn't gone as well as I'd wanted it to, and I'd ended up going back over film for a lot longer than I'd planned on, skipping lunch.

Sonja and I had been trying to meet, but being busy with the team all week, I hadn't had a chance until now. I also hadn't been able to see much of anything outside of my hotel room, the school, and Caribou Coffee. Dinner out at a real restaurant sounded great.

"Hi, are you Charlie?"

I tipped my head back to see two women, one pale with red hair and big green eyes, the other short with golden-brown skin and black curly hair. She pushed big sunglasses up onto her head. "I'm Sonja."

"Yes. Nice to meet you," I said, moving the menus and utensils around the table as they sat down.

"I'm excited to meet you," the redhead said, smiling widely. She moved her long hair to the side and leaned forward. "I've heard so much about you. I mean, I haven't heard *so* much about you, just that you're the new Otters coach. And I have to tell you, I think that's pretty much the coolest thing ever."

I looked between the two women, a bit overwhelmed.

"I'm Piper," she said.

"No filter." Sonja shook her head with a smile. "Pipes lives in the house now, but will be moving out shortly."

Piper nodded, and Sonja placed her arms on the table, hands together with her elbows out. The pose showed off her defined, powerful muscles. "Thanks for meeting us here."

"Of course," I said, playing with the hair tie on my wrist. "Thank *you*."

"Jim told me just a little bit about you. You're from Atlanta?"

"From just outside, yeah."

A gray-haired waitress stopped at our booth and passed out waters. "Are you ready to order?"

Piper stared at the beer menu, lips pursed, and Sonja shook her head. "I think we'll need a few more minutes." When the waitress walked away, Sonja looked at me. "What do you think of Minneapolis?"

"I haven't gotten to see a whole lot, but what I have seen is nice."

Piper kept her eyes on the beer list as she asked. "What'd you see?"

"The Mall of America."

"You didn't," Sonja said, balling up the paper from the straw in her water glass.

"I did." I shrugged. "The Travel Channel told me to go there, and to try a Juicy Lucy—whatever that is."

"It's a burger, and you should definitely go to Matt's Bar," Piper said.

Sonja shook her head. "No. Five-Eight Club is better for a Juicy Lucy."

Piper started to argue, but Sonja cut her off, eyes on me. "Never mind. You live here now. You can skip all the touristy stuff."

"It doesn't feel like I live here yet."

"After we eat, we'll show you around a bit, how about that?"

I paused, taking in the excitement in their expressions. How odd to immediately take in a practical stranger, an acquaintance of an acquaintance. "No, that's okay. I'm sure you're both busy."

"I'm not," Piper said.

"Me either. I cleared my schedule for tonight."

Piper smirked, pointing at her friend while focused on me. "That's a first. You really shouldn't pass up the offer."

When I didn't respond, she persisted. "It'll be fun. Girls' night out."

I pushed a few stray hairs behind my ears, still hesitant to go out with them. "Really?"

"Of course," Sonja said. "What kind of Minnesotans would we be if we didn't take you out?"

Piper nodded in mock seriousness. "They kick you out of the state if you aren't nice enough. First thing I learned when I moved here."

The two of them made me laugh, their easy friendship obvious. It would be nice to make some girlfriends here since I'd had to leave my friends in Georgia. Not that I had a ton—apparently my resting bitch face turned people off.

"So, the stereotype is true then, huh? Y'all really are nice up here—well, most of you."

"Most? Who wasn't nice to you?" Sonja asked, drumming her neon-orange nails on the table.

I was about to answer, but the waitress showed back up, and we paused our conversation to order. Sonja got a salad with the dressing on the side, while Piper ordered the cheese board and some kind of pasta, along with a fancy beer.

"I like your style," Piper said to me, laughing, when I ordered a steak and a red wine. "It's nice to dine with someone who doesn't eat like a rabbit."

Sonja didn't seem fazed by her comment. Whatever she ate, it was paying off. She could've been on the cover of *Sports Illustrated*.

Once our menus were collected and the waitress was gone, Sonja tilted her head at me. "Who wasn't nice to you?"

I looked above to the metalwork and newspaper photos that decorated the wall. "I'm not afraid of someone being rude to me, if that's what you think."

"I wouldn't think that at all," Sonja said.

"I'm sure you put up with a lot of crap all day long," Piper added. "We both know how that can be."

"And we're being a little dishonest," Sonja admitted with a tiny frown. "We do know a little bit more about you than you know about us."

I looked between the two women in front of me. Sonja seemed a little shy, while Piper was about to burst.

"Connor. We know Connor," she let out in a tumble of words. "He's best friends with my boyfriend, Blake, so we know each other really well. We all hang out all the time, including our other friend, Bear, who's also Connor's friend. Bear, Thomas Behr, the hockey player, anyway—"

"Anyway," Sonja said, cutting her off with an exasperated laugh, "what Piper is saying is that we heard a lot about you. But not from Jim."

"From McGuire?"

Their silence was my answer.

"What did he say?"

"Not a lot."

"Which isn't unlike Connor," Piper added. "But you could probably imagine what he did tell us."

I huffed. "That I couldn't possibly be good at coaching

football, and that I only got the job because of my famous daddy. That I stole the job from him. And that I don't know the school or the kids or that Sam Long pukes before every game, even if it's just a scrimmage, because of nerves—I found that one out the hard way."

Sonja's eyebrows rose high on her forehead. "He's told you a lot more than he's told us."

"I told him a lot too. To basically shut the fuck up and do his job or get out."

They both grinned, but I cringed. "I'm sorry. My gram always told me my mouth would get me in trouble one day. Mostly it just scares people off."

"I'm not offended," Sonja said with a flick of her wrist.

Piper gestured to herself. "I've been known to throw around an f-bomb or two. I mean, it's a verb, noun, and adjective. There is no better curse word in the English language."

I laughed, truly relaxing for the first time in what felt like months.

We talked for a long time, through dinner, another drink, and the dessert Piper and I split. Sonja told me about some of the highs and lows of being a female boxer and her upcoming bout in Chicago. She had her eye on the next Summer Olympics, and I was truly amazed at a woman who could literally get knocked down and back up for a living.

Piper was a craft beer brewer and in the midst of expanding her business. She showed me pictures of her gorgeous boyfriend and regaled me with all kinds of stories of how they met, how he taught her how to swim—or really, doggy-paddle, as Sonja said—and how he had most recently bought her a *Golden Girls* T-shirt, which she sported now. Clearly, she was head over heels in love.

I didn't know what that was like.

Not since Dustin Jacobs broke my heart junior year of high school. He was a soccer player with long, shaggy hair that flew out by his ears when he'd run down the field. We'd sat next to each other in math class, and I was so in love with him I'd hung on his every word and had let him cheat off me on all the tests. One day I'd finally gotten up the courage to tell him how I felt, and he'd said, "You're cool. I don't want to ruin our friendship. You're like one of the guys, you know. One of my best friends."

And then the next week, I'd found out he had hooked up with Jana Teke, the pretty cheerleading captain, at Ryan Taylor's party. It was the first time I'd realized what it meant to be "one of the guys." That I fit in, but only in a very specific role, and only until they didn't want me anymore.

"So, what's it really like being a female football coach?" Piper asked, tipping her beer glass on its edge.

"It's great," I said, my usual answer, but they didn't fall for it. Both of them stared at me, waiting.

"Most people don't have a problem with me coachin' football, not with my skills or how I work. In my opinion, they have a problem with everythin' else. My looks, my sexuality, whether I'm too weak or too tough. Too masculine or too feminine. I don't fit into the right boxes for certain people, and it makes them nervous."

Sonja and Piper smiled ruefully as if they understood.

"One time I had an alumnus from the college tell me I shouldn't coach because I was a distraction." Hearing the words in my head even years later didn't take the sting out of them. "As if I was just a body, you know? Like all my years on the field, all my work meant nothin' because I have boobs."

Piper clucked her tongue. "I hear that."

I went on, happy to get all this off my chest to women who knew where I was coming from. "When I was a kid, I tried to blend in as much as possible. I had short hair and wore real baggy clothes, but eventually I realized I shouldn't have to act or look any different than I wanted to. I wasn't the problem. They were."

"Got that right," Sonja said, gesturing to the waitress for another water with lemon.

"But to answer your question, sometimes it's very isolating being a woman and a football coach. I'm surrounded by a lot of people, but I stick out like a sore thumb. And relationships are even worse. A man who is confident enough in himself to not be intimidated by what I do is difficult to find."

"Maybe you'll find him here." Piper smiled.

I huffed. "Yeah, right. Besides, I'm not here for that. I'm here for football, for the field, the sounds, the smell of sweat and dirt."

Piper's nose wrinkled. "I have an aversion to dirt and sweat."

Sonja laughed and pointed her thumb between the two of them. "We've got an opposites-attract kind of thing going on."

"Uh-huh," I said.

"So, when can you move in?" Piper asked, sitting on the edge of her seat.

Sonja backhanded Piper's arm.

"Ow. What?"

"You don't get to decide. You're moving out in, like, two weeks."

Piper rolled her eyes.

Sonja grinned, and leaned toward me. "So, when can you move in?"

"Is tonight too soon?"

We all laughed. And I knew that I wanted these women on my team.

CHAPTER

7

Connor

Like a lot of kids, I'd dreamed of the NFL. I'd wanted the money and the fame and my name on ESPN. I had wanted to be the player everyone drafted on their fantasy football teams. In my high school and college years, I naïvely thought it was possible for me. I thought if I wanted it bad enough, I'd get it.

I didn't account for my actual talent, which wasn't anywhere near the elite level I arrogantly thought I was at. With time and maturity, I could admit I was never meant for that life.

And that was okay. I was a simple guy, and I made myself happy with teaching and coaching. It suited me. I enjoyed teaching history, even if the kids constantly asked to listen to that Broadway musical on a loop. I'd learned a long time ago to pick my battles with students, and the *Hamilton* soundtrack was one I'd lost.

I actually looked forward to the first day of school. It wasn't all that different from the first day of practice, filled with skills assessments and team-building. I had my own routine that started with introducing myself and the year of academics, and ended with handing out American history textbooks. Before I knew it, fifth period rolled around, and with it, lunch duty.

I gave a couple of fist bumps to a few players as I passed them toward the back of the cafeteria. There were two sets of doors, in the front and the back, and for some unlucky reason I got stuck with lunch duty every year, so I'd come to think of the back doors as my usual post. I tucked my hands in my pockets and leaned against the wall, scanning the long rectangular room. Lunch was always uproarious, but after a while it sort of settled to a loud white noise.

"Hey, Connor."

I turned around to find Tina, the home economics teacher and head of the teachers' union. Gibb towered behind her.

"You know Charlie already. Can you show her the ropes of lunch duty?"

I briefly raised my eyes to Gibb before looking back down at Tina, so short I often stared down at the top of her brown hair. "You don't have lunch duty this year?"

"Nope." She touched my arm. "I've got study hall this semester. Could you help Charlie out today?"

"Help, huh?" I raised my eyebrow at Gibb, and her lip curled like a mean dog's. A smirk tugged at my lip, but I turned away because of a commotion by the snack machine. A kid had jokingly lifted up another one, feet in the air. Students laughed and took pictures. Exactly how heads split open.

I whistled through my teeth. "Hey!"

They all stopped and turned.

"Sit down!"

They quieted and sat at the nearest table.

By the time I faced back around, Tina was gone, but Gibb was still there. I unconsciously skimmed her over from head to toe. Her hair was down and a lighter color than I remembered—I didn't know why I'd remember that to begin with. I didn't usually notice much about her. I just wasn't used to seeing her with some makeup on her eyes. Or in the fitted purple shirt that clung to her body.

I was a team player by make, but I didn't want to play nice with her. And I certainly didn't want to look at her any differently than I would at any of the other coaches. But, good God, it was hard not to. She was a woman after all. With a bad habit of snarling at me. Not to say I didn't deserve it.

On the other hand, she didn't deserve *my* job.

We were rivals. And teammates. A bizarre structure.

"Are you havin' a good first day?" she asked, making conversation I wasn't interested in.

I nodded.

"You know, some people think it's polite to answer when you're asked a question."

"I am not one of those people," I said without looking at her.

From the corner of my eye, I saw her fold her arms across her chest.

"I don't know how you're a teacher," she said, her accent getting the best of her. "What with your delightful personality. Must be a joy to be in your class."

"My students love me."

"With all your charm and wit, I bet they do."

I turned to her. "Do you know what they say about gym teachers?"

"No, what do they say?"

I took my time saying the words. "Those who can't teach, teach gym."

Her fists balled up, and I imagined she was thinking about hitting me. It's not that I *liked* when she got all riled up, but I didn't hate it either. This baiting between us was easy, almost natural. As if we were meant to compete with each other.

We didn't speak for a while, but she stayed in my peripheral vision, her hands twisted together. It struck me that she might've actually been nervous on her first day of school, but I refused to feel any sympathy. We weren't friends like that.

Instead, I focused on what was comfortable. Football.

"We need to watch that defensive back on Friday," I said, referring to our first game this weekend.

"I know. We watched the same film."

"Spencer tends to not check down the receivers. He's got to—"

"Connor." She had her hands on her hips, one eyebrow raised. "I know."

It was the first time she'd used my first name, and the sound of it took me by surprise. So much so that I found myself apologizing with a quick, "Sorry."

"You're a good coach, you know," she said softly, and I almost didn't hear it over the din of the cafeteria. "You're patient and knowledgeable. The kids listen to you."

I jerked my head back in surprise at the compliment.

"Don't look at me like that," she said, her perturbed face melting a bit. "Game recognizes game."

I laughed. A real laugh. The picture of a five-foot-ten blond woman telling me *game recognizes game* was too funny.

"What?" Her own smile crawled across her face. "Andre Valentine said that to me once."

And then my laughter died down real quick. Andre Valentine, former Georgia Tech player and current wide receiver for the Bills. He had one of the highest total receiving yards in the league. A reminder that Charlie Gibb had a long history with the sport, with more experience than I could have hoped for.

Jealousy was a dangerous game.

And it gnawed at me for the rest of the day until I grabbed a few minutes to call my brother before practice began.

I closed the door to my classroom and pulled out my

cell phone. If there was one person who could distract me, it was him.

He picked up after a few rings. "Nono!"

"Seanie, what's up?"

"Not so much," he said with his usual lisp. "What's up with you?"

"Just hanging out before practice, thought I'd give you a call."

"Practice? You have it now?"

"In a few minutes, yeah."

I heard a noise that sounded like a slap. He'd probably hit his thigh like he always did when he was excited. "Awesome."

My brother was the opposite of me, happy-go-lucky all the time. He'd make a conversation with anyone and everyone. There was a seven-year age difference between us, but we got along great. He was everything I wished I was more of, open and courageous. He said whatever he felt without fear. Maybe it was his naïveté, or that he hadn't been jaded by the world yet, but it was one of the reasons I looked up to him even though he was my little brother.

"I saw a picture of Charlie Gibb. She's pretty."

I rolled my eyes. My brother, the ladies' man.

"I brought it to school and showed Ava, and she got mad at me when I said Charlie was pretty."

For the past three years, Sean had attended an adult program for people with disabilities in the Twin Cities. He loved it there, loved the girls there more.

"Which one is Ava again?"

"My girlfriend with black hair."

"Well, you can't go around showing your girlfriend a picture of another woman. Of course she's going to get mad. What did you expect, man?"

"Chelsea didn't get mad when I showed her."

"Chelsea? Who's that?"

"My girlfriend with pink shoes. She loves pink shoes."

I shook my head. My brother did better with women than I did. "How many girlfriends do you have?"

"Three."

"I think you should not show them pictures of another girl. And I think you should also just have one girlfriend at a time. It's not okay to date more than one at a time. It's not nice."

"Oh."

"Yeah, oh." I chuckled. "Are you coming to the game on Friday?"

"Yes! Gonna kick butt. You have to tell them to play good."

"I will."

"And tell Charlie Gibb she's pretty, and I hope she coaches good. I want them to win this year."

My brother, the voice of reason.

"We'll try," I said.

"Hold on, Nono, hold on." I heard him saying something in the background before he got back to me. "Mom asked if you wanna come to dinner tonight. It's meat loaf night."

"Well, I guess I could pencil you in."

"You need a pencil?"

"No, it's a saying. You know, like, I'll put it in my schedule."

"Ooh. Oh, okay. I'll pencil you in too."

"You do that."

"Okay, see you later. We'll play Mario Kart, 'kay?"

"Definitely. See you later."

"Love you, Nono."

"Love you too, Seanie."

I hung up with a smile on my face, as usual after talking to Sean. When it seemed like my life sucked, I could talk to him and he'd make me feel better. I could never be upset when I was with him.

Sean had been to all my games since I was in high school and he was the ball boy. Now he sat in the front row, cheering the loudest of everyone. He'd become kind of a legend at Douglass and made himself right at home, next to the band, in front of the cheerleaders. The team and everyone in the stands had come to know him. Sometimes it seemed they liked him more than they liked me.

Probably true.

I shoved my cell phone in my pocket and grabbed my duffel bag before heading toward the gym for practice. With a promise to keep to my brother, I needed to make sure we kicked butt this year. And to do that, I'd have to try to put my feelings about Charlie Gibb aside.

CHAPTER 8

Charlie

We lost.

When the final buzzer sounded at the end of our first game, the scoreboard showed 14–12. A loss on our home turf, and I couldn't have felt worse.

My first game as the Otters head coach, and I'd failed them. I ripped my headset off and tossed it in the case, stepping over the pile of lollipop sticks that littered the sideline.

Everybody had a nervous tic. Some people chewed their fingernails or clicked pens. But the most annoying of all these habits was lollipop chewing, by none other than Connor McGuire. He'd brought a bag of Dum Dums and methodically chomped on each and every single lollipop in the bag until there was nothing left except tiny white sticks surrounding his feet.

"You've got to be fuckin' kiddin' me," I'd said to him when I first heard the sound in my ear through the headphones during the first quarter.

He'd barely spared me a glance as he stuck a little blue sucker in his mouth.

And now, as he bent down picking up his trash, I met his eyes while I sat for a moment on the bench.

"Tough game," he said, putting all the sticks back into the bag. "They're a good team."

"They aren't better than us." I curled and uncurled the list of plays in my hand. "They just outplayed us. We could've won."

He didn't say anything as he threw the bag into the trash and walked off toward the track. The boys had all made their way back to the field house, their heads hanging in defeat. But McGuire didn't follow. Instead, he went to the bleachers. He met a woman with shoulder-length blond hair, wearing an Otters sweatshirt, and a younger man with Down syndrome, who was decked out in the school colors of blue and yellow.

He excitedly jumped at McGuire, alternating between hugging him and patting his shoulders. McGuire, for his part, acted just as happy to see him. It was the most emotion I'd ever witnessed out of him, even during this game when he shouted instructions to players and held their attention in huddles.

Curious, I walked over to Ken, who had made his way down from the booth and was putting all the headsets back in their cases. "Hey, who is that?"

He followed my gaze over to the stands. "That's Mrs. Mc-Guire and Connor's brother, Sean. They come to every game."

"What do you mean, they come to every game?"

Ken huffed out a laugh like he didn't understand why I didn't get it. "They come to every game. Home and away games. Sean wouldn't miss it."

I watched them for a minute longer, trying to comprehend how this seemingly gentle and smiling Connor Mc-Guire meshed with the sour-faced and irritable one I knew. I had a lot of questions but couldn't ask them. It wasn't my business. *He* wasn't my business. He'd made it known he didn't want me in this position to begin with, and now that I had a loss under my belt as our first game, I was sure it wouldn't take him long to try to boot me out.

My curiosity about his family wasn't important when I, quite literally, had a job I needed to defend.

"Hey, can I ask you a quick question?"

I turned, finding the voice belonged to a man who stood a few feet away by the water tanks with a bag over his arm and a cell phone in his hand—a journalist.

"Not right now, thanks."

I pivoted away from him, only to be met by Philander, approaching me at a fast clip. "Miss Gibb! Good game, Miss Gibb," he said, meeting me with a tight, fake smile. I didn't offer him one in return. "This is Ralph Goldberg from *Morning*—"

"Nice to see you, but I gotta get to the locker room to talk to the team."

"But Ralph here is doing a piece on—"

I stopped him with a shake of my head, then turned to this Ralph Goldberg guy. "Listen, I don't do interviews. I have no comment on my history at Georgia Tech or my career in the IWFL. I'm here to rebuild the football program at Douglass, and this loss is a minor setback. We're going to work hard and come back next week with a win against Edison."

I offered him a pleasant wave before grabbing my clipboard to head back to the field house, where I was met with the usual scent of sweat and grass, but what I wasn't prepared for was so many ruddy cheeks, eyes wide with sadness.

Marcus sat on the bench closest to me. He had good instincts and fast feet. He just needed better blocking to give him time to complete his routes. I hit his shoulder pad and walked toward the center of the benches, which were shaped in a U around me. Jaylin sat opposite, his uniform clean. With his ankle still not 100 percent, I'd kept him out of the game. He wasn't happy about it, but his health came first.

"You played well tonight. Just not well enough. I won't coddle you. We have a lot of work to do, a lot of improvement, but we can use this first game as a learnin' experience. For all of us." I paused for a moment to look around, the coaches standing here and there among the team. Al leaned up against a locker, utterly bored. McGuire, though, who'd come in right after me, stood just off to my left, staring at the ground, almost imperceptibly nodding along with what I had said.

I caught some of the players' eyes and held their attention before I went on. "I know what it's like to be the underdog. It's pretty much been my life," I said, and some of them laughed. "The thing about bein' the underdog is that the others let their guard down. They don't expect you to be great. So that's what we'll be, great. Let's give them a little shock and awe."

Heads nodded, and I clapped a few times. "Bring it in. Let's go."

A couple kids yelled out sounds and words of encouragement as they crowded in around me, hands in the middle. I started the chant, which had become commonplace now.

"Work!"

"Hard!" They called.

"Be!"

"Better!"

"Douglass on three. One, two, three!"

"Douglass!"

We all broke up, and they went to shower off the grime as I escaped to the hallway. Once in my office, I jotted down a few notes on a legal pad, things to watch for during film tomorrow morning. I'd meant it when I'd said the opposing team tonight wasn't any better than we were. We'd just been outplayed and outcoached.

And some things needed to change.

But before I could finish writing down my last thought, I

overheard the coaches in the hall making plans to go somewhere called the Public. I assumed it was a bar, and that I wouldn't get an invitation. After a few seconds, the voices passed and my assumptions were proved correct.

They left, and I was alone in my closet. In no rush to go back to my new house, I called my father. It was late and I knew he wouldn't pick up, but I left a voicemail anyway. I might be the head coach of the Otters, yet sometimes I needed a little pep talk from *my* coach.

"Hey, Daddy. I know you're probably asleep by now and you have a game tomorrow, but I was calling to fill you in on what's been going on here. . . . You can probably guess it hasn't been smooth. We had our first game tonight and lost by two points—might as well have been two hundred though." I tapped an Expo marker on my desk. "Anyway, I'll talk to you soon. Good luck tomorrow."

I hung up and tossed my phone on the desk. My father and I weren't big talkers. Outside of football and the Falcons, we didn't have much to say to each other. But I guess when you're raised by a single father, that wasn't unusual.

I grabbed my bag and headed out to my car. The parking lot was empty, since I was the last one to leave. Of course. I drove to Sonja's house in silence and quietly unlocked the front door, making sure to keep my footsteps light so as not to wake her. I didn't mind.

I was comfortable being on my own and had learned to stick to myself, but as I sat in my new bedroom, I glanced around the bare walls and it made me sad. Was this what my life had become? A lonely existence with no pictures to hang, no memories to relive.

I flopped back on my mattress, the idea of being truly alone haunting me until well into the night.

BY THE next morning, I was ready to get back to work with the team. I called a brief meeting before film to talk about the changes I wanted to make. We were all there, stuffed in my closet office, except for Al and McGuire.

Surprise, surprise.

I reached for my frozen coffee, my eyes watering with yet another yawn.

"Late night?" Ken asked, eyeing me with playful suspicion from the corner of the room.

"Late night, but not for what you're alluding to."

"Oh no?" We all turned to Connor, who stood in the doorway. His angry glare was perceptible even under the brim of his hat.

I narrowed my brows at him. "Excuse me?"

"I'd think the beauty queen coach would have men falling at her feet."

Al stepped forward and tossed a few pieces of paper on my desk. I didn't need to see what was on them to know what he was referring to, but I pulled them toward me with my index finger anyway.

There it was in big bold letters.

Georgia Beauty Queen Becomes Douglass High's New Football Coach, Loses First Matchup

All the coaches grabbed at the extra copies.

"You were in a pageant?" Erik asked, laughing. "Look at you! You're a woman. Like, a real woman."

"Of course I'm a real woman, Johnson. I'm not Pinocchio," I snapped.

Ronnie snickered to himself.

"What do you have to say, Rosario?" I asked, hoping the sharpness of my tone would wipe the grin off his face. It did, and his cheeks turned an embarrassed shade of red.

"Say it," I said, standing up.

"Coach . . . you're kind of . . ."

"What?"

"You're kind of . . . hot," he said, holding up the picture of me from when I was in college, wearing a sparkly blue dress with my hair all tousled. I hadn't even made it to the second round, which wasn't unexpected, although my competitive nature had been disappointed.

"For fuck's sake." I threw my pen on the desk and glared at McGuire. Al smirked next him. "I don't need to explain myself to you," I said. "To any of you."

But as I looked them all in the eyes, I knew I'd lost my credibility.

"Yes, I was in a beauty pageant. I grew up in the South, pageants and debutante parties were a big thing. My grandma wanted me to do it, so I did it to make her happy. Now, all y'all satisfied?"

"There's nothing to be ashamed of," Ken said.

McGuire shifted his weight, drawing my attention back to him. "You said you don't like the cameras, but this"—he pointed to the paper—"says otherwise."

I snatched all the papers out of their hands and tore them up before tossing them in the garbage. "We're makin' changes on the squad startin' today." I looked at Al. "Defense played like shit yesterday. You better get it together out there. Xavier missed every tackle. Spencer's movin' to safety and Anderson will start quarterback."

"What?" McGuire and Al said at the same time.

"You didn't talk about this with me," McGuire said, moving closer to me.

"I don't need to. I'm the head coach. Spencer is too arrogant on and off the field to be quarterback. He holds on to the ball too long and thinks he's better than he is. Nate is a hard worker, and the team will listen to him. He just hasn't been given the chance to show off his arm."

"Spencer doesn't know any of the defensive plays," Al argued.

"Then teach him!" I waved my arm toward the door. "Do your job, Al. We have lazy players on this team, and I can only assume it's because they were allowed to be."

He opened his mouth, but I held my hand up. He was on my last nerve.

"Al, I spoke to you last week about this. I'm not gonna have my decisions questioned at every turn. You're either gonna do what's best for the team or you leave."

"You don't know what's best for the team!" Al roared.

"I do. And you're not it. Get out. I don't want to see you on my field again."

Al's mouth dropped open like a fish.

"Rosario, you're on defense today."

Rosario stuttered.

"Everyone out of my office. Now."

They all moved in silence except for Al, who mumbled about how I would regret this, but I was too irate to care.

"McGuire, stay."

He turned, took his hat off, and crumpled it in his hands, his eyes boring into mine. "Why'd you do that?"

"You know why I did that," I said, my voice nearly a whisper through gritted teeth. "Al was the laziest person on this team. He didn't do anything for the players."

"He's been here forever. He's a teacher here."

"So what? He's been here too long. He needed to go. I know you aren't dim-witted enough to think otherwise. Because as much as you hate me, you *know* I know what I'm doin'."

He crossed his arms. "What do you want?"

"I want you to back me up. The more you try to tear me down, the more motivated you make me. So if you want to keep bringin' these stupid pictures and articles in, go for it. You'll find your ass out on the curb with Al."

His jaw worked as we stood off, neither one backing down. I knew he was a good coach, and a more than half-decent player in his time. I also knew that he wouldn't leave this team in the lurch. He simply needed to not be an asshole.

"I have one question for you," he said after a while.

"What?"

"Why are you here? Why this team? Why Minneapolis?"

"That's more than one question."

He shook his head. "Smart-ass."

"You think I got to this position by bein' nice? By rollin' over?"

He scrubbed a hand over his jaw. "Just answer me, why are you here?"

"Because I live in the real world. I, unlike everyone else on this staff, am not afforded the luxury of bein' lazy. I can't just pass, I need to excel. I hit my ceiling at Tech. Football is still a man's world, and I've barely got my toe in the door. I needed to go where I was wanted, and where I'd be able to shine. Where I could show everyone what I can do. That's why I'm here. Because I can turn this team around."

His eyes narrowed briefly before he dropped his arms.

"And I'd really like your help with that," I added.

After a beat, he put his hat back on his head. "I still don't like you."

"I don't like you either."

The idea crossed my mind that I should tell him I'd moved in with his friend, but the hell with it. He'd find out sooner or later. Save that fight for a different day.

CHAPTER
9

Charlie

Parking my car in front of a brick twin townhouse, I checked the address on the slip of paper again before turning my car off. It was late, right in the middle of dinnertime, but I felt I owed Jaylin an explanation. After his obvious disappointment during and after the game on Friday and his slow performance at practice the past two days, I wanted to have a conversation with him away from the other players and in a room that wasn't my tiny office.

A light in the front window illuminated the living room and an orange-tinted wreath with ribbon woven around it hung on the door. When I rang the doorbell, a woman in purple scrubs, with dark skin and hair in a neat bun, opened the door. "Hi, I'm right in the middle of making dinner. Can I help you?"

"Ms. Bose, I'm Charlie Gibb, Jaylin's coach."

"Oh, hello." She tilted her head.

"I wanted to talk to Jaylin."

Worry etched itself on her face. "Is everything all right? Did something happen?"

"Yes—I mean, no . . ."

Her confused look told me I was screwing this up already, and a voice in the back of my head that sounded a lot like McGuire's reminded me how all the players and their parents were used to talking with him.

"I wanted to sit down with Jaylin and talk to him about the game on Friday and his ankle."

Ms. Bose nodded and opened the door wider for me to enter her house. "I've been on night shift for the past two weeks and I missed the game. He told me he didn't play at all." She gestured me toward a beige couch in the living room as she went to turn off the burners in the kitchen before joining me. "He was really upset."

"I know," I said, leaning forward. "That's why I wanted to come here to speak to him."

She shook her head, eyes on a framed photo of Jaylin. "I told him he had to be careful and give himself time to rest, but of course he didn't listen to me."

Her exasperated smile made me smile. "High ankle sprains are tricky injuries—"

"Oh, I know," she said, raising her hand. "I had multiple doctors explain it to him. But Jay's got a thick head, like his father." She rolled her eyes.

"Ms. Bose—"

"Call me Deb."

"Deb," I started again, "I know Jaylin's upset with me, but I know what he's capable of when he's completely healthy. I've watched film from last year, and he's got a lot of natural talent. He just has to be patient while he fully heals so he doesn't injure himself further."

Deb nodded. "And you came all the way over here to say that?"

I lifted a shoulder. "I know I have to earn trust from the players, and I'm not afraid of that."

She eyed me in that way only a mother could. "How's it going for you at the school? I have to say I've never heard of a woman football coach."

"Yeah, you and a lot of other people," I said with a bitter laugh. "I'm really just trying to work hard. We're all trying."

Deb winked. "I like that." She got up and called up the stairs. "Jaylin, come down here, please."

Seconds later, quick steps trotted downstairs. Jaylin's eyes found his mother, and then me. "Hey, Coach."

"Hi. I wanted to talk to you for a couple minutes."

"I'm going to go finish supper," Deb said, ducking out of the room.

Jaylin sat down across from me, in the seat his mother had vacated. "What's up?"

"You have a lot of good qualities that I admire." When he raised his brows, I continued, "You wear your heart on your sleeve. You're smart. You're energetic. But you're also really stubborn."

He hmmed and put his chin in his palm.

"I might know a little somethin' about being stubborn," I added.

That made him laugh.

"Look, Jaylin, you are a leader on this team. The other kids obviously look up to you, and they should. But that means you need to lead them by example."

He started to roll his eyes, so I leaned forward to catch his attention. "Don't make that face. You know they do. The question is, what are you going to do about it?"

Deb's head popped out from around the kitchen wall. She pointedly cleared her throat at Jaylin. I went on, "Are you going to step up and be the captain they need, or are you going to lie back, do the same old thing? You know what it's been like, you want it to stay the same?"

Jaylin clapped his palm around his fist. "I want to win, Coach."

"Me too. I need you to show it in practice. Even when you're mad at me for not playing you."

Deb walked back into the living room and put a hand on her son's shoulder. "Coach Gibb knows what she's doing. If she didn't think you were physically ready, then you need to accept that. What would've happened if you had played and hurt yourself worse, huh?"

I nodded. "I've seen a lot of players get held back by going into the game too early. I understand that you wanted to play last weekend, but I wanted to make sure you were completely healed. Now that I know you are, I promise you will start, but you need to start acting like the player I know you are. If you are at your best, the rest of the team will follow along. But if you half-ass it—" I glanced up at Deb. "Excuse my language."

She shrugged.

I turned back to Jaylin. "If you practice half-speed, so will the others, and we'll end up where y'all were last year."

"I get it. I get it," he said, nodding.

"This is your senior year, you've been on this varsity team for three years now, I know you must be getting some letters from colleges now."

"A few," he said with a shy smile.

Deb pointed to a desk in the corner. "We have a couple, but I'm not sure what I'm supposed to do with them."

"Mind if I take a look?"

She grabbed a couple of envelopes from a drawer and handed them to me. "Jaylin's dad and I divorced a few years ago, and he's not always in the picture. I try to be there for him as much as I can, but I also need to pay the bills, and I take on a lot of extra shifts at the hospital to make sure Jay has everything he needs." She waved her hands to the papers. "I want to help him with this, but . . ."

I stood up and patted her on the back. "I would be happy to help. I did a lot of recruiting in Georgia. Don't worry."

She hugged me, whispering, "Thank you. Thank you."

Jaylin stood up, and I hugged him too. "Just focus on keeping your grades up and doing your best on the field, and we'll get you there."

"Thanks, Coach."

I made my way to the door, but Deb stopped me. "Want to stay for dinner? I've got a casserole in the oven."

"Oh no, thank you, though. I appreciate that. Y'all enjoy your night. Jaylin, see you tomorrow."

When I got in my car, Deb and Jaylin were by the front door, waving at me. I grinned. I'd do whatever I could to get him a scholarship.

Back at the house, I dropped my bag inside the door as I kicked my sneakers off to put them in the closet.

"Hey."

I glanced over my shoulder to find Piper splayed out on the sofa.

"Hi. What're you doing here?"

"Sonja talked me into yoga." She grabbed at her workout pants, making a face. "It's hot yoga, she said it's supposed to be great." She sat up with a smile pasted on her face. "Want to come?"

I shook my head. "I have laundry to do."

"You're going to make me put up with all of Sonja's perfect poses and breathing on my own?" As Sonja came downstairs, with her hair back behind a headband, Piper pointed to her and breathed deeply with her eyes closed.

"It's good for your mind and body," Sonja said, grabbing a green yoga mat from the closet. "Mindful breathing."

Piper waved her off. "I invited Charlie, but she said she has laundry." She sat up. "We should switch. I'll do your laundry while you breathe mindfully."

"Nah, I'm good. Thanks."

Sonja elbowed me. "Come on, it'll be fun."

Piper stood up and made a slashing movement across her throat. "It won't be fun. But you should still come. Oh! We can go out for drinks after."

I gestured upstairs. "I have stuff to do." Sonja and Piper both stared at me, and I laughed. "Really. I do."

Sonja crossed her arms. "You know, I hear you sneaking around at night, trying not to make any noise."

"I know you go to bed early. I don't want to wake you up."

"This is your house too, you don't need to worry about that. Piper certainly didn't."

Piper nodded.

"You also don't have to hide in your room," Sonja added.

"I know."

"Do you?"

"I'm getting the feeling you don't really like us," Piper said, making sad puppy-dog eyes.

I clucked my tongue. "You're silly."

"We invite you to come out and you never do," Sonja said, moving to tie her sneakers.

"Yeah, and when you're turning down Sonja's social invitations, you know you've moved into hermit territory."

With them laying out all the evidence of my fear to venture out into the world and open myself up to their friendship, I suddenly felt ashamed. They were right. They had only ever been kind to me, but in return, I'd declined every invitation to dinner or anything. I'd been here for weeks now, and hadn't managed to make any new friends. Here were two women freely offering up their time, and I was too afraid to say yes.

Silly.

"I guess I could do laundry tomorrow."

"Yes! Put off to tomorrow whatever you could do today." Sonja leveled a glare at Piper. "That's not how that goes."

"Whatever." Piper handed me my sneakers back. "To a sauna we go."

I slipped my sneakers back on and followed Piper out the front door as Sonja locked up. "We really should get that drink after," I said. "We'll have to replenish liquids."

Sonja growled good-naturedly behind us as Piper threw her hands up. "That's what I'm saying!"

CHAPTER
10

Charlie

Tossing the cork of the 2015 Malbec on the counter, I felt my mouth water as the purple-red liquid filled up the face of Idris Elba. I picked up the green glass and smelled the wine before taking a sip.

Sonja leaned over the counter. "You're a professional."

"No, I just like wine." I twisted my hand, facing the painted gaze of Idris out to her. "Where'd you get these glasses?"

"A Christmas present from Piper. One year it was David Beckham's body on a pillowcase. And the year before that it was a watch with Channing Tatum's face on the face." She showed off said watch with the hour and minute marks surrounding Channing's smiling face.

I laughed and took Idris to the living room. Sonja followed.

"My favorite thing to do on Sundays is drink a nice glass of red and watch a little bit of football. Relax," I said as I turned on the TV, searching for the Vikings versus Packers game. I threw my feet up on an ottoman and settled my head back against a pillow—exactly what I needed.

This past week of practice had been challenging, to say the least.

I'd brought up a coach from junior varsity, Dave Watson, to help out on defense, and it had made a world of difference. Al was deadweight, and the kids responded much better to someone with energy and motivation.

Brett had pitched a fit when I'd informed him he'd no longer be starting QB, but after I'd made him run a few laps, he was too exhausted to do anything but stand on the sideline. With Nate in, the rest of the players seemed to fall into line. They understood that big changes needed to be made to make some big gains.

The downside was the blowback I'd received. I had gotten an earful from Jack Spencer, Brett's dad, on the phone, telling me his son was a great hockey player, but they'd chosen for him to play football instead. I'd told him they were both welcome to go back to the rink if they'd like. And then he'd called me a bitch.

Apparently, Spencer men didn't handle being told what to do by women very well.

But by the end of the week, the team had improved immensely. So much so that we won our game on Friday. Mr. Spencer had nothing to say to me after that.

The Otters actually looked like they could pull out a winning season after all. My red wine was well earned.

"Would you mind if I invited some others to come over and relax here too?"

"No." I took another sip of wine. Nothing could take me out of my zone today.

"Great." Sonja went back to the kitchen as she said, "Piper and Blake should be here any second, but I know Connor had a thing, he won't get here for about another hour. Bear's—"

Nothing could take me out of my zone today. Except *that*. "McGuire's coming over?"

"Yeah." She poked her head around the doorway to look at me. "Is that okay? I figured since you work together and all . . ."

"Yeah," I started, murmuring into my glass. "I never told him I moved in. We don't talk much."

Sonja came back to sit next to me with a water bottle. "Sometimes the best relationships are those that challenge us."

"That sounds like it should be embroidered on a pillow."

"It probably is." She smiled. "He's a nice guy beneath all the . . ." She narrowed her eyebrows and pursed her lips in an imitation of McGuire.

I choked on a sip of wine when I laughed. "That looks nothing like him."

"Hey, hey. Sunday fun-day." A thick Minnesota-accented voice barreled through the front door before the body did.

The man had to be at least six foot three, 280 pounds easy. His arms were covered in tattoos, and his long hair hung loose below his chin. His big, cheesy grin slowly left his face when he turned to his left and spied us—me—on the couch.

Sonja stood up and punched his waiting, outstretched palm as if they greeted each other that way all the time. "Best behavior," she said quietly to him before tipping her head to me. "Charlie, Bear. Bear, Charlie."

I waved. "Hey, how's it going?"

"Good." He sat down in the corner of the couch, taking up as little space as possible with his thick legs. As if I had a disease.

"What's your squat?" I asked, looking him up and down, and he loosened up a bit.

He scratched his chin. "Uh, three fifty, three sixty-five."

I nodded, impressed. He was quite the specimen. I pointed to him with my glass. "You're the ex–hockey player."

"You're the football coach."

"You're the best friend."

"And you're the enemy."

"I like a man who shoots straight." I pointed a finger gun at him.

He reluctantly smiled. "That's me. Straight shooter." He gave me a little brow wiggle that had Sonja slapping the back of his head. He jerked away from her, but then pulled her close to him, resting his head against her torso. "It's the Lord's day. No hitting on the Lord's day."

She ran her hand through his hair, the intimate action piquing my interest as to the exact nature of their relationship. I stored the questions away to ask later, and put my empty glass down on the side table next to me. "That sounds like something my gram would've said."

"Smart woman, your gram," Bear said with a pat to the side of Sonja's thigh before he let her go and settled more comfortably into the couch. We fell into easy conversation. He might've been big, but he wasn't nearly as hard to get to know as his friend. He, as Sonja had described him, was a giant teddy bear.

Piper and Blake showed up not too long after, and I received the same suspicious treatment from Blake when we were introduced. But I didn't mind his glare. The pictures, truly, didn't do him justice. Blake Reed was one good-looking man.

"Piper, you did fine for yourself with that one," I whispered once we were alone in the kitchen.

She giggled. "I know, right? God, he's just . . ." She bit her lip. "Sometimes I can't believe that we ended up together. After I struggled for so long with my business and had terrible luck with guys, I never thought I'd find somebody like him."

"Like who?" Blake popped out of nowhere, and she startled.

Piper swiveled around, putting her hand on his chest. "I told you, you have to stop sneaking up on me like that. It's not good for my heart."

He pouted slightly, saying, "Sorry, Sunshine," and kissed her sweetly on the neck. He hung his arm around her shoulders as she opened up a couple of her own beers. "And I wanted to apologize to you too," he said to me. "Bear, Connor, and I have all been friends for a really long time, and we're protective of each other. Him not getting the desk was a big bummer, but that's not to say it's anything against you. It's just, he's our friend, we have to stick up for him."

"I respect that." I took one of the dark bottles Piper offered me. "I'd want my friends to do the same for me. If I had any," I added with a pathetic laugh.

Piper looked at me with such sympathy I thought she'd cry. "You have me and Sonja now."

"I'm joking, I'm joking," I said. "I have friends . . . a few." I didn't like admitting that I'd always had a hard time making friends because I put my job before most of my relationships; to avoid having an intervention, I changed the subject to the bottle in my hand. "So, what's this?"

"That is my Platinum Blonde. Like you."

I fingered my grocery-store-color-dyed hair as I tilted the bottle, admiring the Out of the Bottle Brewery logo, which looked like a bottle but in the shape of a woman. "I'm really more of a wine drinker," I said honestly.

Blake took his own beer from Piper. "Try it. You may like it."

I took a small sip and held back a wince. It was way too bitter for me.

"Don't like the hops?" Piper asked.

"Uh, yeah, I guess."

She nodded. "Next time I'll bring over my blueberry. It's a new one I'm working on, much fruitier than anything I usually make."

I shrugged. "I'll give it a shot."

The three of us made our way back into the living room and had just settled down for a nice chat when the front door opened.

"Aye, there he is," Bear boomed.

Connor's eyes took in the room, at first glancing right over me as if I were invisible before crashing back into me.

"Surprise," I said with jazz hands.

"Gibb?"

"Charlie," Piper corrected.

"What are you doing here?"

"She lives here," Sonja told him.

"And you didn't tell me?"

"Didn't think I had to," I answered.

"So, what, you're all pals now?" He pointed to Sonja, Piper, and me sitting together. The three of us laughed at his ridiculous question.

He turned to Bear and Blake, both enthralled with something on their phones at the moment. He sat on the teal ottoman with a huff. "Traitors."

"How was the game?" Piper asked, leaning over to poke Blake in the leg so he'd put his phone away.

Connor fiddled with his hat. "Eight–three."

I sat forward, trying to get his attention. "Game? What game?"

He hesitated before telling me, "My brother plays soccer."

"Your brother who was at our game on Friday?"

"How do you know my brother?"

It was really more of an accusation than a question, and the air in the living room changed. I glanced around. The others' faces displayed varying degrees of concern or embarrassment.

"Now that we're all here, how 'bout we get dinner started?" Sonja stood up, probably to cut the tension.

Blake hopped right up, tugging Piper along. "We got the grill."

Bear clapped. "I'm ready for some barbecue."

McGuire made a move to follow as they all left, but I held my hand up. "Wait. Can you wait?"

"Actually, no." He shook his head. "I may have to listen to you on the field, but I don't here."

I stood up and reached for his arm, but he backed away before I got close. "What's your problem with me?" When he didn't answer, I stepped into his space. "No, really. What is it? I'm here now, here's your chance. Lay it out there."

He breathed deep through his nose, his eyes bouncing around the room. He took his hat off and ran his hand over his short hair a few times before sitting down on the couch opposite me. "You're really good, okay? That's what pisses me off. It'd be much easier to believe this whole thing was a publicity stunt if you didn't know what you were doing, but, shocker, you do."

I rubbed my forehead. Was he serious? "You don't like me because I'm good at what I do?"

"Well, when you say it like that, I sound like an asshole."

"You are an asshole."

His gaze met mine, searing me for a few moments. His jaw worked back and forth before he finally broke, his mouth opening wide for a laugh I'd never heard before. An honest-to-goodness laugh. Not a huff or a rude snort, but a real laugh.

And it felt good.

"I am," he said eventually, then leaned over, his hat hanging from the tips of his fingers. "I'm not always. It seems just with you."

The confession hit me hard. It was the first time he'd expressed any kind of genuine emotion toward me that wasn't rage. He wasn't lying when he said he was a quiet person, which made his words all the more powerful when he did speak. They were measured, the definition of *say what you mean and mean what you say*.

His honesty with me was unexpected, but not unwanted.

"It doesn't have anything to do with you being . . ." He motioned his hand down my body. "A girl."

"A woman, you mean."

He inhaled heavily as if it was such a chore to talk to me, a familiar sound. "Yes, a woman."

Our eyes met again, and if I didn't know better I'd have

thought they briefly drifted down to my legs, exposed below my shorts. But then those electric-blue eyes flickered up to where my T-shirt hung loosely off my shoulder.

And I knew *that* wasn't by accident.

"What about your own stunt with the article in my office?" I asked, crossing my legs, a little unnerved by this new friction between us. The kind that wasn't angry.

"I didn't find that. Al did."

"I can't stand that guy." I let out an annoyed groan and reached for my empty wineglass.

"What are you drinking?" McGuire stood up and held his hand out to me, wiggling his fingers up and down.

I tilted my head to the side. "Does this mean you've changed your mind about me? We're going to be best friends now?"

He dropped his arm and rolled his head in a circle. "Never mind."

When he turned, I stood up and followed him to the kitchen, not wanting the teasing to end quite yet. We could see the other four outside, chatting and laughing; but instead of going to them, McGuire opened up a beer and leaned against the wall by the refrigerator.

I refilled my wine, avoiding his gaze while I sipped, but by the time I put the glass down, I found Connor's attention on the label of his beer bottle as he picked at it with his thumb.

"It was a good call," he said, "moving Nate up."

My insides warmed, but I played it cool. "A compliment? From you?"

He smirked. "Are you going to write it down in your diary?"

"September fifteenth, the day the Grinch's heart grew three sizes."

"How do you even know I have a heart?" he asked as I walked to the door.

I looked over my shoulder. "Just a hunch."

CHAPTER
11

Connor

How do you even know I have a heart?

Just a hunch.

A day later, Charlie's words still followed me.

I did have a heart. I just didn't show it very often. Not after I'd seen how people could be cruel to my brother. Not after my dad died. And especially not after what had happened with Alison.

But I wouldn't tell that to Gibb. We were nowhere near trading secrets over chocolate and nail polish, we were barely even . . . friends?

"Hey."

Speak of the devil.

I glanced away from the crowded cafeteria to Gibb, who sported a long-sleeved black shirt and athletic pants that did nothing to camouflage the curve of her ass. She tossed her hair over her shoulder, and I swore I could smell some kind of perfume on her.

It wasn't like I didn't know she was a woman, but there were times it was more apparent than others. Like when she stood right next to me, her arm brushing mine.

"Hey yourself."

We'd had lunch duty together every day since the start of school, but the way she looked at me was different today. Her features were relaxed, not that usual hard-stone look. I actually forgot I was supposed to hate her.

"Did you—" She stopped whatever she was about to say to me to wave at a pair of boys. "Hey, y'all! Put that chair down! What do you think you're doing with that?"

When they didn't immediately comply, she took two steps toward them, and they quickly put the chair down. She faced me, and I tipped my chin to her.

"You almost sound like a real teacher."

"And you almost sound like a homo sapien."

"Me talk good," I said, moving over slightly to give her more room when she stood next to me again.

"Now jokes too? After yesterday, we might just be telling each other secrets by next week."

I froze. It was as if she knew exactly what I'd been thinking. But I quickly played it off and skimmed my gaze around the room.

"Don't worry, I won't tell anyone you're warming up to me," she whispered conspiratorially.

"And I won't tell anyone I saw your *NSYNC T-shirt on the bathroom floor."

"How do you know it's mine?"

"Because Sonja has better taste."

"Hey now." She whipped her head around to me. "Those five guys were the soundtrack to my adolescence. JC has the voice of an angel."

I smirked.

So did she.

"What was your soundtrack?" she asked, eyes back on the kids.

I thought about it. "Eminem, I guess."

"Angry music for an angry boy?"

The question threw me for a loop. "I'm angry?"

She made a face. "Yeah. Obviously." She held her palms up, making a silent point with herself as evidence. "I mean . . ."

Yes, I was upset about not being head coach. Yes, I'd taken it out on her. But was my past that obvious? Did I not hide it as well as I thought I did? "I *was* angry, yeah. But not anymore." When she raised one eyebrow, I backtracked. "Not really."

"What happened? Your stocks in Apple went down?"

"My dad died when I was fourteen."

Her eyebrows rose, and I knew I'd surprised her. Hell, I'd surprised myself with the admission.

I never talked about my dad or my family. Talking led to

emotion, and I preferred to avoid sentiment. The fact that this life tidbit had spilled out of me was completely out of character. And I didn't know how to take it back.

Or if I even wanted to.

Gibb tied her hair low on her neck with one of the elastic bands on her wrist. Her brown eyes were filled with something I'd never seen before: empathy. "I'm sorry. That's a tough time to lose a parent." She paused just long enough for me to feel awkward before she said, "I never knew my mother. The only thing I have of her is pictures of us together when I was a baby. She died when I was two. Her car collided with a tractor trailer."

She said it so unaffectedly, I wasn't sure what to say. I wasn't good with these kinds of conversations to begin with, and I was totally out of my league with this particular one.

Thank God she spoke so I didn't have to. "I don't know what it's like to grieve a parent, but I know what it's like to miss one. The only things I know about my mom are stories from my dad and grandmother, and I'm sad I never got the chance to have her. Maybe I would've turned out differently."

She looked off into the distance and crossed her arms. "Maybe I would've turned out more of a lady like Gram always wanted me to be. Maybe I wouldn't have played football." She shrugged. "Maybe I would've gotten my first kiss before someone had to dare Ryan Lipton to do it when I was eighteen. Who knows."

She smiled good-naturedly, and I didn't know if I should laugh with her or not. That was a lot of information to unpack from a woman I barely knew off the field. But in this noisy cafeteria, it felt easier to say things like, "My dad owned a little hardware store. Ironic that he died when he fell off one of the ladders he sold there."

"That's awful." She cringed. "I'm sorry for you and your family. Is it just you, your brother, and your mom?"

"I'm the oldest of four," I said, stuffing my hands in my pockets. "There's Siobhan, Brigid, and Sean."

"Wow."

"Good Catholic family." I suppressed my smile. "I miss my dad every day. He was the one who taught me how to throw, but he never got to see me start any games."

She touched my elbow, and I glanced down to where her fingers were on my skin.

"Sean had a really hard time. We all did, but him especially. He didn't get that his dad was gone forever."

"That must've been really hard to deal with."

I nodded. "I sort of became the man of the house . . . that sounds lame when I say it out loud." I kept talking, as if I were in some kind of vortex that sucked words out of my brain, my mouth refusing to shut up. "Sean was only in first grade. By proxy, I became his dad."

Her hand lightly rubbed up and down my arm before dropping. "That's a lot of responsibility to put on a kid in high school."

"Yeah, but it's not like I wasn't going to do what I had to. We had to figure out how to be a family without my dad. There's no way you don't do whatever you have to when you find your mom quietly crying in her closet so her kids don't hear."

By habit, I reached up to my head for my hat, but it wasn't there. Instead I skimmed my hand through my hair before shaking my head. I felt dizzy, as if spilling my guts took a physical toll. "It's not—I didn't mean to say all this."

She pivoted away from me like she knew I was embarrassed and afforded me some privacy in my discomfort. I cleared my throat and straightened my already straight tie.

After a few moments, Gibb looked over, head tilted, studying me with unreadable dark eyes.

"What?" I asked.

"You're a bit of a puzzle, Connor McGuire."

She wagged her head back and forth as if deciding her next words, and I waited patiently to hear them. But instead of her Georgia peach voice, I got an earsplitting buzzer.

Time for next period.

And just like that, the spell was broken.

"Hey, Coach," Orlando Reyes said as he slung his backpack on his shoulder, walking out the door.

Gibb and I answered at the same time: "Hey."

Our eyes met. We were both coaches.

On the same football team.

She had the title.

I was left with *assistant coach* next to my name.

And I wanted to punch myself because of everything I'd just revealed.

I hauled ass back to my classroom, needing to get away.

A woman I'd dated had once told me I was cold. She was a therapist and said I hadn't reached the top of Maslow's hierarchy, and that if I wanted to be a self-actualized person I needed to work on my intimate relationships and self-esteem. I told her she was full of shit.

I was an actualized person. I just *actually* didn't care to talk about my personal life to other people. That conversation in the middle of a crowded high school cafeteria was definitely a first.

But once practice started, we went back to our usual routine. It was a relief not to have to think about Gibb as a friend, or how weak I'd looked when I told her those personal details about my life. At practice, we were football coaches. There was no silence between us to interpret.

After a particularly bad play, Gibb raised her hand to me. "McGuire, what's your offense doing out there? Are they taking this week off after winning a game?"

I tugged my hat farther down my head and called Nate over. "You're bouncing all over the place, and it's slowing you down."

He stuck his mouth guard in his helmet. "I'm trying to get rid of the ball. Bernie missed the block and—"

"Forget Bernie. Hopping around in the pocket isn't going to help you. You're off-balance, and you can't find your receiver under pressure. Drop back, keep your knees bent, plant your foot, find your target."

I mimed the last two steps, accentuating how to settle into his knees and plant his foot before the release.

"Stay on your toes but keep those knees bent as you move or else you might as well be standing still. Got it?"

"Yeah, Coach, yeah."

"Good. Show me." I smacked his helmet twice, and he ran back onto the field to the huddle.

Gibb clapped a few times. "Let's go! Simpson, stay on your man. If Anderson gets sacked one more time, everyone's running laps."

A collective groan rolled over the players.

"On your toes, knees bent!" I reminded Nate through cupped hands as he set up behind Krajewski on the line.

He took the snap and dropped back, and I zeroed in on his feet, watching as he did exactly as I'd told him. He released for twenty yards, straight to Marcus.

I raised my eyebrows to Gibb in a challenge. She waved me off before circling her finger in the air. "Run it again!"

CHAPTER

12

Charlie

We were down by one with a minute some left on the clock, but we'd just scored. The opposing team's defense was fast; twice they'd intercepted Nate's passes for touchdowns, pushing us to move to a running game at the beginning of the second half. But with literal seconds left, we needed to go for the two-point conversion to win the game.

"Take the kick," McGuire said in my ear through the headphones, crunching on a lollipop.

I clenched my fist, tempted to slap the candy out of his mouth. "I'm not confident we can get the W with the extra time."

"Well, I'm not confident Jaylin can get through that line. Sixty-two's been on him all night." *Crunch. Crunch. Crunch.* "Remember what happened in game one?"

"Thanks for the reminder." I pulled my headphones off. "Anderson!"

Nate turned, and I gave him the signal for the conversion play. He nodded, and set the team up at the line.

I glanced over to McGuire, who shook his head. I fantasized about strangling him.

Nate called the play, took the snap, and tossed to Jaylin, who had miraculously sprouted wings like Icarus and flew over the heads of the defense right into the end zone.

There wasn't much time for cheering because the other team was already taking positions for kickoff, clearly anxious to try to take it back. Joel Cooper, the skinny-ass kicker, took his place, and landed an onside in perfect placement for us to recover it. Nate took a knee and the clock ran down.

The team went wild.

Another W in the books.

I marched directly over to McGuire and shoved my headphones into his chest, digging my knuckles into his pec. "Next time, I will choke you with those lollipops."

He caught the headphones when I let them fall before I spun away from him. When would he learn? I had gotten this job for a reason.

I grabbed Jaylin by his jersey and pulled him close to me. "You earned this one. You earned it!"

He grinned through his face mask. "Thanks, Coach."

I bumped my forearm to his before congratulating a couple of other players, the whole time sensing eyes on me. I glanced around until I saw him, the other team's coach blatantly glaring at me. I ignored it and lined up behind my players, shaking hands, hearing murmurs of "Good game" all around me.

Until I got to him.

This guy, Brad, who I read had come from Alabama, sneered at me. "What're you doing out on this field?"

By habit, I met his extended hand. "Excuse me?"

He squeezed hard, and I ground my teeth together to keep from flinching. He dragged me in close to him to whisper, "Go back to the kitchen where you belong."

I smiled as politely as possible, knowing our players surrounded us. "Hey, let me ask you a question. What's it like for your mama to also be your cousin? I heard you like to keep it all in the family where you're from."

"Somebody should shut up that smart mouth of yours."

I yanked out of his grip. "Don't ever t—"

A hard grip around my bicep dragged me to the side, and I flipped around to find it was McGuire, who took my place in front of Brad. I didn't hear what he said to the older man, but whatever it was made Brad back up two steps.

"You wanna run with the big dogs, but you can't even fight your own battles?" Brad said to me, his face bright red, his index finger pointed at me.

I started to make another retort, but McGuire forced me to move, shoving me back, saying, "Leave it. The jackass isn't worth it."

I growled and pulled my wrist out of his grip, torn between appreciation for him sticking up for me and fury for him sticking up for me. A couple of the kids caught the scuffle, but I couldn't look at them, the shame and anger of what the other coach had said washing over me. I knew his small-mindedness wasn't my problem, but it affected me. Made me feel two inches tall, like I was back in middle school when the principal had sat me down to tell me I couldn't play on the football team because "it's just not what girls do."

I'd won that particular fight, but that didn't mean I wanted to keep having it over and over.

A girl got tired after a while.

I could barely muster up a smile for the team in the locker room, so McGuire took over, congratulating them and instructing them to get on the bus as fast as they could. He glanced at me over his shoulder, his face blank but eyes full of emotion. I think he was just as angry as I was.

Normally I didn't mind the smell of sweat and grass once we were trapped on the bus, but tonight I did. I sat in my usual seat in the front and dragged the window down, letting the chilly air cool me down. I leaned my head back against the seat and closed my eyes, listening to the players sing stupid songs and make jokes. I couldn't laugh along tonight.

The seat dipped next to me, and I lifted my head.

"You need something, McGuire?"

"I wanted to check on you."

"Check on me?" I jerked my head back. "Since when?"

He didn't answer.

"I don't need you to fight battles for me," I told him.

"I know that."

"I can take care of myself."

"I know that too."

"Then why did you do it?"

Our eyes met in the glow from the passing streetlights. "Because even though you *can* do it doesn't mean you should have to." And after a few moments he said, "We're on the same team, aren't we?"

And in spite of myself, my lips curled up in a small smile. He patted my knee twice, then folded his arms across his chest and turned his head to watch out the front of the bus.

"We weren't expected to win that game," he said after a while.

"I try not to read the papers or the analysis."

"You should. You would've seen the write-up on our improving offense." When I didn't show gratitude, he rolled his head toward me. "You're welcome."

I backhanded him in the stomach, noting that it wasn't the first time my hands had found him tonight.

"Hey," Ken said from behind us.

My head popped up. The bubble that had formed around McGuire and me had burst.

"You coming to the bar tonight, Gibb?" Ken asked.

I looked to McGuire next to me, not for permission but to see if he had any opinions on the matter.

"We go to Blake's bar," McGuire said. "You should come."

I kept my face straight while my heart danced. Maybe it was a little immature, like that time I was invited to Lindy

Crane's birthday party in sixth grade, but I was finally being accepted into the club. And by Connor, no less.

"I'll be there." I nodded to Ken and turned back around in my seat.

McGuire and I didn't say anything again until we ended up next to each other at the Public. The place was pretty crowded, the brick of the walls and metallic of the exposed pipes and décor melding to provide a trendy but welcoming atmosphere.

We were all seated in the corner next to the windows, still in our clothes from the game, except for Ken, who'd changed into a button-down and jeans, earning some mocking from the rest of the guys about his GQ fashion. Apparently, he wasn't one to ever sport his Otters uniform off the field.

"Blue and yellow just aren't my colors," he said with a laugh.

"What is your color?" I asked.

Dave leaned in and answered for him. "Anything that takes away from his fat head."

"All my smarts have to go somewhere," Ken said.

"What do you do again?" I asked.

"Chemical engineer. My company separates elements in different gases to sell them to other companies."

I shook my head. "I don't even know what that means."

"Join the club," Ronnie said, sipping his dark beer.

They were all more than halfway done with their drinks, while I hadn't really touched mine.

"Not a fan of beer?" Erik asked, digging into a basket of food.

"I'm more of a wine drinker myself," I said. "Red wine."

"Fancy," Erik joked after stuffing a couple of freshly made chips in his mouth.

"Here." McGuire slid his light-colored beer bottle to me with one finger. "Try this one."

"What is it?"

"It's a . . ." His eyes went off into the distance until he snapped his fingers a moment later. "Grisette. Piper said it means gray . . . or something. I don't know."

I picked up the beer and raised my brow to make sure he really wanted me to share his drink. He nodded and watched as I brought it to my lips to take a sip. I swallowed, and his eyes followed. When I licked my lips, his gaze stayed there as he asked, "So?"

I shook my head. "Nope. Still don't like it."

He scooted the bottle back in front of him, leaving a trail of condensation on the dark wooden table. He wiped it away with the palm of his hand, and I stared at the way his long fingers curled in toward his palm. Noticed the small scab by his knuckle. The muscle of his forearm.

I'd been around athletes for as long as I could remember. I'd seen plenty of muscular men in my lifetime, shirts off, or even only in their underwear, and I'd been unfazed. Walls of muscle all sort of blur together after a while, so not being able to take my eyes off of his forearm was new. Wondering what the weight of his arm would feel like had me thinking that maybe a few sips of beer was a few too many.

Before I could completely lose myself in these crazy thoughts, Blake made his way over to our table. He greeted everyone with a "Next round on me, fellas." Then he grinned down at me. "And lady. Another big win, huh?"

"Five more games until playoffs."

"Think you'll get there?"

"Next week's game will put us in contention if we win."

He nodded. "Nice." He pointed to my nearly full beer. "Not a fan of the Natural Red?"

I wrinkled my nose. I hated to admit that I didn't like Piper's beers.

"She likes red wine," Connor interjected, and I flicked my eyes to him, still unnerved by the awareness buzzing between us.

"That's all right," Blake said, putting his hand on my shoulder as he picked the bottle up. "This happens to be my favorite from Out of the Bottle." The way he said the name of Piper's business exuded pride in every syllable.

And it made me a little sad that I'd never experienced the love of a man like that.

"Can I get you anything else? We've got a few choice liquors, soda, water . . . ?"

I waved the offer away. "Nah. I should be heading home anyway. Big day tomorrow."

"Yeah?" Blake asked. "Doing what?"

My chin bobbed up and down—caught in my fib. "Well,

we have films tomorrow morning, and then I've got to go to Target."

"Big day . . . at Target?"

"I love Target," I said, moving to grab my car keys.

"Who doesn't? But that's your big day?"

I jingled my keys. "I've got to get my car checked. It's been making a funny sound."

Blake's brows narrowed, one hand on his chin. Piper had told me that in his previous life, he was an attorney, and I could see that in how he stared at me. I began to sweat.

He looked to McGuire, then back at me. "Why don't you get your car checked out and then come over to our place tomorrow night? Piper has been bugging me to have a game night."

"I won't have a car," I lied, the words coming out before I even thought of them.

"Connor can take you," he suggested.

I blanched. My gram had a saying about liars: *I don't tolerate liars. I'm a nice person, not a stupid one.*

But in this case, *I* was the stupid one. If I told them I was lying about my *big day* tomorrow, they'd think I was a loser. But if I kept it to myself, I'd have to be in a car with Connor.

"Thank you for the invitation, but I don't think so."

For a second, Blake's focus split to Connor, who was silent behind me. I half hoped he'd jump in to say there was no way I was allowed in his car. Would've saved me from all this floundering.

Blake shifted his weight, staring at me until I gave in.

"Fine. I'll come over for game night. Although I refuse to play charades."

"You've got yourself a deal. Connor," he said, snapping, "pick the lady up at seven. We'll have dinner."

He left, and McGuire still hadn't said anything by the time I stood up. I lifted my arms in question to the eternally stoic guy next to me.

He shrugged in answer. "I like Clue."

I rolled my eyes. "I'm going to murder you in the library with the wrench."

"I don't mind playing dirty," he said with a smirk that said a million more words than he ever would.

And I made it all the way to my car before I took a real breath.

CHAPTER
13

Charlie

With Sonja away for the weekend, I was able to enjoy my *big day* in peace. I got to play Britney Spears as loud as I wanted, soak in a chamomile bath for over an hour, and paint my toenails bubblegum pink.

Eventually my day of self-indulgence had to come to an end. And my night of strange had to begin.

With one single knock.

I opened the front door to find the bill of a cap in my line of vision. "What's with the hats all the time?" I asked. "I know you don't have a misshapen head, what are you hiding?"

He tipped his head up, and our eyes met. In the dark, they seemed much more silver. And scary. They moved from the top of my ponytail, down my leggings, to the tips of my gray tennis shoes. "What's with the baggy sweater? What are *you* trying to hide?"

I pulled at the oversize knit bargain I'd found on sale that suddenly strangled me. The foot of distance between us was so narrow yet oddly too far.

"It's cozy," I said, averting my eyes, refusing to give anything away. I grabbed my coat and scarf because balmy Atlanta had spoiled me for Arctic tundra Minneapolis. I locked the door behind me, mumbling, "I'm not built for this weather."

He sniffed a laugh next to me.

"What?"

"Guess no ice fishing for you." He flipped his car keys in his hand.

"Absolutely not. The only thing worse than sitting for eight hours in a boat hoping to hook a fish is sitting on the ice for eight hours hoping to hook a fish."

"I go every year with Sean," he said as he opened the passenger-side door of his truck.

I stopped at the gentlemanly act, and he gestured up toward the seat. "You waiting for me to throw you in or what?"

"I'm sure you'd love to get your hands on me," I said, then immediately tried to reel it back in. "I mean—I meant it like I'm sure you'd love to throw me around." I shook my head. "You know, because we don't like each other, so—"

He gave me a bored expression and, leaving the door hanging open, strolled around the hood to the driver's side. I stepped up into the cab at the same time he did and buckled in. The radio turned on to some annoying fast-paced punk song, and I reached out to tune in to a different station. He slapped my hand away.

"Hey! I'm a guest in this vehicle."

"And I'm the driver," he said, starting down the road.

"Will we ever agree on anything outside of football?" I asked.

He ventured a glance at me. "We don't always agree even on the field."

"Oh, right," I said. "Because you hate that I'm in charge."

At a red light, he cut his eyes to me. Could've melted steel.

"Now you're wishing you could toss me out of the car?" I guessed.

The light turned green, and he shrugged. "Something like that."

I folded my arms and stared out the window, wondering if it should feel comfortable to be sitting next to my assistant coach and self-described enemy, doing this weird push-pull.

"I know you lied," he said after a while.

"Huh?" I turned to him.

"About your car and whatever else you said you had to do today."

"How do you know?"

"You're a terrible liar."

I huffed defensively. "Am not."

"I saw your car parked on the next block back."

"Damn, I thought I'd gotten away with it."

"Why?" he asked as we drove down a street with a rainbow of businesses lighting up the dark sky.

"I don't know."

He waited in perfect silence until I couldn't stand it anymore.

"So you wouldn't think I was a loser who sat at home by herself," I confessed. But as proof of my loserdom, after two months of living in this city I had no idea where we were.

He hmmed, but didn't actually speak any words. Honestly, his silence was the worst form of torture.

"Just say what you want to say! Jeez, you'd make Mother Teresa lose her temper."

"Don't yell at me in my own truck."

"I'm not yelling."

"Your voice is raised."

I clucked my tongue. "You are impossible."

"And you have no chill." He kept his eyes on the road the whole time, even more irritating that he could argue with me like he was listing his grocery order.

I pressed my hand to my chest. "I have no chill?" I remembered the group of girls in my third-period gym class who hated to participate and thought I couldn't see them fiddling with their cell phones. They'd told me I had no chill when I made them hand 'em over. "I am chill. *You* have no chill," I countered, sounding beyond lame.

He laughed, and then I laughed, and then we sat smiling at each other once he'd parked.

"You ready for me to kick your ass?" he asked, swinging his door open.

"Ha. Like you could."

Turned out neither one of us could, not with Piper offering Blake sexual favors in return for his Boardwalk real estate. They were sickeningly sweet. And I envied it.

Blake whispered something in Piper's ear, making her crack up just as McGuire's phone rang. He breathed out a silent sigh of relief that I don't think they noticed. He didn't seem to find their antics as romantic as I did. He peeked down at the screen and answered quickly: "Hey Kim." He stepped a few feet away, and I barely caught it when he said, "Tonight? I might be able . . ."

"Who actually calls anyone anymore?" Bear asked no one in particular.

Blake moved his hand to Piper's back. "It's probably that chick he's been hooking up with."

"Which one?" Piper asked, as if it was a common occurrence.

He shrugged, and I tried to sound as nonchalant as possible when I asked, "Does he hook up with a lot of women?"

"Well, you know him, doesn't say much. Especially about that."

"But he gets it more than I do," Bear added.

"Anyone gets it more than you do," Piper teased, and Blake high-fived her. "Why are you even here? I thought you were going to Chicago with Sonja."

He kept his attention on the colored paper money in his hands. "Her coach said she needed to focus on the fight." He didn't seem happy about missing it when he rolled his eyes. "Whatever."

Piper and Blake exchanged a glance that I didn't understand before he said, "I'm getting a drink. Anybody want anything?"

I shook my head as Piper lifted up her glass. Bear stood up too, saying something about chips and dip. I took a moment to gaze at a couple of the pictures hung by clothespins on a string along the wall.

"Pinterest?" I guessed, surveying the arrangement, and Piper laughed.

"Of course. I'm not a great cook, but I like to make things. Do you Pinterest?"

I reached for a pretzel. "Not really. I have an account, but it's mostly sayings from wise women and recipes for fried chicken."

"I can get down with that." Piper smiled, then tilted her head in the direction of McGuire, who had put his phone away. "How's it going with him?"

"Fine." When she eyed me suspiciously, I inwardly pondered how truthful I should be. "We coach. We fight. We coach. We fight. We've got a good routine going."

She nodded, pushing the game board over a few centimeters. "Should we play a different game? Monopoly takes forever."

Piper might have been done with the McGuire conversation, but I wasn't.

"Are there are a lot of women?" I asked, the words racing off my tongue. "With Connor, I mean." His first name felt foreign when I said it.

Her green eyes flicked up to mine, lighting with interest.

She held back a smile as best she could. "You guys never talk about that?"

I shook my head. "We talk about the I and shotgun formations, but never girlfriends."

Piper blinked. "I have no idea what you just said about shotguns and eyes, but Connor doesn't have girlfriends."

"No?" I sipped my wine.

"Not really, no. Just hookups. I don't know much but"— she leaned closer, whispering—"I've heard stories. Like this one woman was a sex columnist for a women's magazine and tested out some BDSM tips on him for her article."

My cheeks heated, but I remained quiet as Piper went on.

"I don't know the details because it was a while ago, but could you just imagine Connor with chains and whips?" She laughed to herself.

I forced myself to laugh to cover up the odd feeling in my belly that gurgled and bubbled as if I'd drunk too much soda and the fizz was going straight to my head. It didn't feel good, thinking about him with other women.

Piper's attention floated to the kitchen for a moment. "This is all secondhand knowledge through Blake, but apparently some girl named Alison broke his heart, and now he tends to go for divorcées and women who've seen something of the world. You know what I mean?"

I didn't, but I tucked that bit of information away. Bowls and glasses clinked behind us, and I glanced back to see the trio of men returning. Connor's hat was turned backward, giving him a boyish appearance, and a fist squeezed my heart. As he sat down next to me with a nudge to my shoulder, I wondered if he thought I was just one of the guys. Or, with his gaze settling somewhere around my thigh, if maybe he saw me as something more.

Or maybe he just had a thing for leggings.

Monopoly dragged on for another hour before we all finally gave up, too mentally exhausted to try another game. We said good-bye, and I got hugs from Piper, Blake, and Bear, like I was one of the gang.

"Looks like you won't have to make up plans next time," Connor said, once we were back in his truck.

I nodded. "Maybe we can finally get around to playing Clue."

"So you can murder me with a wrench?"

"I heard you prefer ropes."

He glanced at me with a confused face.

I'd learned a lot about him tonight, and I didn't know where or how to begin dissecting it. "A little birdie told me you might be into a little kink."

"A little birdie named Piper?" When I didn't answer, he grumbled, "This is exactly why I don't tell people shit." And then went silent for six minutes.

I watched each one pass on the digital clock on his dashboard.

"You've got a lot of notches in your bedpost?"

His grip tightened on the steering wheel. I couldn't see it in the dark, but I heard the whine of the leather. "That's none of your goddamn business."

"What did I tell you about taking the Lord's name in vain around me? God has nothing to do with this."

"You're a real piece of work, you know that?" he bit out. "You're pushy with other people, but stubborn as hell when other people try to push you. You've got no problem speaking your mind, but you don't know when to shut your mouth. You curse like a sailor but are offended by saying G-O-D. What is your deal?"

I inwardly flinched at his accusations, more examples of how I didn't make sense to other people, to him. I swallowed. I couldn't—wouldn't—let it affect me.

"You're the one who refuses to answer any questions. What does that make you?"

He parked in front of my house and breathed audibly. The leather creaked again. I touched the button above our heads to turn the light on, determined. "Who is Alison?"

He kept still as a statue. A beautifully irate, sharp-jawed statue.

"Connor."

At his name, he whipped around to face me, and I swallowed, the thought to stop baiting him running out of my mind as quickly as it'd raced in.

"No one," he said finally.

I circled my finger around his face. "She's obviously someone if you're making your angry face."

"I don't have an angry face."

"Yes, you do," I said breezily. This was what we were good at, lobbing barbs back and forth. This was comfortable.

The other stuff, the soft gazes and slight touches—that was the new, awkward stuff. "It's not obvious to someone who isn't trained in the art of conducting animosity from you. But I am a professional in earning your hate-filled glares."

"I don't hate you, Charlotte." He seemed to enjoy my discomfort at his use of my given name. "I just dislike a lot of things about you."

"I'm sure you stay up every night thinking about me, listing all the things you dislike."

He barked out a single laugh and shook his head. "You have no idea." He took his hat off and dropped it on the dash with a sigh, then considered me seriously. "You really have no idea."

I refrained from combing my fingers through the light-colored strands that stuck straight up in the back like Alfalfa's. I had some idea.

I tried again. "Who is Alison?"

"A woman."

"I assumed as much. Who was she to you?"

"An ex. We broke up a lifetime ago."

"Oh." I played with the hair ties on my wrist, and two long, thick fingers lined up next to my own. I gulped in a breath of air.

"How many of these do you actually need at a time?"

I kept my gaze down so he couldn't read anything on my face as his calloused fingers skimmed over my skin. "One, but that's not the point. You never know when you'll need another." I shook him off, not to be distracted, no matter how good he was at it. "Are you going to tell me about her?"

"No."

"What about Kim?"

"What about her?"

I sighed. "Your newest hookup who called you. Are you going to see her tonight?"

His lips ticked up in the corner like he'd caught me stealing a cookie from the jar. "Why do you care?"

"I don't."

"You're a terrible liar."

"I am not."

His mouth spread to a wicked smile. "What's that quote? 'The lady doth protest too much'?"

I growled and, like a child, resorted to violence. I thumped his shoulder with the side of my fist, but he didn't let me pull back. I felt the distinct pressure of each of his fingertips as they wrapped around my wrist, and before I knew it, his mouth was on mine, kissing me.

Then I kissed him back.

And the world was upside down.

But with his lips—a little velvety, a lot demanding—I didn't care if I floated away into space. We were already in a different dimension.

He let go of my arm and moved both hands to my head, pulling my hair tie out with ease to let my hair drape against my shoulders. His fingers dug into it. Weeks of resentment, irritation, and fury had bubbled up and burst through our bodies, and I couldn't get enough, finding my own hold on him. I squeezed the soft material of the T-shirt over his chest, yanking him closer, anchoring me to him. Like every argument we'd had, we fought with everything—lips, teeth, tongue—caressing, nibbling, and sucking.

He tilted my head, allowing me to catch my breath and, along with it, my brain. We came back to earth slowly, and I released my fingers from his shirt.

My offensive coordinator had kissed me. I'd kissed him back. "What the hell was that?"

He blinked and backed away from me by an inch, but not enough for me to escape the heat from his body. He blinked again, his eyes finding focus, then licked his bottom lip. Purposefully.

"I don't know, but stop staring at my mouth."

I zipped my attention up, and he laughed. A deep, rich sound I didn't know he'd been hiding.

"If I knew that would shut you up, I would've done it a long time ago. You're much less aggravating when otherwise occupied."

"Only you could turn a good kiss sour." I got out of the car, half expecting him to stop me, to do something. He didn't. I refused to look at him until I was at the door. He was leaning forward in his seat, watching me. Once I was inside, I heard his truck rumble and drive away.

"Bastard."

CHAPTER
14

Connor

H oly shit.

Holy fucking shit.

It'd been a constant chant in my head since Saturday night.

I'd been so wrapped up in trying to keep Charlie Gibb at arm's length that she sneaked up on me.

Or I on her.

I didn't know who'd done what anymore.

For sure, though, this wasn't a one-way street. We'd been going full-tilt at one another for a while now. I suppose we had to collide at some point. I just never thought it'd be with our lips.

Jesus, her lips.

And this time it wasn't in vain. Her mouth, which she usually used to toss a few sharp words at me, was a miracle, and I offered up thanks. She was right about me: I did stay up thinking of her, just not in the way she assumed. And now, after I'd had a taste, a tease of what she had inside her, I wanted more.

When, where, or how didn't matter. But it did give me a lot of grief.

We taught at the same school. We coached the same football team. She was the head coach. My boss. I didn't know what I was thinking.

Because I *wasn't* thinking.

One minute we were arguing, the next kissing, and I'd been suffering from whiplash ever since. I was restless, buzzing with angst, not used to feeling out-of-control. This was why I kept my romantic encounters short, a few weeks at most. And with women who were usually older than me, who knew what they wanted. No questions, no thinking. A simple yes or no.

With Charlie? There were no easy answers.

And after tossing and turning for a second night in a row, I got up early and packed my work clothes. Normally I exercised at night, but I needed to work out some of this energy, so I headed to the weight room at school. At this time of day, it'd be empty.

I got my keys out to unlock the door, and promptly dropped them on the floor as soon as I opened it. "What are you doing here?"

Charlie jumped up from where she was bent over. "What are *you* doing here?"

I picked up my keys and shut the door behind me. "I'm here to work out."

"Me too." She pushed a twenty-five-pound plate onto a bar at the squat rack. "I come here every morning."

"You do?" I put my bag down in the corner, next to the speaker her phone was plugged into, playing an annoyingly upbeat song.

"Yeah." She gave me a reproachful frown in the mirror's reflection. "If I'm going to ask the kids to give it their all, I'm going to too."

"Your music is garbage. How do you work out to this?"

She flipped me off, and I watched her set up, bare arms on display as she held on to the bar on either side as it rested across her back and shoulders. She stood up, lifting the bar off the rack, and squatted nice and deep. Impressive.

Not only her physical strength, but her commitment to a work ethic people would never know about. She wasn't all talk or hired for the job because of her father. She was here at six-thirty in the morning because of her dedication to the team and the sport.

She finished her set, the bar clanging onto the rack. "You're staring." My gaze raced up to find hers in the mirror, and she rolled her eyes. "I knew you had a thing for leggings."

"What?" I put hundred-pound plates on the straight bar.

"My leggings." She plucked at the stretchy material on her thighs, doing nothing to help keep my attention away from them.

I lay on the bench and gripped the bar above my shoulders. "No. Your legs."

"You like my legs?" Her voice was uncharacteristically high, as if she thought it'd be impossible that I admired her legs.

I lowered the bar to my chest, breathing in, then pushed it back up on an exhale. "And your ass."

A minute passed in silence as I mentally counted reps to ten.

"You do?" she finally squeaked out.

"Is it that much of a shock?" I sat up, waving my hand down her body. "You're fit. You've got a really nice body. Face isn't bad either."

She snorted, hands on her hips, her confidence back. "Aren't you sweet," she said, accent put on thick. "No wonder you have a bevy of women."

"You're pretty," I said, all kidding aside as I lay back down for another set. Charlie moved back to the squat rack. We each completed our second set, the terrible singsongy pop music as our soundtrack. "But your music really does suck."

"It's cute how you think I care what you think."

God, I loved when she flicked her tongue against her teeth like that. She did it whenever she wanted to prove a point.

I pointed my finger at her. "But you think I'm cute."

She held her palm up. "Don't get ahead of yourself there, bucko. And don't look at me like that."

"Like what?" I stood up and closed the gap between us.

"Like a villain with one side of your mouth curled up." She took a step back, right into the squat bar, and I crowded her. We studied each other, eyes, noses, lips. Definitely lips.

"If I'm the villain, what are you?"

Her eyes went to the ceiling for a moment before she grinned at me. "The princess in the tower."

"Ha. You are no princess."

She shoved me away and ducked under the bar, lining up for another set. "Spot me or get out of the way."

I leaned against the rack, watching as she completed her first four reps before slowing down. Her face twisted as she breathed deeply, her legs wobbling slightly from the strain. I stepped behind her, holding my palms out underneath her arms, just in case. "You got it. How many more?"

She breathed. "Four."

"Let's go. Nice and easy."

Her face turned pink and then red as she worked through another rep.

"Three more. Keep it up . . . two . . ." I noticed her back beginning to fall, her shoulders bending in, and I got a bit closer, one hand on her lower back. "Don't give in. Keep the form."

One more breath, and a push to stand up straight. I patted her on the back before making sure she got the bar back on the rack okay. "Good job."

"Thanks." She lifted her tank top to wipe the bottom of her face, exposing some of her stomach, flat and tan. The first time I'd ever had the hots for a workout buddy made for some awkward silence.

I shook my head and went back to my bench for another set, firing off ten quick reps, the heat in my muscles taking my mind off the woman a few feet away from me.

We continued our separate regimens, ignoring the big, fat elephant in the room. But if she wasn't going to bring up what had happened between us, I wasn't going to either. Not to say that this cat-and-mouse game wasn't fun.

We passed the time by teasing each other. I called her Rambo when she made some kind of guttural sound on an especially hard rep with a dead lift. She challenged me to do twenty pull-ups "like Henry Cavill." I didn't know who this Henry Cavill was, but I wasn't going to back down . . . although I only got through eleven pull-ups before losing my grip. She gave me two thumbs down, and I yanked at the bottom of her ponytail. It might have been childish, but it felt better than angst-ridden silence.

We finished up and grabbed our bags.

"See you for lunch duty," she said.

"Try to relax during your difficult day of gym classes," I said, and locked the weight room door behind us.

"Try not to bore your classes to death."

We started off toward the locker rooms. "I'm never boring. It's *Oregon Trail* game day."

"That old computer game?"

"Yeah. It's a Wii game now."

"I figured you for the write-a-vocab-definition-ten-times-each type of teacher."

I clutched at my chest at the horror. "Now, that's offensive. History is really interesting, especially when you get the kids to realize it's all our shared history. None of us would be here now if not for something that happened three hundred years ago, or three thousand before that."

She stared at me for a moment, her head tilted and brow raised. "You really do surprise me sometimes."

"I'm not all bad," I said, and a tiny smile appeared on her perfect lips.

"Just about two-thirds." She laughed at her own joke, and I turned to my right to the men's locker room, watching her walk to the women's locker room, the curves of her body retreating from me. My eyes and my feet wanted to move in opposite directions, but if my feet knew the view my eyes had, they'd want to stay in place too.

It was much easier to ignore her when she wore ugly polo shirts and khaki shorts, not that tight purple and black getup that was practically painted on. It was easier to be mad at her when she was sarcastic and full of bravado, not when she showed her soft and sweet side. It was easy to not kiss her when she was just Gibb, but when she was Charlie . . . that was a different story.

Whenever I had a free moment between classes and quiet moments during the lessons, I thought of her. How her soft brown eyes seemed out of place among her hard features, her pin-straight hair and sharp mouth. I thought about the contrast between her witty comebacks and her nervous shifting when I got close to her—almost imperceptible, but I noticed.

I definitely noticed.

That's what made her Charlie.

But it didn't change the fact that she was Charlie Gibb. Coach.

That afternoon's practice was dominated by focusing on defensive plays. But it didn't go well.

"Spencer, did you eat too much at lunch today? You're moving slow, Marcus is getting by you on every run. It's like you're not even trying." She smacked him on the arm with her folded papers. "Come on, now, you're better than that." She turned her back to him and walked toward Dave, not seeing how Spencer rolled his eyes before heading back to the defensive huddle.

I ran my hand over my mouth as Nate passed for yet another touchdown, Brett giving no coverage at all.

"Oh, come on! Spencer, get over here!" Charlie threw her arms out.

He rolled his head back on his neck like he was too tired to move, and Charlie stalked out onto the field. "Move it, Spencer."

He started to walk.

"We run on this field. Do you need a reminder?" He must've mumbled something, because she yanked on his jersey. "Excuse me?" She got right up against his face mask and said quiet but irate words to him, face red. She pointed her thumb behind her, and his feet were sluggish as he made his way to the track. "You know what to do!" she called after him.

Then on Wednesday while I stood in the hall, I heard her slamming around in her office before practice. I poked my head in the door. "Everything okay in here?"

"No. Everything is not okay in here." She ground her fist into her desk. "Get Spencer in here, will you?"

I nodded, and brought him back to her office a minute later. I didn't stay, but stood just outside the closed door, listening as she said, "Why did I just find out you have detention tomorrow?"

Brett didn't say anything.

"You don't care you're missing practice?"

"Well, I can't do anything ab—"

"You better think very carefully about the next words out of your mouth. If they're anything other than an apology for acting like a jackass, you're going to be missing more than practice."

"It was just a joke."

"Snapping a girl's bra is not a joke. Making someone cry is not a joke."

I shook my head. This kid was a grade A asshole, and I was glad Charlie wasn't holding back.

"Chill—"

"I swear to God, one more excuse from you, and you will be benched on Friday. I expect everyone on this team to be better on the field and off. Snapping a girl's bra strap and making fun of her is not being better."

"It wasn't that big of a deal," he said.

"You're benched Friday."

I was actually surprised she kept it together. I didn't know if I would've given him that much latitude.

"You can't do that!"

"I can. And I don't want to believe that you really aren't sorry at all, so before you say something you'll regret, get out of my office."

"Fine!"

The door opened and he stormed past me. I was tempted to grab him by the scruff of his neck and throw him up against the wall, but I let him go and moved back into Charlie's office.

She sat at her desk, eyes closed.

"Hey." When she didn't respond, I gave her shoulder a reassuring squeeze. "You did the right thing."

She opened her eyes and pulled away from me. "I know I did. But I'm the bitch again," she grumbled, then grabbed her baseball cap and stomped over to the locker room in a fit of rage. She yelled inside to the players, "Y'all better be out on the field in five or you're running!"

CHAPTER

15

Charlie

I shook my head, arms folded, as I stared at the scoreboard. Another loss. This one 21–7. Our biggest loss yet, and totally unacceptable. The defense had been sloppy, slow off the line, and our offense barely had any time on the field to even try to score.

"Hey, Gibb! Hey!"

I refused to turn to the man yelling at me. I wasn't in the mood to talk to any parents tonight.

"You're not going to talk to me after what you did to my son?"

Especially *this* parent. I took a breath, tossed my clipboard and hat on the bench before slowly turning around to Mr. Spencer at the chest-high chain-link fence. I'd thought it odd I hadn't heard from him over my benching Brett. I supposed he wanted to have that conversation now.

I didn't.

"How can I help you?"

"You can help me by doing your damn job." His fingers curled around the metal diamonds like an animal in a cage.

"I am, sir," I said as calmly as I could. "And I'm gonna ask that you lower your voice. We're not at a zoo."

"And I'm going to ask that you watch what the hell you say to me. You don't know who I am."

"I do. You're Brett Spencer's father."

"That's right. And if you think you can pull my kid, *my* kid, from QB and put him on defense, in a position he's never played—"

"I'll stop you right there. Brett is much better suited for free safety than quarterback. He's excelled there. We've already discussed this."

He stuck a foot on the fence as if he was going to try to climb it to get to me. "Then why did you bench him?"

"Disciplinary reasons."

"Dis . . . disciplinary reasons?" He dragged his hands through his hair so it stood on end. "You've *got* to be kidding me."

"He missed practice because of detention and has had a bad attitude on the field. Brett needs to fix that if he wants to continue to play for me."

He made a noise, a mix of a huff and a maniacal laugh. "Play for you, huh? You just lost this game, and my son wasn't playing. Seems like you need him more than he needs you."

The field was almost empty, but I noticed Connor stand-ing about twenty yards away, talking to Ronnie, acting as if he wasn't listening. I kept myself together. I wasn't going to give him or Jack Spencer the satisfaction of seeing me fall apart.

"You've got another think coming if you think you're going to continue to treat my son this way. And if I were you, I'd try very hard to win or you might be hauling your ass back to your daddy's house."

"I don't take kindly to idle threats."

"It wasn't idle," he said ominously with a stubby finger pointed at me before whirling away. I watched him walk to-ward a group of parents, most of whom I'd only spoken to on a few occasions, enough to know that their kids were ju-niors. They eyed me up, and I'd like to say I didn't care, but I had to work with their children. It'd be different if they were graduating; then I wouldn't have to worry about them in a few months. But these parents? I'd see them for a long time. And they could make things hard for me.

"Hey!" Connor waved to me with a whistle. "Let's go."

If I could've screamed, I would've. I grabbed my stuff and walked toward the goalposts, pausing next to Connor to say curtly, "I'm not a fucking dog."

His eyes rounded and he looked as if he wanted to say something, maybe an apology, but I didn't stick around for it.

I sat at the front of the bus, my foul mood a physical blockade around me. None of the other coaches even attempted to talk to me on the ride home, and that was all right with me. I slammed the door of my office, rubbing at my eyes once I sat down. Between the loss and the totally inappropriate dressing-down I'd received, I felt awful. I'd been talked down to before, that wasn't anything new. But to have it done in front of other coaches and the players' parents, that was embarrassing.

I really, really hated to admit that it got to me. But it did.

I picked up my cell phone to call my dad.

He answered after a few rings. "Hey, Charlie, a little late to be calling. How was the game?"

"We lost." I sighed. "We're two and two and might be out of contention for the division."

"Ah. That's tough. I watched your game that you sent me from last week. You made a good call with the conversion."

"Thank you. I'm trying my best." My voice cracked, and I cleared my throat, wishing that for once my dad would ask me what was wrong. That he'd understand I needed more from him than sports talk. But he couldn't and didn't.

"We have Wake Forest tomorrow. They've got a good spread," he said.

When I didn't respond, he rattled off the stats of some of his players. He said their kicker had injured his knee, and how they could've used my expertise with the backup. Again, I stayed quiet. Right now, the last thing I wanted to talk about was football.

"Well, I'll let you go. I'm going to watch some more film before bed, and I'm sure you have a lot to do."

"Yeah." I glanced around my office, to the charts of plays on the whiteboard, to the windowless walls, to the sad plant on the tiny bookcase in the corner. I had nothing to do. And no one to talk to.

"Talk later," he said before hanging up, and I dropped my phone on my desk before the tears fell from my eyes.

My father was the only parent I had, and as far as parents went, I couldn't complain. He didn't treat me badly and had kept a roof over my head. He'd let me tag along to his practices and games, and eventually gave in to letting me try it for myself.

Still, there were no *I love yous*.

I was sure it had been difficult for him to be a single parent with a little girl after his wife died in a tragic accident, but it was difficult for me too. My grandmother was there to help raise me, try to tame me into the southern belle she wanted me to be. Gram and I were like oil and water; for as much as we got along, we also fought. About everything. And she was the sole female in my life, a great role model, but not exactly my number one fan.

What I didn't ever have was a confidante. I'd never had anyone to talk to about my mother, or how I didn't feel especially close to my dad or my gram.

I wasn't my father's son or my grandmother's granddaughter. I didn't check any of the right boxes. I was too wild to be a proper girl, and the wrong gender to play football. And sometimes when I felt out-of-place and sad, I wanted someone to ask me how I was doing, but because I never seemed to be able to build a bridge out of my in-between space, I had no one.

I wiped my eyes with the backs of my hands before gathering my coat and bag. A glass of wine and a bath sounded great right about now. I turned off the light and opened the door, smacking right into McGuire's chest.

He grunted, and I actually hoped I'd hurt him a little bit.

"You practicing to become a wall?" I asked.

"No."

"What are you doing here? Why aren't you at the bar?"

"We didn't feel much like going out tonight," he said, then fixed his hat and focused over my shoulder, back into my dark office. "I, uh, I heard you crying and thought I'd stick around."

"Great," I grumbled, and tugged my bag over my shoulder.

"Want to talk about it?"

"*You* want to talk about feelings?" I said with a skeptical laugh.

He shrugged. When I didn't move or open my mouth, he tipped his head back. "How about food then?"

Even though a nice Shiraz in the Idris Elba glass along with a Big Blue bath bomb was the plan, his company seemed better. "I could eat."

We walked out to the parking lot in silence, the wind whipping hard against me, and I huddled into my coat. He wore only a jacket and baseball cap. "What are you, part polar bear or somethin'?" I asked, peering up at Connor out of my thick scarf. "Penguin, maybe?"

"Penguin," he said, straight-faced, but moved in closer to me, shielding me a bit from the wind. "This isn't even the worst of it. How will you last when we hit January?"

"Never leave the house. Possibly buy a Snuggie."

"Good plan." He pointed to his pickup. "Want me to drive?"

"Sure." I hopped into the truck and buckled in, rotating all of the air vents toward me when he turned the engine over.

"You make yourself right at home, don't you?" he said, and I reluctantly twisted one vent to him to share some heat. He rolled his eyes. "Gee, thanks."

"You're welcome," I said, and sank into the seat as he drove.

"You're not going to fight me over what we listen to?" he asked, his voice almost sounding let down.

"I don't feel like fightin' tonight."

He tuned the satellite radio to a pop station that happened to be playing Britney Spears, and I sang along. He laughed to himself. "I never thought you'd like this kind of stuff. Pink T-shirts and Britney Spears and wine from a glass with a guy's face on it."

I held my breath, steeling myself for the inevitable. Of course he hadn't thought I'd be into other things, because how could a football coach like "girlie" things? Everyone assumed things about my personality, even my sexual preference. The stereotypes were endless.

"I thought you southern girls all wore cowboy boots and listened to country."

I let out a relieved laugh that it wasn't any of the other stereotypes generally cast on me.

"What?" he asked, making a left by a strip mall.

"I just thought you were going to say something else."

"Like what?"

"Like . . . you'd assumed wrong things about me." I studied him, his jaw cutting a harsh shadow along his neck under the fluorescent lights above us at a drive-thru. "People expect me to be a certain way. Sometimes they don't bother to get to know me beyond their own assumptions. And other times, they don't like what they find when they do get to know me."

He nodded and put the car in park as we waited in line.

"Like how I'd assumed we would eat at a real restaurant. A place with tables, chairs, and physical menus." I raised my eyebrow at him.

He held up his hand. "Well, you know what they say about assumptions . . ."

"That sometimes they're right, and it makes you look like an ass when you take a girl to a drive-thru?" I bit my bottom lip, which drew his attention. His eyes stayed there for a long moment before meeting mine.

"Greasy french fries always cheer me up," he said with a shrug.

"Really?" I took off my scarf and coat, finally warmed up. "You seem like the type who never indulges in fast food. You probably survive on raw almonds and a couple ounces of plain chicken."

"Assumptions make an ass out of you and me," he said in a singsong voice, pulling forward for our turn at the speaker. "What do you want?"

"Fries. Obviously."

He smiled at me and poked his head out the window to order two large fries and two sodas. He paid, got our food, and pulled off to the side by a gas station that was closed for the night. We settled into our food, and after a minute or two, Connor turned to me. "Gonna tell me what Spencer senior said to you?"

I shoved a couple of fries in my mouth. "Nothing, really. Just your average asshole-type stuff."

"But you're upset."

I sipped my Coke, giving myself time to think. "I'm upset over a lot of things."

"Want to talk about any of those things?" He shifted in his seat like he expected me to start spilling.

I pointed at him with a fry. "You don't strike me as the type who is good with emotions."

He bit my fry. "You don't strike me as the type to be afraid."

"I'm not afraid," I said, pouting at my half-eaten fry before popping it in my mouth.

"You're upset." He became absorbed in something on the road. No car was in sight, but a streetlamp kept us illuminated. "I don't want you to be upset," he said quietly, clearly a secret he didn't want to share too loudly.

I swallowed thickly. "First, we lost the game, which might take us out of division playoffs. Second, Spencer was—"

"Totally out of line," he cut me off, shoving his drink into the cup holder with an audible thud. "I'd really like to punch that guy in the throat."

"Huh. You and me both." I polished off the rest of my french fries, and Connor handed me a couple of napkins.

"Is there a number three?"

I put my garbage back into the paper bag. "My dad."

"You don't get along?"

I played with the straw in my soda. "We get along fine."

"Sounds real convincing."

"Sarcasm is not one of my favorite qualities of yours."

"No?" He smirked. "What is?"

I huffed haughtily. "The arrogance that you think I even have a favorite."

He elbowed me. "I know you go home and write in your diary about me. Stop pretending."

I mushed his face with my hand, and he took hold of it, keeping it in his grasp. There was something about the roughness of his fingers grazing my palm that I loved. I stared at our hands together, my fingers obviously feminine next to his. I loved that too.

"My dad and I have nothing in common outside of football. Sometimes I feel like if I hadn't played as well as I did, he would've totally ignored me."

Connor's thumb smoothed the back of my hand, encouraging me to keep talking.

"I know he was heartbroken when my mother died, still is, and I think he didn't know how to deal with me without her. So on one hand, it's good we have this connection, but on the other hand, it's not enough. For me, at least."

He nodded, his eyes on mine, and I realized he might often be irritatingly quiet, but he was also an excellent listener. I supposed that was my favorite quality of his.

"Must be kind of lonely," he said.

Lonely. That word hit a chord within me. It could have described my life, always on the outskirts. I had friends, but none I was really close to. And my family wasn't much better. "It's why I appreciated Sonja and Piper accepting me into their group, and Bear and Blake too."

"Not me?" He actually seemed hurt.

"Aren't you the one who wants my job? You said it yourself, you don't like me."

He let go of my hand and rolled his head back to the headrest behind him. I watched his lips work as if he was going to speak. When he didn't, I gave in to my desire to take him in. And I did so leisurely, noticing things I hadn't before.

Like the freckles that dotted his cheekbones, barely there, softening all his hard angles. The sleek muscle of his shoulders meeting the slope of his pectorals, the sign of his past as a quarterback, was shown off by his long-sleeved T-shirt as if it was made to contour his body. I imagined what his skin might feel like under that soft material, under my fingers. What the weight of his body might feel like over me. His kisses on me. His stubble scratching me.

He moved, turning his face to mine, and my cheeks burned. He couldn't see inside my head, but with the way he surveyed me, it seemed like he somehow knew. Maybe from the way I breathed or how I molded my legs together.

I prayed he couldn't detect the impure thoughts running through my mind.

It'd been a long time since I'd been with a man.

And with the way his gaze roamed over my face, I questioned everything I knew about this man. Every sarcastic comment and mean look we'd ever given each other was now suspect.

I asked myself it if was all some sort of weird foreplay— sexual tension wrapped up in pretending to hate one another.

Or maybe he really did hate me, and I'd just been out of the game for so long I hoped it meant something else.

"I do want your job," he said, lifting me from my fantasies. He shrugged one shoulder, totally cool. "And your fancy office."

I refused to smile at his teasing. "If I were a man, I'd have a fancy office."

He nodded without looking at me, and I went on.

"You want my job, but you want me to forget all that and be best friends with you?"

"Best friends? I don't know about that." He shook his head.

I leaned in close. "What do you want?"

He remained infuriatingly quiet.

"Honestly, sometimes I could kill you," I said, fisting his shirt in my right hand. If he was going to make me take the first step, I would. I yanked him to me and pushed the hat off his head. Maybe it was what had happened tonight, or maybe it'd been building with our antagonism, but whatever was causing this, I felt unleashed. I scrambled into his lap, kissing him like my life depended on it.

He didn't seem to mind. With his mouth on my throat, he scooted back against the door, giving us both room to explore. One of his hands went to my hair, the other to my back, scrunching up my shirt, and his palm pressed against my spine. I ran my fingers up and down his chest, alternating petting and scratching, and he sucked in a breath through his teeth. The sound pushed me to dig my nails into his shoulders, and he rewarded me by holding me tighter.

We were overly eager, like a couple of kids, bumbling in our excitement. It didn't take long for the windows to fog up, my heart beating just as wildly as my breathing, but I eventually broke away from him. His hands slipped out from under my shirt, taking the heat of his fingers away. But instead of letting me go completely, he hung on to my hips, pressing me down on his hardness underneath me.

"What now?" I asked, knowing my hair was a mess, my lips swollen.

He shook his head, eyes blinking at me as if in a haze. "I don't know."

CHAPTER
16

Connor

I t was déjà vu.

After Charlie and I spent Friday night together talking and making out in my truck like we were sixteen, it'd been weird. Admittedly, I wasn't great at relationships, which was why I didn't have them, but we were already in one. Charlie and I *had* to be around each other.

Saturday during films, we were both aware of one another, but neither of us approached the other. And the only words out of our mouths were about routes, sacks, and downs. Saturday night, I caught a hockey game with Bear, and that nosy shit wouldn't stop asking me about her. About how she was getting along, if she was fitting in well at school, whether or not she was dating anyone. I gave him one-word answers: "Fine," "Yeah," and "Why?"

Bear talked a big game about girls like he had them

crawling in and out of his bed, which wasn't at all true. We all knew he was not-so-secretly in love with Sonja, but him even asking about Charlie had me defensive.

"I'm just curious," he said. "Anyway, she's not my type. She's kind of . . . plain."

"Plain?" I lurched back.

He ignored me, clapping when one of the players checked another into the boards by us, but I couldn't pay attention. I was too busy stewing.

Charlie wasn't plain.

Sure, she was blond, not unusual, and her brown eyes might be dark, but they gave her a sense of mystery. They covered for her, and I never knew what would come out of her mouth. It was a surprise.

She was a surprise.

"She's not plain," I said.

"Huh?" Bear laughed at me. "What are you talking about?"

"You said Charlie was plain. She's not."

He raised his eyebrows. "Bro. That was like half an hour ago."

I leaned forward, elbows on my knees, refusing to acknowledge him. I didn't want to give him any more fodder. Gossipy son of a bitch.

But it had me thinking of her all night long. Again.

And I ended up back in the weight room early Monday morning. Again.

When I opened the door, Charlie didn't seem the least bit startled. "We meet again," she said, hands on her hips.

Today she wore long black leggings and a white tank top. "Eyes up, McGuire."

I raised my gaze, but took my time in doing so.

"Come here just to gawk?"

"Arm day," I said, peeling my sweatshirt off. My T-shirt lifted a bit, and Charlie's attention snagged somewhere around my waist. I tugged my shirt down. "Eyes up, Gibb."

She rolled said eyes at me, the corner of her mouth lifting in a sexy slant.

No, Charlie wasn't plain at all.

We worked out together, saying nothing in particular, walking small circles around the big issue between us, but we buried it by fighting over what we listened to and a push-up contest. She did more in a minute than me, but her form was crap. We finished up, a sheen of sweat on both of our faces. She twisted open a blue aluminum water bottle, and without something to do, we fell into loaded silence.

The first kiss was a chance. The second was on purpose. But neither of us was going to be the one to acknowledge it. Instead, we agreed to meet tomorrow morning at the same time, and I started my day with a hop in my step. With no definable terms or any particular plays in mind, Charlie and I had made a silent deal to not make it a big deal.

Relaxed, just how I liked it.

Which was why Al caught me off guard.

I'd always found the teachers' lounge too busy. Whether it was the clank of the copier, somebody cursing something like not having enough resources, or the crinkle of plastic and snap of carrots while people ate, there was always so much noise. But today I'd claimed my spot in the corner, away from the long table where most teachers ate, and opposite Mrs. Fay's big art cart that had caught me in the side one too many times. Fourth period was the forty-three minutes of the day I had to myself, and I took them to eat and read the newspaper in peace.

"A bit old-fashioned, don't you think?" Al said, tugging the corner of the paper.

I snatched it out of his hands. "You should know—you were around when it was invented. What're you doing here, Al?"

He laughed, pulling up a chair next to mine. "I like to see that fire in you. Good, we're going to need it."

I opened the paper back up.

"Hey, put that down, wouldya?"

"I'm reading about our game on Friday."

Al huffed. "You mean that humiliation."

"Hey," I snapped, putting the paper down. "I don't—"

"I know, I know," he said, shushing me with his hand. "If you were head coach, you would've won. I know." He shook his head sadly, and I cocked mine. That wasn't what I was going to say or what I was even thinking. "Listen." He got up close to me to whisper, "I talked to Jack Spencer."

I refused to whisper, knowing that whatever Al had up his sleeve, I wanted no part of it. "What does this have to do with me?"

"Shh. Keep your voice down," he said, looking around conspicuously. No one was paying attention to us.

"Al, what do you want?" I checked my watch, annoyed.

"I want you to keep your head down and keep doing what you're doing. Those kids do well with you. Keep it up."

"Okay. Will do." I rubbed at my eyes. There were only a few minutes left of my lunch, and I didn't want to be bothered. I picked up my paper, and he smacked my shoulder.

"We'll take care of the rest. Don't you worry about it."

"Yeah, okay," I said, back to reading already. "See ya later."

He walked away, and I followed him out of the corner of my eye. The conversation was odd, definitely laced with a disturbing undertone, yet Al was no sinister villain. He was a guy who counted down the days to his retirement. I knew he still felt ill will toward Charlie for firing him, but he was no serious threat to anyone. He could barely stay awake during his classes; he didn't have it in him to overthrow the regime or whatever stupid idea he was floating around.

Before I could think too much of it, the bell rang and I headed to lunch duty, which was fast becoming my favorite part of the day.

I met Charlie at our usual spot by the side doors.

"Long time, no see," I said in greeting, and she stood up from where she leaned against the wall.

I didn't tell her how the few hours apart were starting to feel like a long time. We'd known each other for about two months now and had spent the better part of that either arguing or glaring at one another. I figured all this time together was catch-up.

"You seem so happy about it," she said, sarcasm getting the best of her tone.

"I am happy. Do I not seem happy?"

"Your happy looks like this." She stared straight ahead of her, mouth in a line. "And your sad looks like this." She made that same face again. "And your angry looks like this." She made the face with a slight frown, her eyes a tad bigger this time. She held it for a few seconds before looking at me. "Subtle difference, but most people wouldn't notice."

"You notice," I said, and she nodded, shrugging as if it was no big thing. It didn't take a rocket scientist to recognize that I was difficult to read. God knows I'd heard it enough times in my life.

"I am happy to see you," I said after a while, and she waved me off.

"You're going to try to charm me now? Be sweet to me after all this time?" She shook her head exasperatedly, and I watched as her eyes drifted around the cafeteria, landing on a couple of girls at the end of the table fiddling with what looked like a small robot, a tiny smile flirting with her lips.

Charlie wasn't exactly an open book either. She put up a tough front, and I knew she wasn't happy that I'd seen all the tender stuff she was made of when I caught her crying this past weekend. But I wasn't going to tell. I'd keep her secret.

"Is it too late?" I asked, and she turned back to me, lifting one shoulder like she didn't care, but her smile told me otherwise. "I was reading the analysis of the game on Friday."

"Ugh." She raised her palm. "Don't tell me."

"Said it was a fluke."

"I told you not to tell me."

"They said the Otters are a different team, and are improving with every game. At this rate, we'll make it to state."

She dragged the hair tie out from the way her hair was done up all sloppy on the top of her head, only to redo that same knot. "Oh, great. The newspaper guy thinks we'll make it to the end. My life is complete."

"I thought you'd be happy to hear that."

"It's just more pressure." She shook her head and exhaled deeply before shaking her head again. "If I'm a bad coach, it's because I'm a woman. But if I'm a good coach, I've got to be undefeated to prove that I am. I can't be so-so. I'll either be the experiment gone wrong, or the coincidence. There is no average for me."

And when she looked at me with those brown eyes filled with all that emotion—good, bad, and everything in between—it clicked for me. Her whole life she'd been trying to fit in the right box, and she'd never even gotten a chance to know if it was the right shape. A loss for any other team might have gotten a paragraph or two mention. For Charlie Gibb, daughter of Lloyd Gibb, it got a whole page write-up.

"*Average* is not the word I'd use to describe you."

She shouldered me. "What word would you use?"

I thought about it for a while, fixing my tie so it lay flat against my torso, but she flipped it back out of place. "*Antagonizer.*"

She nodded slowly, hands folded primly. "Sounds about right. Can't be afraid to upset the apple cart when you're in my position."

Yeah, she'd sure upset mine.

Charlie

Game five brought another check in the W column, and Connor and I found ourselves making some lame excuse to leave the Public early to meet back up at a park. This time there were no streetlights above us or fast food between us, only the dark of his truck as we overlooked old sawmills on the water. The calming sound of the quiet rushing water and the pretty sight of the moon reflecting off the canal escaped me. It became white noise with all of my concentration on Connor.

"This is becoming a pattern," I said in between breathy pants. The way he flicked his tongue against my ear made me sound like a sex-crazed woman. And we still had our clothes on—for the most part.

He kissed my neck and fiddled with the back of my bra. "I don't mind."

"I do." I pressed my palms against his bare chest to shove away from him. I couldn't even appreciate his body with no light. "I may be from Georgia, but I don't find a dirty pickup truck swoon-worthy."

He huffed, his hands flying out at his sides as if what I was asking for was *so* difficult. "What do you want?"

"I don't know. A little romance, at least." I slid off his lap and grabbed my shirt to hold it up in front of me. "I know this . . . whatever you want to call it, an illicit affair—"

"An illicit affair. Are we living in some kind of soap opera?" He laughed, and I punched his arm.

"When we sneak around, that's what it feels like." Dirty. Cheap. I wasn't asking for champagne or diamonds or anything life-altering. Just something that felt more . . . *more*. "Am I to believe you make all your women suffer with the gearshift in their backs?"

He sighed heavily and put his shirt back on, shifting in his seat. If he was as worked up as I was, I guessed it wasn't easy to do, but this conversation needed to be had. I sat next to him, waiting for his answer.

I waited a long damn time.

"First of all, I don't have *a lot* of women. It's not like I'm out with different women every night."

"That's nice of you," I said, a little haughtier than I'd meant it to be.

He ran his hand over his head a couple of times. "I don't mean for this to happen. It just does."

"When you found me by the bathroom tonight and said,

'Meet me at Mill Ruins Park in twenty minutes,' what did you think was gonna happen?"

He growled and threw his hands up. "I don't know, Charlie. I was looking at you, and you said some stupidly cute saying and I thought, *Goddamn, I want to kiss that girl.* That's as far as I'd planned."

I stared pointedly at him before tossing my shirt over my head, hurrying to cover up my old-lady bra.

"Sorry," he apologized insincerely, and I crossed my arms. He was infuriating. Sometimes sweet, but always infuriating.

"If it ain't ants, it's fleas."

"Huh?"

"That's what I said to Ken. If it ain't ants, it's fleas."

"Yeah. What does that mean?"

"If it's not one thing, it's another."

He reached for me, extending a physical olive branch when he curled his index finger around mine.

"You think I sound funny, but I think you sound funny. Y'all up here are 'ooohhhhh goooosh.'" I pulled my vowels, overenunciating each one. "'You betcha like this hotdish and pop up north in Fargo.'"

His laugh bellowed around us, the whites of his teeth on full display. A rare sight. "Hey, now. We don't sound like that at all."

I got caught up in giggling with him. "Totally. Y'all sound like you're from a different country. But, sure, *I* have an accent." With his arm around me, we became quiet, the faint sound of water rushing below us. A question nagged at the back of my mind, and I couldn't let it go. "Are you gonna tell me about those other women?"

"We were having such a good moment."

I ignored his attempt to throw me off the scent. "And?"

"What difference does it make?"

"What are you hidin'?"

"Nothing. Why are you so pushy?"

"Why are *you* so cagey?"

He lifted his arm from my shoulders, putting distance between us. "What do you want to hear? That I go home alone every night, holed up like a monk? Would that make you feel better?"

I frowned. There were plenty of ways to interpret those words, to insinuate meaning into his tone, but I took them at face value. "I'm not dumb or a prude. Forgive me for wantin' to know a little bit about your personal life. I thought I was owed that much since not twenty minutes ago you were moanin' against my collarbone about how soft my skin is and how good I smell."

With his elbow against the window, he rubbed his hand over his mouth.

"And it's perfume, by the way. I keep it in my office to spritz on. For you," I snapped, wanting him to hear how I tried, how I put myself out there. Yet here he was, acting like a lackadaisical shithead. I told him so.

"No need to call names," he said, and I swore if he made

one more sound of impatience, I'd slap him. "The woman who called me during game night, Kim, you asked me about her that night. Remember?"

I nodded. Of course I remembered. It had lit some kind of spark inside me. Made me realize I wanted him for more than a verbal sparring partner.

"I met her a few months ago. Her kid needed tutoring."

"Oh, Jesus," I said, dropping my head into my hands.

"Hey. Jesus has got nothing to do with this," he said, a smile in his voice.

"That's for sure." My imagination raced with all kinds of images of how "tutoring" could go. "So, what, you went to her house and made the kid fill out worksheets while you banged his mom?"

He jerked his head back. "*Bang*? I don't bang. And I have some professional ethics. I waited until after the kid's sessions were done."

"And then you banged her?"

"Stop saying *bang*, will you?"

"For someone who bangs moms he meets while tutorin' children, you're awful shy about admittin' what you're doing."

He pried my hands from where they were crossed on my arms and pulled them to him, bringing our faces a few inches apart. It was the first time I could see his eyes since I'd stepped into his truck tonight, and they danced into my own.

"I don't have a problem admitting what I do. But understand me when I say I don't do anything frivolously. I was open with everyone I've been with, clear about what we each wanted. The last time I spoke to Kim was when I got home that night. I didn't think it was fair to her to continue what we had after I'd kissed you."

His tumble of honesty left me speechless. I'd figured he didn't talk about his personal life to anyone because he didn't particularly care, but it was the opposite. I should've known.

Connor didn't do anything lightly. And with that revelation, a wave of unease hit me. If he was clear with those other women, why wasn't he with me? What made me different? Why had we been hanging in this limbo for the past three weeks?

He dropped his head for a moment. "Do you want to go somewhere with me on Sunday?"

"Yeah."

He chuckled. "You answered quick." He kissed my cheek sweetly. "I'll pick you up at three."

That night, I locked myself in the bathroom for a soak, during which I ran through every short-lived relationship of my life. They were few and far between, and I'd never felt really good about myself with any of those guys. For one reason or another, I had trouble being myself. It went one of two ways: either they wanted a woman with a more traditional job with regular hours that didn't involve football, or they wanted a guy's girl, totally cool with beer and wings every day while we talked shop endlessly.

I didn't want to be either of those women. I wanted to be me.

And Connor allowed me to do that, potty mouth and all.

Yet when films rolled around the next morning and he basically ignored me yet again, I wondered what we were actually doing. I wasn't as experienced as he was in relationships, maybe sexually too. But I didn't want to think about that. I couldn't think about that. My innate competitiveness made me a jealous person.

That aside, I considered whether I was setting myself up to be hurt. I wasn't necessarily looking for him to pass a note to me that asked if I'd be his girlfriend, but I had hoped for something. Especially since he'd said he was open with the other women before. I waited for him to be that way with me, but getting anything from him was like pulling teeth. I wondered if I was so starved for attention from a man that I was shortchanging myself. That I was settling for less.

'Cause I sure as shit wasn't a settler.

I was a fighter.

It just so happened that I delighted in fighting with Connor.

SUNDAY ARRIVED before I had any answers to my questions, and Sonja happened to be home when he came to pick me up. She answered the door just as I reached the bottom of the steps, able to see her brows raise to her hairline.

"Connor? What are you doing here?"

He looked past her shoulder to me, fumbling for an answer. "Oh, we're running out for a bit."

Sonja quirked her mouth at me, and I pretended I didn't see the flicker of understanding in her eyes.

"Okay," she said, backing away from the door. "I guess I'll see you later?"

"Yeah, won't be gone long." I smiled and closed the door on her knowing grin and cocked head.

"I hope you dressed warmly," Connor said once we were on the road. "We're going to be outside."

"What are we talkin' here? Ice fishin'?"

He nodded, and terror must've been written on my face because he backtracked. "I'm kidding. We're going to a soccer game. You want to stop for something warm to drink first?"

"I thought you'd never ask."

I fought his fingers for control of the radio, and ended up losing to some ridiculous punk station with blaring drums. "These songs all sound the same," I said. "How can you listen to it?"

"Same could be said about your music choices." He pulled into a Caribou Coffee, the same one where he almost ran me over.

"Back to the scene of the crime?"

"Hey," he said, lining up at the drive-thru, "I didn't actually hit you."

"No, but I was seconds away from murdering you."

He tipped his head to me. "You'd never."

"Don't tempt me."

He wrapped his hand around me, his fingers warm and tight at the nape of my neck. A challenge. I put my own hand just under his jaw, the base of my palm on his Adam's apple. I squeezed, our eyes boring into one another. I felt him swallow; his lips parted slightly.

"You'd make one good-lookin' corpse," I said, and he grinned. I thought myself victorious for making him break first.

"What do you want?"

I didn't even have to think. "Medium dark chocolate mocha latte, two percent, extra whip with mocha drizzle, hold the lid."

His eyes glazed over. "What?"

"Medium dark chocolate mocha latte—you know what? Never mind. I'll order." I unbuckled my seat belt and leaned over him to stick my head out the window, my body practically draped over his. He didn't move an inch, made no room for me, and I swear I saw him smirk out of the corner of my eye as I ordered. "What do you want?" I asked him.

"Large black coffee."

"You would," I said, and relayed his order to the disconnected voice at the speaker. "Can we also have two oatmeal chocolate chip cookies, please?"

The voice told us to pull around, and I shuffled back into place, reaching into my bag for my wallet. He pushed my hand away, refusing the payment. "Does this qualify as a date if you pay?" I asked, and he sniffed.

"I don't think a drive-thru ever qualifies as a date."

I tried not to analyze that statement and got my seat belt back in order just in time to see Nate at the window. I was sure his shocked expression mimicked ours.

"Coach?" he said, slowly.

"Yeah," Connor and I both answered, and I shut my eyes, mortification coursing through my body. The possibility of being caught with my offensive coordinator had flitted through my mind from time to time, but it was mostly a vague idea. The complicated nature of our relationship had been in the forefront of my mind. Until now.

Connor paid for our drinks and handed me the cookies. "Thanks, Nate. See you tomorrow," he said, and drove off before I could come up with any words to say to my quarterback.

"Dear Lord in heaven," I said, sinking down. "Why have you forsaken me?"

"All right over there?" he asked, one hand on the steering wheel, the other holding his coffee.

"Am I all right?" I whipped my head to him. "No. Nate Anderson just saw us together."

"Yep."

"Why are you not freakin' out?"

"What is there to freak out about?" He sipped his coffee leisurely.

"We're in a car together."

"Correct observation."

"Here's another observation," I said, sitting up straight,

flicking his ear. He threw me a glare before tracking his attention back to the road. "We coach together. What would people think if they heard about us?"

"If they heard we were in a car together, getting coffee? Scandalous." He took another long sip, and I wanted to knock the cup out of his hand.

"Don't be obtuse."

"Don't be dramatic. We're adults."

I grumbled, "Is condescension your normal disposition, or do you try to be this way?"

"I think you're blowing this way out of proportion."

"I'm not. Certain people would love, *love* to hear a juicy piece of gossip about me. I have enough trouble keepin' the wolves at bay, they'd use whatever this is against me. For sure."

"Whatever this is? We're getting coffee and going to a soccer game, that's what this is."

"We've also dry-humped right where you're sittin'."

He eyed me sternly. "*Dry-hump, bang* . . . you have the vocabulary of a thirteen-year-old boy."

"I'm tryin' to be serious with you right now. Don't make jokes!"

"I'm being serious too. There is no rule at school about fraternizing. That being said, I don't plan on blabbing around to anyone about what we do, coffee or no coffee." He lifted my drink from where it sat in the cup holder. "Your disgusting coffee is getting cold. Maybe you could warm it up with those laser eyes."

I took it from him. "Rude."

I stuffed half a cookie in my mouth, the sugar softening me up again. I tilted the rest of it up to him, silently offering to share.

"I'm not big on chocolate," he said.

"Ah. That's why you're the way you are."

A slow grin spread across his face. "Hasn't helped you much either."

Connor

I parked the car and waited for Charlie to pack away her second cookie, her cheeks puffing out like a chipmunk's. I resisted laughing at her and climbed out, yanking my hat farther down on my head. It was a sunny afternoon, but that didn't help the chill that seeped through my coat. Charlie immediately sidled up to me, her ridiculous coffee between her hands like a cavewoman with fire.

"Warm enough?"

She swallowed down a healthy gulp before saying, "It's colder than a witch's tit."

I barked out a laugh. "You're familiar with witches' tits?"

"I have been called one before." There was no bitterness in her voice, like she was used to being called names. I'm sure *witch* was on the nicer side of what she'd experienced.

"Some people are assholes," I said.

"Yeah." She smiled up at me. "Takes one to know one."

I curled my arm around her, jostling her against me.

"Hey! Hey! Don't spill my latte."

I let go and she took a drink, the mountain of whipped cream halfway melted. A bit of it stuck to the corner of her mouth when she pulled the cup away. I wiped it off with my knuckle, and the tip of her tongue darted out, licking the spot just after. The temptation to kiss her there was almost too much to ignore, but a whistle sounded behind me and shook me from my impulse.

"Come on," I said, moving my hand to her back. She wore a long black parka, covering up what I knew were her usual sporty clothes, fitted to her body like they were made for her. That was the bad part about living up north: the weather forced women to wear layers upon layers to stay warm. On the flip side, it was like unwrapping a present, and from the small glimpses I'd seen of Charlie's body in the weight room, I knew she had a pretty good gift under there.

"Connor!" I raised my head, searching for where my mom's voice came from. I spotted her on the sideline of the soccer field. I waved and she grinned, watching Charlie and me make our way to her. She couldn't have looked happier, her eyes, the same color as mine, toggling back and forth between us.

"Hey, Mom."

She reached up and kissed my cheek. "Hiya, Monkey."

I was a thirty-one-year-old man who lived on his own

and benched 225, yet my mother still called me Monkey. Charlie snickered. I paid her no mind.

"Well, look here," Mom said, practically dancing in place as she ran her gaze over Charlie.

"This is—"

"Charlie, I know." Mom clapped her hands once, her mouth opening wide. "The infamous Charlie Gibb. It's nice to meet you." She hugged her immediately, patting her back. "I've been to all of your games."

"Hi, Mrs. McGuire. Nice to meet you." Charlie peered at me, her arms reluctantly wrapping about my mother, one hand holding her drink away to keep it from spilling.

"Call me Theresa, please."

My mother was a force of her own. There was no way to ease into it; meeting my family was a jump-into-the-deep-end kind of event, which was why I didn't introduce people to them very often. But Charlie wasn't afraid of a big leap.

"Wait until Sean sees you're here. He's going to be really excited." Mom released Charlie, but held on to her arm, pointing to my brother warming up on the field with his team. This was the championship game for the adult soccer league he was in.

"Uncle Connor!" I heard my name screeched from the trees before Liam beelined it straight for my legs. He crashed, almost taking me out in the process, and I reached down with one arm to pick him up and throw him over my shoulder.

Siobhan waddled after, shaking her head, one hand on

her very pregnant stomach. "Liam, what have I told you about running? You need to watch where you're going."

"He's all right," I said, pretending to drop the four-year-old, causing him to yelp in delight.

Siobhan rolled her eyes at me, spotting Charlie with Mom in the process. She did a double take.

I gave a quick introduction. "Charlie, this is my sister Siobhan."

Charlie smiled at my sister, who in turn raised her eyebrows at me. It wasn't exactly run of the mill for me to bring a woman to my brother's game.

"Nice to meet you, Charlie," Siobhan finally said, hugging Charlie, although her big belly didn't let them get too close. "Connor, please don't make him puke. He just had a Go-Gurt."

I righted my nephew and set him on his feet before moving next to Charlie. She gazed up at me, eyes wide.

"Overwhelmed?"

"Are you kiddin'? I love bein' around people who like me. I'm thinkin' of askin' your mom to adopt me."

The idea of bringing Charlie around my family for other reasons formed like a cloud in my brain before scattering away.

"Hey, Seanie," Mom called. "Look who's here!"

Sean spied me and darted over, ringing his arms around my neck. "Nono!"

"Hey, buddy." I laughed, patting him on the back. "Are you ready for this? Got your head in the game?"

Sean nodded, fixing the band of his sports glasses at the

back of his head. He jumped up and down, his long sleeves covering his hands. His cheeks were already red, probably from a combination of the temperature and him doing jumping jacks to warm up.

"I'm ready! So ready!" He slapped his thigh a few times, then glanced over to Charlie next to me and positively lit up. "Charlie Gibb?"

Charlie nodded, and Sean hugged her. This time she wasn't apprehensive, somewhat expecting it from my family by now, I supposed.

"Charlie, you coach the Otters. You won three games!"

"We did," she said with a laugh. "But I don't care about that right now. I'm here for *your* game. What position do you play?"

"Sweeper," he said, pointing to a spot on the field. "I kick it like . . ." He demonstrated a kick, his leg going waist-high with a hop.

"All right." She raised her hand for a high five, and Sean slapped it before running back to his team, all in red. "Good luck!"

He waved to her, and she gave him a thumbs-up.

I smiled to myself at how they got along. I should've known my family would love her. Between my mom's silly grin and my sister's hopeful expression, their feelings were obvious. But I didn't mind that I'd be getting multiple phone calls and texts from them tonight about her. I was just happy that Charlie was here. She'd made my family's day. And mine.

The game started, and Charlie and I both stepped closer

to the field, shouting directions, "Get the ball up the field!" and "Good kick, number four! Keep it up!"

At one point, my mother looked over to me, meaningfully raising her eyebrows. I pretended I didn't know what her questioning look meant, and turned back to the game with a "Let's go, red!"

It didn't escape me that I hadn't brought a girl around my family since Alison. And I was sure they were assuming things about the two of us, but it wasn't like I was getting down on one knee either. I simply liked being with Charlie. Plus I owed her something more than the cab of my truck, which she had so indelicately pointed out Friday night.

So here we were, cheering on my brother as he kicked the ball up the field to another player in red. Charlie jumped up and down, her drink completely forgotten, and I wished I'd let go of my resentment about her coming to Douglass as soon as I'd felt it. It certainly would have made for a more enjoyable couple of months.

Sean's team scored and Charlie absolutely lost her mind, grabbing my shoulders as she jumped up and down. Whenever the Otters scored, she barely even smiled.

My brother hopped up and down as well. I cupped my hands around my mouth. "Nice work, buddy!"

The ref brought the ball back to the center of the field, and I turned to Charlie. She'd been staring at me, not even trying to hide it. There were only a few inches of height difference between us, and with her standing so close I could count each of the caramel-colored flecks in her eyes.

I changed my mind. My word for her was *unforeseen*.

I hadn't seen Charlie coming. But before I could tell her, the final whistle blew.

The final score was 5–4.

The soccer coach had medals for each of the players, and Sean zipped right over to me. "Did you see it? Did you see me?"

"I did, man. That was awesome." I slapped his back. "Let me look at this thing," I said, holding his medal. Sean's proud grin was contagious, and I slung my arm around him for a hug. "I'm really proud of you."

"Mom," he said, holding on to me. "Can I have my phone?"

Mom grabbed his phone from her purse, and I already knew what he was up to. Sean was obsessed with taking selfies. He had pictures all over his room, his toothy smile starring in each one. "Nono, take a picture."

I bent my knees, sinking down to fit both our heads into the picture, and Sean pressed the button. The picture was slightly blurred, but he didn't care. With his medal in one hand and his phone in the other, he took pictures with all of his friends, Mom, Siobhan, Liam, and finally Charlie.

"You want your picture with me?" she asked.

"Yeah. Yeah. Come on." Sean tugged her down to his height, mushing his cheek with hers. "Cheese," he crowed, and she followed suit.

"Aww. What a good picture," she said, looking over his shoulder at the phone that he cradled.

He nodded, his eyes on Charlie, and I could tell he was already in love.

"Hey," I said with my hand on his shoulder, "don't go showing that picture to other girls. Remember what happened the last time?"

"Oh. Uh. Yeah." He frowned. "They got mad."

"Yeah. And remember what I said about your girlfriends?"

"Uh. That I should have one. Even if I like more than one, I could only have one. 'Cause it's not nice to have more."

"Yep. It's disrespectful. And you need to respect women, right?"

"Right." My brother nodded, and looked between Charlie and his phone, the picture of the two of them still showing. "But can I keep this picture? I won't show it to Ava."

"Sure," she said, tucking her hands into her pockets. "Mind if I have a copy of it too? Can you send it to me?"

His face brightened as if he'd won the lottery. He held his phone out, carefully punching in each number as she gave it to him. He hugged her once more before running off to his friends, probably to show them the picture.

"We're going to get something to eat. Want to come?" Mom asked us, Liam hanging off her leg.

I deferred to Charlie. "I appreciate that, Theresa, but I've got to get home."

"Next time," my mom said, and hugged her. And then, to my horror, petted her hair and cheek. "I'm so glad to meet you."

"Me too," Charlie said, almost leaning into Mom's touch.

We said good-bye to Siobhan and headed back to the car. "Sorry," I said, unlocking my truck. "I honestly didn't think they'd be all over you like that. Your fan club."

She bumped her elbow into mine before opening her door. "You mean, *your* fan club. It's obvious the sun rises and sets with you. Liam and Sean can't get enough of you, and your mom might as well wear a neon sign above her head that blinks CONNOR MCGUIRE IS MY SON."

We settled into our seats, and she continued, "Your family is really sweet. It's nice to have that kind of support system. Thanks for allowin' me to come with you today."

"Thanks for being here. You made more than one person's day today." I didn't tell her that one of those persons was me as I drove her home. No, I kept my mouth shut and my thoughts to myself. The last time I'd let go, I'd been a kid, young and in love, who freely told his girl every thought and feeling that crossed his mind. I'd ended up giving her a ring and a promise to love her forever. She'd given me a Dear John note the night before our wedding.

And I had no plans to relive any part of that. I'd learned my lesson the first time around. If I could keep my feelings bottled up, they'd never have a chance to breathe and grow. I'd smother them before they could live.

When I pulled up in front of her house, Charlie pointed to her front door, asking, "Want to come in? I've got leftover pizza and *Sunday Night Football*."

"You turned my mother down for leftover pizza?"

She rolled her eyes. "We were having such a nice time, and you gotta go and ruin it."

She hopped out of the truck before I could respond and didn't look back when she opened her door. I slapped my palm on the steering wheel.

The more I tried to keep it uncomplicated, the more convoluted it became. We were like kids on the playground, pulling hair and pinching each other for attention. I just wasn't sure how to make us grow up.

I opened up the text thread with Bear and Blake. What are you guys up to?

Bear responded almost immediately. Depends. What do you have in mind?

Blake answered with a picture of Fresh Wok's delivery menu. Piper's working late.

Be over in a bit I replied, and put my truck in gear.

Blake's condo was only a few minutes away, close to his pub downtown. I was used to it being clean, everything in its place, because of the three of us Blake was the neat freak. But since Piper had moved in, his normally spotless home had become a little more . . . animated. Her imprint was everywhere. I found a pair of mismatched socks underneath a pillow on the sofa and dirty Converse under the coffee table. But he didn't seem to mind.

Blake threw a coaster down in front of me for my beer. "What'd you get up to today?"

"Sean had his championship game. They won, he got a medal." I skipped the part about Charlie being at the game and how my family had fallen in love with her.

"Nice. Bet he loved that."

"Yeah, you know him."

I looked over the menu for our delivery order as we waited for Bear to show up. He was always the life of the party and the first one to arrive, so it was unlike him to open the door almost twenty minutes after I did.

"Way to finally show up," I said, sitting up from my sprawled-out position on the couch.

He waved me off and tossed his coat on one of the stools at the kitchen counter before helping himself to a beer from the fridge. "I was on the phone with my mom."

"How's she doing?" Blake asked.

"Okay." He sat down with a big sigh, and Blake and I exchanged a glance. His mom had been diagnosed with breast cancer about two years ago, and Bear had retired at the height of his hockey career to take care of her. It had been pretty bleak for a while, but she was in remission now. "She's thinking about getting reconstruction surgery. I never *ever* thought I'd talk to my mom about her getting a new pair of boobs, but I did tonight."

He ran a hand through his long hair, looking wiped out, but I supposed I would too if I had to have that conversation. He reached for the menu. "I'm starved. Gimme that."

"Wait. Real quick before we order, I wanted to talk to you guys about something." Blake got up and disappeared down the hall to the bedroom, returning with a small box in his hand. "What do you think?"

He opened the box to reveal an engagement ring.

"You're proposing to me?" Bear asked, his hand on his heart, but Blake rolled his eyes.

"Seriously. I want to know what you think, honestly."

"I honestly think you and Piper are the real deal, man," Bear said, and stood up to give Blake a hug before they turned to me.

I pointed to the ring. "It's pink."

"Rose gold," Blake said.

"Pink."

"Dude. It's, like, a fancy gold. It's cool, right? Do you think Piper will like it?"

"I think she'll love it," Bear said, supplying all the right comments.

I, on the other hand, stumbled as memories of the engagement ring I'd bought flooded my mind. Envy wrapped itself around my gut that my friend had found what I'd thought I had, but I pushed it aside to stand up.

"Hey," I said, clapping Blake on the shoulder a few times as I hugged him. "I'm happy for you guys. Really, I am. You're perfect for each other."

A momentary apologetic expression crossed his features before he smiled, all goofy-like. "Happens when you least expect it."

Since Alison, I'd carefully curated my life to avoid the unexpected, but the last few months had been like one giant prank. First with the arrival of Charlie. Then finding out we actually had the same outlook for the team and coaching styles. I'd realized we got along great. And she had really good legs, toned and muscular, that felt perfect when she straddled my lap.

And her lips . . .

Charlie Gibb was what I'd least expected.

And I didn't know what the hell to do about it.

CHAPTER
19

Charlie

Today was in-service day, otherwise known as the seventh circle of hell.

I sat toward the back of the auditorium, trying to stay awake as a woman from the state board of education flipped through a PowerPoint on data analysis. This was definitely important information, but as Connor unfailingly pointed out, I didn't teach much. Sure, I made plans and had standards to follow, but I wasn't collecting data to help on state and national tests. I had the task of getting kids to participate minimally in class in order to "earn" their physical education credits to graduate. I tried to stop Tristan in second period from hitting on every girl in class and urged Madison in eighth period to talk to someone, gain some confidence in herself.

After taking one of the handouts that were passed around,

I followed the instructions to find my assigned team for discussion. Group Five gathered down in the front, and I made my way there only to find Connor walking in that direction as well.

I kept my features impassive, refusing to let him know how affected I was by him. In the past I'd been made a fool of by men, but it wasn't going to happen with him. I refused to fall for his stupid smirk and hop in his truck to explore the weird sexual tension between us.

Not anymore.

"Hey, Charlie," he said, standing at an angle behind me. I spared him one single glance. Normally he wore a button-down and tie to work, which always looked slightly ill-fitting, like a teenager who'd bought the first thing he saw on the mannequin. It was annoyingly endearing.

But because of the in-service, everyone had dressed casually. And Connor was born to wear the light denim he had on today. His jeans were worn in all the right places and fit him like a glove.

I focused on my orange tennis shoes. "Hi."

"How are you?"

"Fine."

He sat down, stretching forward to rest his arms on the back of the seat next to me. "Cat got your tongue?"

I didn't look at his face, only his jaw. A day's worth of stubble there. "Nope. I don't like cats."

"No? But Sonja has a cat."

"And he knows not to get in my way."

"How?" When I glared at him, Connor smirked. "I'm not scared of that look, if that's what you're trying to do."

I knocked his elbow away from me, causing him to tip off-balance. "You know, I don't appreciate what *you're* trying to do."

He cocked his head to the side. "What is that exactly?"

"Flirt. I don't like whiplash."

He frowned and moved out of my space when Tina arrived. I smiled at her, inviting her to sit next to me. As instructed, our group discussed the best ways to integrate data collection into curriculum. I didn't have much to contribute, but Connor, as usual, surprised me, having good ideas about using other assessments besides tests. He really did seem to be an excellent teacher. I didn't know what he was like in the classroom, but the way he interacted with students during lunch proved they respected him. So did the other teachers. Maybe a little too much. I didn't especially like the way Sandy Harrison, the geometry teacher, was looking at him with come-hither eyes.

But he was oblivious, taking copious notes on his handout.

At one point Mr. Philander stopped by to listen to our discussion. He wore a dark suit, even on a day with no students, and with the arch of his brow, it appeared as if he was judging all of us. Once he left, headed toward Group Three, Tina said under her breath, "Can't stand that guy."

"No? I thought it was just me."

She shook her head. "There's something off about him.

It's weird how he's always putting himself out there, you know? I teach because I love it, because I want to educate. But he's a climber. It seems like he's a principal for the pat on the back."

"Sometimes I wonder if he hired me for the publicity," I confessed quietly.

Tina patted my hand. "You were hired because you were the right person for the job. But I'm sure he doesn't hate that there's always a gaggle of photographers and journalists at your games."

"I know. I hate it." I huffed and folded my arms.

She smiled kindly at me and returned to the discussion at hand. At break time, I stood up to stretch, and Connor touched my arm. "You have plans for lunch?"

I'd hoped to tag along with Tina, but she was already off talking to two older teachers.

"Can I buy you lunch?"

I didn't answer.

"Please?" He leaned in close, begging me with his eyes. When he was sincere like this, not one ounce of overconfidence in his face or voice, it was impossible to say no.

"Not if it's a drive-thru," I said, and he smiled.

"Your choice."

"And I'm driving this time." I pointed a warning finger at him: there would be no fooling around in his truck like some sad country song about a girl who kept coming back for more.

We grabbed our things, and he followed me out to my car. It was rare to see him without a baseball cap on, and I found myself staring at him as he fiddled with the seat to adjust it to fit his six-two frame.

"Stop ogling me," he said, his attention on the seat belt while he buckled it. "Makes me think you only want me for my body."

"Well, I certainly don't want you for your sparkling personality."

"Yeah." He scratched his cheek, his focus everywhere but on me. "I wanted to talk to you."

"Okay." I started the car and pulled out of the parking lot to turn left, acting as if I'd never heard *those* words before, in *that* tone. If he was going to tell me he'd made a mistake in kissing me all those times or that he really wanted to keep me as his "friend," I wasn't going to give him any more attention than necessary.

Two minutes passed before he spoke again while we were stopped at a red light. "It's like we're going around in this circle. And it's stupid."

"What do you mean?"

He ran his hand over his hair, going silent again as I made another turn into the little parking lot of the bistro. I parked the car and took a deep breath. If he didn't have the balls to say something, I would. "Listen, I feel—"

"Let's stop this fucking runaround."

"What?" I froze.

"We got something going on here, right?" He didn't wait for me to answer. "We're both grown adults, so let's stop acting like children on the playground."

"Wow."

He turned in his seat to face me. "You look confused."

"Yeah. I'm confused that you're admitting this to me out loud."

He smiled, proud of himself, but it slowly melted. "What's wrong?"

I shrugged, refusing to answer, and fiddled with the two bands on my wrist, my sticky self-esteem and bad history with men rearing its head. But Connor wasn't as patient as me. He laced his fingers in mine and tugged my arm over, making me raise my eyes to his.

"What is it?"

"We work together. Coach together . . ."

"Yeah, and?"

I sighed. He was really going to make me point out the obvious. "And I'm a football *player*."

He rolled his finger in a motion for me to get to the point.

"And you like that?"

He tilted his head playfully. "It's one of your better qualities, yeah."

"Is this a trick?" I asked, wondering if he was trying to throw me off my game to somehow steal my job.

He brushed away a few of the hairs that had fallen in my face. "No, it's not a trick. I like a lot of things about you. Do I need to list them?"

I allowed the smallest of smiles. "It wouldn't hurt."

"Well, I'll start with those tight pants you wear to work

out in. I like it when you get all huffy and mad at me with your finger against my chest. And I like it when you kiss me. I think about your lips . . . a lot. More than I should think about another coach's lips." He touched the corner of my mouth with the pad of his thumb. "Okay?"

I swallowed thickly. "I think that's the most words you've ever said to me at one time."

He bent his head toward me conspiratorially. "And what did you think of them?" Stunned into silence, I didn't answer, and he reached up to take the elastic out of my hair. "Just say it."

"I didn't think you'd want me," I confessed softly after a while.

He brushed that off as if what I'd admitted was dumb. Inevitably, it all came back to a fight. He capped it off with: "Don't talk stupid."

"I'm not stupid," I said, lurching away from him.

He rolled his eyes. "I didn't say you were stupid. I said, 'Don't *talk* stupid.'"

"You are the worst."

"And you don't see yourself clearly."

"And you—"

"Just shut up and kiss me," he said, grabbing me by my shoulders.

And I did.

I kissed him until there was nothing else to do, nowhere to go. I pulled away from him, both of us breathing hard. "Your truck is much bigger than my car."

"I didn't mean to end up like this again." He pulled at his pants, and when I laughed, he tossed his hands up. "Let's go. I gotta get out of this tight space. I've been walking around with blue balls for a couple weeks now, I don't need you laughing at me for it."

"Drama king," I teased, and got out of the car.

A colorful sign greeted us for the Middle Eastern restaurant. Inside, a handful of tables dotted the small space, and we occupied the solitary one available in the corner by the window. Yara, a young girl I'd come to know, handed us glasses of water.

"Roasted red pepper hummus?" she asked.

"Please. Thank you."

She smiled and went back to the kitchen.

"You come here a lot?" Connor asked, looking over the small menu.

"Yeah," I said, pointing to the falafel panini. "That's my favorite. The family who own this place are from Damascus. Delicious food, good people."

He nodded as Yara came back with a plate of hummus and pita. Over the past few weeks, I had gotten to know the family pretty well. Enough to know that Alfred had one more semester of community college before he transferred out, and that his mother, Talitha, wasn't looking forward to her son moving away. And that Yara had had a second date with a guy last weekend.

"So, how was it?" I asked, and she grinned, tossing her dark hair over her shoulder.

"Good. Really good. He's coming over this weekend to meet the family."

I put my chin in my hand. "Ooh. That was fast."

"Well, you know, they need to vet everybody," she said with a resigned raise of her shoulder, "no matter how quick things are moving. But, yeah, he's special."

"That's exciting. I'm happy for you."

"Thanks." Yara's eyes flitted between me and Connor, inquisitive.

"This is Connor," I said, gesturing to him. "We . . . work together."

She smiled at him. "Nice to meet you. I'll be back in a bit with your food."

As soon as she'd gone, he mumbled, "Work together, make out in cars, one and the same."

"That's how you want me to introduce you from now on? Connor who I make out in cars with?"

He used a piece of pita to scoop up some hummus, avoiding the question.

"You're going to make me ask?"

He popped more food into his mouth.

"Fine," I said, irritated. "What is going on between us?"

"That's up to you." He gestured to where Yara had stood moments ago. "You're the one clearly uncomfortable with this, so you tell me what you want it to be."

I thought about it. "I like being with you."

"But . . . ?" he intoned, obviously picking up on my hesitation.

"But I'm not sure I want to tell people yet."

He nodded. "Okay."

I smiled. He smiled, and our eyes met as he licked a bit of hummus off his thumb. I took my own bite, his eyes going to my mouth, and his words from earlier echoed in my head: *I think about your lips . . . a lot.*

"I like how you pretend you're this pearl-clutching lady in white. You curse more than most men I know, and I heard you calling out some especially crude words the other day when I was in the hall."

"When?" I tried to remember what he was referring to, and snapped my fingers when I got it. "Oh! Sex education week."

His eyebrows raised. "Week?"

"Yeah, you think I'm going to spend just one class period on STDs and pregnancies? These kids are dumber than rocks when it comes to that stuff." I had two periods of health this semester, and the bird and the bees were required teaching.

"How's that working out for you?"

"I've got the basics covered. Insert piece A into piece B hasn't changed, at least I don't think it has."

He absently rubbed his palms together the way he would warm them in front of a fire. "Changed?"

I swallowed back my fear. I wouldn't be a coward. Not when today seemed to be the day we were putting it all out there. "It's been a while . . . for me . . . with that. . . ." When he covered his smile with his hand, I kicked his shin. "It's not funny."

He lowered his hand from his face and dropped it under the table to grab my leg, right under my knee. "You're right. It's not. If you're worried about it, I think I can catch you up."

"Oh, do you, now?"

His thumb stroked up and down the side of my knee. "I'd do anything for education."

"If you don't mind," I stammered, "I guess that'd be good."

We gazed at each other, our eyes gleaming with something yet to be experienced between us, his hand on my leg, my own inching across the table for him. My pulse raced. Heart beat erratically. The inferred promise made me over-eager. Made me weak.

"How am I going to go back to work now?" I asked, my multiple layers of clothing stifling me. I dragged the top of my zip-up shirt down, revealing an inch or two of my neck and collarbone, and his eyes snagged there.

"My question exactly."

Yara arrived with our plates of food, leaving almost no room on the table. Connor let go of my leg to eat, and I actually missed the contact, even though we were mere inches apart. The table was so small we were practically eating in each other's laps, but it wasn't close enough for me.

While I chowed down on my panini and chips, Connor had ordered some plain chicken with a salad, and I wondered if his diet really did affect his mood. Going without carbs would make me cranky too, but boy, did he look good.

When we finished, Connor kept his hands to himself as we walked back to my car, and after having him to myself in close quarters for thirty minutes, being outside with space between us burst my bubble. Too much air and room to breathe put ideas into my head, like he would only show emotion when we were alone and squeezed together.

"Hey, Charlie," he said, and I lifted my head, bringing our faces mere inches apart. He slung his arm around my shoulders and kissed my temple. "Thanks for coming to lunch with me."

I fit well next to him, my head at the right height to lean into his shoulder, and my second thoughts about him disappeared. He opened my door for me, like a well-mannered gentleman, and I let him plug his phone in to cue up his playlist. Like a real couple.

Back at school, we went to the auditorium to sit through Mr. Philander's PowerPoint about our school's test scores with the rest of the faculty, but this time it was with the knowledge that Connor and I had turned a corner. No more running in circles. This was a new game. I didn't know the rules yet, but I sure as hell wanted to play.

CHAPTER
20

Charlie

We were crushing the Patriots from Patrick Henry High, and with one quarter left I put in our second string. Piper and Sonja were in the stands, and I turned at their obnoxious, wild cheering. Piper, decked out in Otters regalia, and Sonja, holding a sign, waved at me. If it were anyone else, I would've been mortified, but with my new friends, I filled with love.

Ironically, they were only a few feet away from Mr. Spencer, who couldn't have been more uncomfortable if he tried. It was almost as if I'd told the girls about him or something. . . .

Connor made his way over to me, stuffing another lollipop in his mouth.

"What did I tell you about those?"

The thing twisted around in his mouth, and he moved

his headset microphone away. "I don't begrudge you playing with the bands on your wrist, do I?"

"Because you can't hear me doing it."

He smirked and pulled a small lollipop from his pocket. He glanced down at it. "Cotton candy. Want it?" When I didn't reach for it, he wiggled it in my face. "It's sweet. Come on, Coach."

I grabbed it and in one motion had the wrapper off and the lollipop in my mouth just in time to watch Johnny Heimer score a touchdown. "Yeah, Johnny, yeah!"

The pipsqueak of a sophomore jumped up and down and the other players all ran to him, chest-bumping and high-fiving, but I overheard Brett Spencer on the sideline say something about what a loser he was. I tore my headset off, ready to go after him, but Connor stopped me with a hand on my arm.

He got hold of Spencer's face mask and dragged him off a few yards to where no one could hear. Brett was tall and muscular, a hell of an athlete, with a great read of the field. Damn shame he had such a piss-poor attitude. Connor spoke to him, his face giving nothing away, but I knew him better than that. I knew by the way his fingers curled at his side that he was on fire. I imagined his voice dangerously low with that acerbic tone.

A minute later, Spencer was at the other end of the sideline and Connor was back at my side.

"What did he say?" I asked.

"He apologized, but he's going to be staying with me

an hour after films tomorrow. He owes the team an extra workout."

Even though I was satisfied—he'd have Spencer running the bleachers the entire time—something still rankled me. Connor had gotten an apology out of him when I never could. Because of my gender, I was sure. It was good Connor could get to him in that way, but I still resented it.

"Don't worry," Connor said. "He'll be happy he can still flap his gums after I'm done with him."

We bumped our fists together, the most we'd touched since our lunch on Monday. And with the final seconds winding down, I knew that the time for us to be together inched closer.

"I see you brought your own cheering section with you tonight?" he said, putting his headset in the box after the final buzzer.

"You have yours all the time. I figured I needed one too."

He waved at his mom and brother before following me over to the fence.

"Hey, girlie!" Piper reached out for a high five. "I don't get football at all, but that was exciting!"

Sonja hugged me. "Quite a blowout."

"The scores aren't usually like that. And our record is only four and two now."

"Four and two is great," Sonja said, pushing my shoulder hard enough that I fell off-balance.

"Not perfect."

Piper scrunched up her nose. "You don't have to be perfect. You're already better than the guy before you. Right, Connor?"

He nodded, but I flicked his agreement away.

"*I* need to be perfect. Dick basically lost every game, and he's still considered a legend. I'm new and a woman, there's a lot riding on whether or not I can take this team to the end. It's state or bust."

Connor made a dubious noise next to me, and I glanced his way to see him shaking his head ever so slightly.

"So, we're going out after?" Sonja asked. "Should we just meet you at the Public, or do you want to go somewhere else?"

Piper bounced on her toes. "Yeah. Birthday girl's choice. Don't let my relationship with the owner sway you."

I laughed at her. "No, the Public is good."

We made plans for me to meet them in about forty-five minutes and said good-bye. When they walked off toward the exit gate, Connor brushed up against me.

"Birthday?"

I looked up at him. "Hmm?"

"Why didn't you tell me it's your birthday? How old are you?"

"First of all, I didn't tell anyone. Second, I didn't know that was a thing we were doing." I supposed it was up to me to set the rules of this *thing we were doing*, but I was way out of my league. "And third, don't you know it's not polite to ask a woman her age?"

"I'm not known for my politeness," he said, and I couldn't

disagree with him there. He shoved his hands in his pockets and we took our time as we sauntered to the end zone. "I'm thirty-one. My birthday is January second." And then he waited me out in silence.

I sighed. "I'm thirty-two today."

"Basically an old hag," he deadpanned.

"Don't joke," I said, the truth falling from my tongue before I could stop it. "I've got anxiety about it."

"Anxiety for what?"

I waved to Jim, who threw me a thumbs-up from his spot by the concessions stand. "I thought I would've accomplished more by now. I'm solidly in adulthood yet have nothing much to show for it. No big success in my career, no house, no man. No nothing. Not even a dog."

He stayed silent, and I wished I could take it all back. I'd revealed too much of myself to him, making us uneven. He knew more about me than I did about him.

"I wouldn't say nothing," he said finally, stopping at the end of the fence. "You've got your own Wikipedia page."

"Oh, so you finally did some research, huh?"

"I have to keep up with you." He elbowed me, then glanced over his shoulder to where his mom and brother waited for him. "The rest will fall into place."

"Nice platitude."

He smiled sadly, a slight tic, only slightly indistinguishable from his other smirks. "I'm still hoping for my puzzle pieces to fit too."

A million and one questions entered my brain, but none

would be answered now, or anytime soon, given his tight-lipped nature. Instead of asking them, I gave a quick hello to his family, including big hugs, and parted ways with him. But before I got too far, he called out to me, "Hey. See you tonight."

His words were friendly, but his tone sharp. A delicious threat. A combustible command that smoldered inside my chest until we met back up at the pub a little while later. The fire in his steely blue eyes then as they coursed over me set off the explosion inside of me, radiating from my finger-tips to my toes.

"You look good," he finally said after I'd greeted the rest of the coaches, who were spread out in the few open spaces available in this big crowd.

"It's just jeans and a sweater," I told him, glad I'd thought ahead to bring a change of clothes to my office, and even more that I'd smeared on ruby-red lipstick with Gram's voice in my head: *If you don't wear red, you might as well be dead.*

My gram, God rest her soul. She'd died right after I grad-uated college, and we'd spent a good ten years before that fighting over my hair and makeup.

I'd never got that line until now, sandwiched between Connor and the bar. He licked his bottom lip, a tease, and grazed his thumb on my hip, a promise.

"Beauty queen."

"Stop." I rolled my eyes and twisted around to gesture to Blake, who was busy behind the bar. He saw me and smiled as he finished up serving another patron before coming to stand in front of me.

"Packed tonight," I said.

He regarded the masses with a proud grin. "Yep." He knocked on the dark wood of the bar. "What can I get for your birthday drink?"

"Who told you?"

He raised his eyebrow, the answer obvious.

"Piper can't keep a secret."

He chuckled. "You're telling me. So, what'll it be?"

"Two fingers of your best bourbon over ice."

"Hey now," a guy said next to me. I dropped my attention from Blake to a man sitting on a stool, his shaggy hair combed to one side, wearing a maroon blazer. Narcissism dripped from his bright white smile. "Bourbon? My kind of girl."

He did look good, in a GQ fashion kind of way, but he wasn't my kind of guy.

"I'm sure you'll find one of them around here somewhere," I said, angling away from him.

"Stone cold." GQ pouted in a way he probably assumed was sexy.

It was not.

Connor's arm slid behind my back to rest his hand on the bar next to me. "You want to sit down?"

He motioned to the stool in front of him that had appeared out of nowhere, seeing as there were none available moments ago. I sat, and he immediately moved, blocking out

GQ's access to me. I didn't mind. Connor was my kind of guy, ratty baseball hat and all.

Blake slid a glass of amber liquid to me as bodies rustled behind us. Bear parted the crowd, followed by Sonja and Piper.

"It's crazy in here tonight," Sonja said, leaning over to kiss my cheek. Piper followed suit, then crooked a finger in a tiny wave to Blake, who practically lay across the bar for a kiss.

Bear high-fived me. "Giblet, how's it going?"

"Good." I pointed to his ever-growing beard. "Going for a Paul Bunyan vibe?"

He tugged at the hair on his face before taking off his knit hat to reveal the mess of hair on his head. "My family *is* from Bemidji."

"Be-what?"

Connor shook his head. "Bemidji." He picked up the beer bottle Blake had placed next to him. "It's supposedly where Paul Bunyan is from."

I nodded, my attention on Piper as she fished a single cupcake from her purse. She handed the plastic container to me, saying, "It's carrot cake."

"My favorite." Truly touched, I almost didn't want to open it and ruin the fancy icing, but Piper pulled out a candle and lighter. My cheeks started to burn in embarrassment. "You're really going to make me do that?"

"Of course," she said, grinning. She took the cupcake out of my hands and set it all up on the bar, lighting the wick. "Make a wish."

I hesitated, and glanced around at the five people surrounding me. Friends in a place that made this city feel like home after years of going it alone, they were my wish. I closed my eyes, not to make a wish but to thank God for them, before blowing out the candle. They all clapped. Normally I'd have been self-conscious about the attention, but I wasn't with them. Until Connor bent to my ear and whispered, "Happy birthday."

I picked up my glass, trying to ignore the flush I felt coloring my neck and face. "Cheers, everyone."

They all clinked glasses and bottles to mine, but Bear was the one to point it out. "You're all red."

I touched my fingers to my cheek. "It's the amount of people, I think."

Connor stepped closer to me, his torso pressing lightly against my back, and I knew he'd done it on purpose. The bastard knew it'd throw me off.

I couldn't pay attention to any of the conversations around me. Not to Piper talking about opening up her dream brewery next month, not to Sonja explaining how she needed to win her next fight to get on the Olympic team, and especially not to Bear rambling on about his reading of Jack Kerouac.

After finishing my drink, I excused myself to go to the bathroom and was both relieved and disappointed to be away from the solid wall of Connor behind me. It'd been four days since we'd had any physical contact that was more than a fist bump or an elbow to the side, and the mere hint of anything else felt earth-shattering. The unspoken understanding of what was to happen had made me hyperaware of him, and with the loss of his contact, I felt overexposed.

I spent an extra minute in front of the mirror, finger-combing my hair over my shoulders as some form of cover. But I couldn't camouflage the flush of my cheeks or my bright eyes, and when I opened the door, he was there.

I couldn't hide anything from him.

"Are you following me or something?"

Instead of answering, he pushed off the brick and leaned over me, forcing my back against the wall, my head tilting up. His thumb dragged along my lower lip.

"Red like a lollipop. Did you wear this for me?"

His hand spread over my jaw and neck, trapping me. One of the things I liked best about Connor was his size—not that he was much taller than me, but he made me feel petite, feminine. He made me feel wanted.

"I think you did," he said.

I wouldn't confirm or deny, but the way he looked like he could eat me made me want to wear it every day. I'd happily sacrifice myself to the Big Bad Wolf.

"What big eyes you have," I murmured, wrapping my fingers around his wrist, closing the tiny distance between us. My lips barely brushed against his when I said, "What big teeth you have."

"Hmm?"

"Little Red Riding Hood."

He pulled back to look at me, not understanding. "You've got a weird sense of humor."

"At least I have one," I said, and pressed a small, chaste kiss on the center of his mouth. The spark of a fire.

Then his hands tangled in my hair, and mine tugged on the waistband of his pants. Those teeth of his scraped against my lower lip, and if I died from his attack I'd be okay with that.

"You think you're about ready to get out of here?" he asked, one hand inching up under my sweater.

"Yes. Please, yes."

"Begging already?" I felt his smile against my throat.

"I'm leaving now." I swallowed, forcing my eyes open. "Meet me at my house in twenty."

I ducked around him, not even making eye contact to be sure of this arrangement. My single goal was to get home as quickly as possible. The crowd had thinned out since it was closing in on midnight, and I beelined to the group. I grabbed my coat. "I'm going to head out."

"Already?" Bear pointed his thumbs down.

"I'm too old to be staying out late."

"You sound like Sonja," Piper said.

Sonja shrugged, unaffected, as she placed her water with lemon on the bar. "Speaking of. I think I'll head home too."

I stopped her. "Are you sure? You should stay, have fun. You've been working hard lately."

"Exactly," she said, looping her arms into her coat. "I'm ready to sleep for ten hours."

I panicked. Sonja being home wasn't part of the game plan. "Oh, um, okay." Connor reappeared at my side, and I stared at him, hoping he'd get my mental message. "Sonja's leaving too."

He slung his jacket on. "That makes three, then." With one single raise of his brows, he looked at me. "I'll see you later."

He changed the play with his audible.

CHAPTER
21

Connor

Despite protests, I left without much more than a few words to Blake, Bear, the girls, and the coaches. I had somewhere to be.

And I knew she'd follow.

For the first time ever, I'd used the contact saved in my phone and texted Charlie my address. She arrived minutes after me, and like the bastard I was, I didn't even say hello before I hauled her to me. We made it exactly four steps to the couch, our clothes only two.

I'd like to say I took my time, that it was romance all the way, but that didn't happen. I skipped all the good stuff and went right for the score. Charlie didn't seem to mind though.

No, she was right there with me, sloppy kisses and even sloppier hands. It was over in minutes, and we sat splayed out, limbs draped loosely over each other. A blanket hung limply over our naked bodies, hardly providing any coverage. But again, she didn't care, a lazy smile crossing her face.

With her head against the cushion, she turned to me, her finger lifting up a few inches. "Nice place you got here."

I swiped a palm down my face.

"Oh, look. A ficus."

I followed her gaze to the tall fake tree in the corner of the living room.

"You have a china cabinet." She sat up, the blanket dropping off of her chest. "You have actual china too. Why? Hosting lots of fancy parties?"

I slanted my eyes away to the blank TV. "People have china."

"I know. But why do you?"

"Why not?"

She snorted. "Because you're you. You've got calluses on your hands and wear baseball hats and jeans with holes in them. You spend most of your time at school, and I'm sure when you come home you always use the same plate and fork for your bland grilled-chicken dinner. You don't use fine china."

After the whirlwind we'd just had, I wasn't ready for her inquisition or her acute description of my life. I'd expected something different, something not so . . . personal. And my defenses went up. "Hey, you're in my house. Isn't it bad manners to ask your host so many questions?"

Her mouth snapped shut, her cheeks red for a reason

other than me, and I immediately wanted to swallow my words back.

"Okay," she said, grabbing her sweater from the floor.

"Charlie, I'm sorry—"

"No." She held up her shoe, pointing it at me. "Don't."

I slipped my pants on, an odd juxtaposition with trying to keep her from getting dressed to leave. "Can you hold on a second?"

"No, Connor, I can't wait a second." She buttoned up her coat, the snaps echoing the anger in her words. "I get that this is our relationship, the arguing and the digs. It's all in good competition. But as soon as I think we're moving beyond that, you remind me we can't. There is no substance with you, only surface-level crap. So I'm leaving now." She turned on her heel, opening my front door with a curt, "Thanks for the fuck."

When it slammed, I sat back on the couch. It was still warm from her body. My skin still burned from the scratches of her nails. And I was still a bastard.

I raked my hands over my head and made a game-time decision. I jumped up and ran after her, needing to apologize or try to explain, but I made it to the sidewalk just in time to see her taillights take off down the street. "Damn it."

I truly hadn't meant to be rude. It was just that explaining the china cabinet, or the light fixtures, or the color of the cabinets couldn't be done without bringing up Alison. And that was one subject I *never* talked about. Instead of telling her that sad, sorry tale, I'd done what I was good at: I deflected.

I wasn't good at making phone calls, and even worse at texting, so I hoped I'd be able to explain things to her face-to-face. My first opportunity was Monday morning in the weight room—but for the first time in weeks, she didn't show up, and I felt lost. I didn't have relationships for this reason. They were hard. Confusing. Emotionally draining.

But I'd do it. I'd do it for Charlie.

On my lunch, I ran out to Caribou Coffee to get her one of the fancy coffees she liked. I figured it couldn't hurt to sweeten her up with sugar, but by the time lunch duty rolled around, it was cold.

She turned her nose up. "What's this?"

"A gift." I held it up until she took it. "An apology." When she didn't drink the coffee, I offered a suggestion. "I know it's not hot anymore, and I know I screwed up the order, but I figured you could put it over some ice. You like iced coffee, right?"

She nodded begrudgingly, and plunked the cup down on the empty table next to her. I had an uphill battle.

"How come you weren't working out this morning?"

"I didn't feel like it, and you can stop trying to get me to talk. I'm not giving you the silent treatment, if that's what you expected."

I played with my tie. I didn't expect anything, and that was the God's honest truth. All of this was new to me.

"Okay," I said. A few minutes passed before I tried again. "Sean has your picture in a frame in his bedroom."

She dropped her arms from where they were wrapped

around her waist, and stared at me with such bored annoyance that she actually made me wish I hadn't said anything. Usually people were mad at me for not talking. But now she glared at me *for* talking.

The confusion never ended.

"This is what I don't get about women. You get mad at us for not doing a thing, then we do the thing, and you get mad at us for doing the thing. It's like . . ." I rolled my hands around each other.

"Don't blame women for your idiocy. I have never gotten mad at you for anything other than being yourself, which is a dick knob."

I glanced around, checking for any ears listening before I looked back at her. "They might be able to hear you cursing."

"Please." She put her palm up to me. "You know the mouths these kids have. Worse than mine."

It was obvious I was getting nowhere, but I tried one last time. "I think you look really pretty today."

She rolled her eyes and walked away toward a group of volleyball players. She didn't speak to me directly for the rest of the day, but I didn't give up.

Tuesday morning, I left her a bag of Skittles on her desk. At lunch, she gave the bag back to me.

"I don't like Skittles."

"What? No. I saw you eating them."

She shook her head. "No. M&M's I'm addicted to. Not Skittles."

I took them back, frustrated.

"Second and ten," she said, and I smiled. Her words meant I had two more chances.

Wednesday she made a return to the weight room. I was prepared, just in case, with Britney already playing and a donut. I showed her the pink-iced "breakfast."

She didn't take it. "Why food?"

"Hmm?" I didn't understand the question.

"Why do you think I want food?"

A few seconds passed before I said, "I'm trying to apologize."

"But why with this? What makes you think I want a donut, or candy, or coffee?"

"Because you like it." But my voice rose in a question, and she shook her head, a soft laugh breaking through.

"Bless your heart."

"What? I'm trying to do something nice for you. I'm being nice!"

"Yes," she said, backing away from me to stand by a bench. "Anyone can bring me candy. I don't want that from *you*."

"What do you want then?"

She kept her eyes on me as she loaded a plate on the bar. "Third down."

I went home that night wondering what the hell I was supposed to do. I had one more chance to prove to her I wasn't the inept asshole she thought I was. I opened my refrigerator to retrieve the portioned meal I'd already prepared of chicken, sweet potatoes, and broccoli.

I hated that Charlie knew details about me without trying and I couldn't do the same for her. She didn't try to figure them out. She had just known. Things that I'd never told her. She could read my face when no one else could.

I microwaved my dinner and grabbed a fork, remembering how she'd said I ate with the same fork and plate all the time. But she was wrong, I owned more than one plate. I ate off of, probably, four.

God, she was irritating.

I sat down in the living room to watch TV while I ate, but a colorful card on the table snagged my attention. I put my food down to pick up the invitation, reading it over. When Sean had given it to me, he'd looked just as nervous as he did every year. As if I wouldn't go. But I'd never miss out on something so important to my brother as the annual costume bash.

That was when I realized what Charlie wanted. To be included. It would be hard to let her into my life, but I could try, because she was important. The affection that had grown between us felt big, at least to me.

I waited until after practice on Thursday, after all the players and coaches had gone and only Charlie was left. She was tapping a green marker on her desk as she watched film on her computer. When I knocked on the doorframe, she didn't lift her head. "Yeah?"

"Can I come in?"

That made her look up. She waved me in and sat back in her chair. "What can I do for you, Coach McGuire?"

I placed the invitation on her desk and pushed it toward her with one finger. "You're cordially invited to the annual Halloween party for the MPLS Adult Education Program."

She turned the invitation in her fingers and read it over before eyeing me. Her gaze gave nothing away. "Sean wants me to come?"

I shook my head. "*I* want you to come. With me."

She rested the corner of the invitation on her chin, inspecting me up and down. For once, her silence made me nervous.

"It's a fund-raiser they have every year. I thought, maybe, you'd want to come with me."

She pursed her lips.

"It's a costume party, though."

She tilted her head. "Let me guess, you don't like Halloween parties."

"I don't, but Sean does. We get matching costumes. Last year we were Mario and Luigi."

"Okay. I'll go."

"You will?"

She shook at her head at me as if I didn't have a clue. "Of course I'll go. I like when you try. It's pretty simple actually."

I fixed my hat. I didn't think it could be simple.

I overthought what women wanted because Alison had left me second-guessing myself and everything I knew about relationships.

"I'll pick you up Saturday at six-thirty?"

"Perfect," she said, and then a few seconds passed where

we both stared at each other as if waiting for the other to speak.

I broke first. "You heading out of here soon?"

"No, I've got some stuff to do."

I waited.

"We have to win tomorrow and next week to make it to the playoffs," she said, her hands up in defense.

"You don't think we will?"

"If Nate can throw past their safety and Jaylin can out-run him, we have a shot."

I pulled up a chair next to her to get a better look at her computer. "The safety isn't the issue. It's the cornerback. We've got to beat him first." I grabbed her mouse to press play, the game turning back on. "See that? Twenty-two's got some legs on him."

I watched the screen, but she watched me. If she was trying to make me uncomfortable, she was doing a great job. "Why are you staring at me?"

"Because I think we make a good team."

"I do too."

We both moved, sitting much closer together than when we'd started, the sleeve of her Georgia Tech hoodie touching my arm. She was forever cold and had taken to wearing layers upon layers, even inside.

She adjusted said layer. "I like to see your passion. Very rarely do you show it, but with this you do."

I nodded, and pointed to the screen. "Clearly you've never seen my lecture on Manifest Destiny."

"Riveting, I'm sure," she said with her chin in her hand.

"It is. I'm telling you, I don't consistently get asked to be class trip supervisor for nothing."

She nodded sarcastically. "I bet. That's a real honor."

I smirked, yanking her to me so I could kiss her temple. "Stick with me, kid, I'll show you the ropes."

CHAPTER
22

Charlie

Connor was right. Washburn's cornerback was the player who gave us a run for our money, but we came out on top, giving us good momentum going into the last regular-season game. One more win and we were headed to the playoffs, and, I hoped, into the state finals. But instead of falling into my old pattern with him, I refused to sit anywhere close to Connor while celebrating at the Public. I made sure to keep the table between us, and didn't return his flirtations, including the quiet invitation to meet him by the bathroom. I didn't go.

Like the lady I was.

I slipped out early to boos from the coaches, but I needed to get home to put some kind of costume together. With Sonja already asleep and Piper busy with Blake getting ready for the brewery opening, I had no friends to turn to, only the Internet. It gave me lots of wacky ideas, but I picked one that wouldn't need much work.

Although I hadn't realized the reaction from Connor would be so positive when I opened up the door Saturday night.

He pushed the dark aviators from his face, his eyes slowly perusing me from my bandanna and curled hair, to my red lipstick, and then to my legs in my skinny jeans. He whistled between his teeth, and I felt the sound reverberate through my body, but I couldn't focus on myself when he stood in front of me. Pure sex in the male form.

I tugged on his fake leather jacket, my thumb rubbing over the *Top Gun* patch on his left shoulder. The V-neck white T-shirt clung to his chest perfectly. I had difficulty looking anywhere else, but after approximately a year and a half of ogling, I raised my eyes.

"I didn't know I had a thing for Rosie the Riveter," he said breathily.

I wrapped myself up in a coat, scarf, hat, and mittens. "I've always known I had a thing for Maverick."

He licked his lips—it was positively sinful, and I had to actually shake my head to focus on locking the door behind me. But just as I put my key in my purse, he had me gathered up in his arms, his mouth on mine. I gasped in surprise and he took advantage, his tongue finding mine, but I quickly caught on. I wound my arms around him, under the jacket. Even with my winter gear on, I melted into the heat radiating from his body. His hands—gentle yet strong—memorized the curves of my face, and I sighed, wanting much more than what a kiss outside my door could give me.

He released me with one more sweet peck before backing away.

"Where's Sonja?" he asked, casually reaching out to take my hand.

"She's with Bear. His mom wanted to go to the ballet, and he got tickets for the three of them. I didn't realize he was so cultured."

He let out a low, teasing laugh. "You mean a pretentious bastard."

"Sounds like you may be a bit jealous of his world knowledge."

"Nah," he said, opening the front passenger door for me. "I'm okay without tutus and classical music. I'll stick with beer and hot wings for a good time."

"Simpleton," I said as I got into the truck. Sean was seated in the back. "Hey."

"Hi!" He slapped his thigh a few times. "You're coming to the party!"

"Yep, I am."

"I'm the Iceman!" He pointed to his green flight suit.

"I know. You look great."

Connor hopped in behind the wheel with a stupid smile, and he pointed to his lips, motioning for me to check mine. I pulled down the overhead mirror to see my lipstick smudged all over my mouth like a clown.

"You jerk," I said, licking my fingers to scrub them over my skin.

"Worth it," he said, and pulled away from the curb. Sean leaned forward toward us, and Connor glanced over his shoulder. "Is your seat belt on?"

"Yes," he answered quickly before tapping me on the shoulder. "Are you my brother's girlfriend?"

I froze, the red massacre still all over my face. "I . . . um . . ."

"That's a personal question," Connor said.

"You kissed and held hands. I kiss Ava and hold her hand and she's my girlfriend. Is she your girlfriend, Nono?"

Connor cleared his throat, and it only made me feel nominally better that he didn't have an answer either.

"Charlie and I are friends," he said after a while.

"I don't kiss my friends," Sean pointed out.

I snapped the mirror shut, holding my tongue about what kind of friends we were, and turned in my seat to ask Sean about Ava. He told me she worked in a pet store and sometimes helped out with dog grooming. He also told me about the dog he'd tried to get Connor to adopt from Ava's store.

"No way," Connor said, briefly looking at me. "It was this little yappy thing. If I'm getting a dog, it'll be a man's dog."

I huffed. "What's that supposed to mean?"

"Ya know." He held his elbows out. "Something big and intimidating, named Diesel or Tank. Not a little white rodent named Ginger."

"I don't know," I said. "I could see you with a Chihuahua or Pomeranian. You could carry it in a backpack."

"Yeah, right."

"I liked her," Sean said.

"I know you did, buddy. But you already have your guinea pig. And since you're going to be moving out on your own soon, I think Bart is good enough for now. Right?"

It took Sean a couple moments to agree, but he did, and my heart softened with every conversation I witnessed between Connor and his brother. He was so sweet and patient, it was hard to remember he was the same guy who used to fight me at every turn. I could picture him with a bunch of kids, throwing them around the way he did Liam, teaching them how to throw a football, and tenderly tucking them in at night.

I'd thought about marriage and children the way I'd thought about winning the lottery—that it would change my life, but the chances of it happening were slim. Didn't deter me from dreaming; and right now Connor seemed like a dream guy.

When we arrived at the center, Sean ran ahead, leaving me with Maverick. He escorted me inside and kept his arm around me the whole time as if we were a couple. Ironic, since Sean made sure to introduce me to everyone as Charlie Gibb, Otters football coach and Connor's *friend*.

"Kissing friend," Sean told Ava behind his hand.

After a lap around the party, Connor and I spent most of the night hanging by the dessert table, watching Sean dance with Ava—and a few other girls, to his big brother's chagrin, but mostly with Ava. I learned that Connor and Sean had a standing bro date every Sunday afternoon, and that Connor was much closer to his family than he'd led me to believe, including random dinners and babysitting duty for Siobhan. His youngest sister, Brigid, lived in Vegas, and he'd flown there to move her in over the summer. Being an only child with a relatively solitary existence, hearing stories about the McGuire family had me wishing I could experience one of their loud and chaotic Christmases.

We waited until the silent auction items were called and the costume contest winners announced before heading out. Sean wanted to stay longer, and Ava's mom volunteered to take him home, so when we got into the truck our sudden isolation hit us at the same time.

"You want to call it a night?" he asked, his eyes giving away his eagerness more than his voice.

"No."

"You want to come over?"

"Yes."

His only acknowledgment was to start the engine. We rode back to his house in silence, and if there was ever a time I wished I could see inside his head, it was now. After this week of him trying to get back into my good graces, I hoped he understood that I wasn't looking for a frenemy with benefits type of situation. I wanted something more, and I wanted it with him.

Connor lived by Audubon Park, and the neighborhood

was filled with single-family homes, all adorned with pump-kins and Halloween decorations at this time of year. The last time I'd been at his house, I'd had too much going through my mind to take any real notice of it, especially after our spat. But now I had the time to admire his cute little house with beige siding and a maroon door. The neighbor to the left had an elaborate scene in the yard with inflatable witches, black cats, and a cauldron. Connor had one sad-looking ghost on a stake in the grass. When I pointed it out to him, he said, "Mrs. Hamil next door felt I lacked spirit." I laughed as he unlocked the front door and opened it for me. "What? You don't seem to be brimming with it either."

"You're wrong there." I stepped into the small foyer with light hardwood floors and set my purse down on a green table. "Piper, Sonja, and I are carving pumpkins tomorrow while drinking pumpkin lattes and eating pumpkin roll. I'm filled with the spirit."

He took my coat and every single one of my winter-weather accessories and put them in the closet next to us. He offered me a drink, but I shook my head, and he turned his palm up to me. I laced my fingers with his as he led me past the kitchen and down the hall to a room painted dark yellow, which I thought surprisingly bright for Connor.

"Did you pick this color?"

He shook his head, lightly gripping my hips, and I didn't have a chance to ask any follow-up questions about any other idiosyncrasies, such as the random painting of a daffo-dil in the living room or the frilly curtains in the kitchen, because his lips were on my neck. Every other time we'd been intimate, we'd been rushed and confined, but this time Connor was utterly leisurely.

He took his time, learning every place I liked to be kissed, every ticklish spot on my skin, as he removed all of my clothing before running his hands over my hair.

"I like you all dressed up, but I like you better without any of that," he said, tugging at my hair.

"Even without the lipstick?"

"Even without the lipstick," he said, before gently pushing me to his mattress. With his T-shirt and jeans still on, he leaned over me, his weight on his hands.

"You going to catch up or leave me here naked and cold?"

"Give me a minute, you'll warm up." That cocky smirk slanted his lips a second before he was kissing me, his mouth and hands moving lower and lower. I tried to pull him up by his shirt, but it was no use, and I kicked at his shoulder. When he looked up at me with raised brows, I fumbled my words. "I, uh, I've never . . ."

He narrowed his eyes. "You've never . . . ?"

I nervously tucked my hair behind my ear and surreptitiously brought my knees in together. "I can't have an orgasm from—"

He cut me off with a sudden slashing motion. "You've never come from someone going down on you?"

"No." I pushed myself up toward the headboard, but he yanked me back down by the ankles.

"Then they've been doing it wrong." He sank down, his eyes burning blue.

He must've felt my tension, the slight movement of my knees fighting him, because he loosened his hold on me and held on to my hips. "Try to relax. I promise you'll like it."

Those were the last words I heard from him for minutes. Hours. Days. Eternities.

I lost track of time, and of how many times I took the Lord's name in vain—God forgive me—and by the time I finally glanced over at his discarded watch on the night table, it was almost one in the morning.

Connor, with all of his perfect muscles, smiled over at me, all lazy and satisfied, and tugged on my index finger. I lifted my arm.

"Don't worry," I said. "As soon as I get feeling back in my body, I'll leave."

"Leave?" He sat up, his abdominals rippling.

I forced my attention up. "Yeah."

"But you look so good in my bed." He made me roll over, draping my arm across his torso.

"How long can I stay?"

"As long as you want." His fingers found my hair. "I'm not going to make you leave in the middle of the night." Seconds ticked by, our soundtrack the sound of his arm moving against the sheets as he petted my head. "I wouldn't make you leave even if it was the middle of the day."

"Look at you. Talkin' all sweet to me. It's almost like you like me."

"Just a little."

Between the sound of his breathing and the soothing rise and fall of his chest, I fell asleep quickly, dreaming of a football game where everyone dressed in Halloween costumes. But woke up just after Frankenstein scored because I was freezing.

I sat up and looked around. Connor was fast asleep, burrowed in the cover with one of the windows open a crack. I jumped out of bed and closed the window before taking the liberty of looking through the closet for a sweatshirt.

My rustling woke him up. "What are you doing?"

"I'm cold. I'm looking for something to wear."

He got up and turned the light on before pulling out sweats and a hoodie. I promptly put them on, noting he was still naked.

"Your window was open," I said.

"I know. I like it open."

"Why? You know it's, like, negative degrees out, right?"

"It's not negative degrees. And I like it a little cooler. I'm always hot."

"But you were buried under the covers." I pointed to the bed. "Why don't you sleep without them instead of opening the window?"

He ran a hand over his face. "Because I like being completely covered."

"Don't." I stopped him from opening the window again. "What aren't you telling me?"

We squared off, and eventually he gave up with a pitiful shrug. "I have to sleep under the covers. I need to be completely covered."

"Why?" I laughed. "You afraid something is going to get you?"

He waved me off and flipped the light off before getting back into bed.

"Don't think you're getting off that easy. You think a lizard man is going to get your ankle if it's exposed?"

"No, I don't believe in monsters. I'm not five." He yanked the covers up to his waist. "I like to be covered. I don't like body parts to stick out. Just in case."

"You're ridiculous."

"Yeah, well, you sleep like you're dead. Like a vampire."

I giggled. "You should probably cover up then so I don't get you."

He grumbled and turned away from me, but I wrapped myself around him, finding space for my arm under his. "This is really backward. You should be spooning me, but I get it, you need protection."

"I hate you," he said, finding my fingers.

"My gram always said if you don't have anything nice to say, don't say anything at all."

He brought my hand to his mouth and kissed my palm, then placed it against his chest. "That's not how we play. Now, shut up so I can sleep."

I closed my eyes, a smile on my face.

CHAPTER
23

Charlie

The next morning, Connor made us egg-white omelets for breakfast and invited me to hang out with him and Sean, but I had my day with the girls planned already. Although saying no to his puppy-dog face was pretty hard. I didn't want my time with him to stop. I'd gotten a small taste, and I'd become greedy.

Connor drove me home and walked me to the front door, where he left me with a kiss that curled my toes. I swore I could feel the imprint of his hand and the scent of his sheets on me as I stepped into the shower. It was all washing away, but I still had the memories, and they made me smile. Like when he'd tucked me into his side with his fingers in my hair as if I was meant to be there. As if the crook of his arm had been created just for me.

Something had changed between us last night. We'd gone from casual hookup to a night cocooned under his covers.

"Hey, where have you been?"

I startled at Sonja's voice as I filled a glass of water in the kitchen. I turned and moved to grab one of the pumpkins she juggled in her arms. "Oh, I went to a party last night."

She eyed me, her curls loose and natural around her head. She had a way of seeing through you, but I blinked away from her, not wanting to give anything away quite yet. Connor was my secret to keep. I'd never had good luck with men, and no matter how illogical and silly, it felt like if I spoke the words out loud, it would be real and then could break. But if I kept it to myself, it couldn't hurt me.

Not to say that I hadn't checked the Douglass handbook to see if relationships between colleagues were off-limits. They weren't. But I was positive if anyone found out, they'd think I needed Connor to somehow help me coach, that I couldn't actually win on my own.

"Where?"

"Huh?"

Sonja playfully rolled her eyes at me. "The party. Where was it?"

"The MPLS Adult Education Center," I tossed out indifferently as I lined up all the pumpkins on the counter, ignoring the little *hmm* of interest Sonja let out.

"Was it fun?"

There seemed to be more implied in the question, but I

was too busy to offer more than a nod, and continued pulling out supplies we'd need for carving: knives, spoons, markers, wine.

"What time did Piper say she'd be here again?" I asked, and almost on cue, the front door opened.

"Marco?" Piper called.

"Polo," Sonja said.

Piper appeared in the doorway of the kitchen with two green reusable grocery bags.

"You just come in the house now? No knock or nothing?"

Piper grinned at Sonja's ribbing. "Still got my key. In case of emergencies."

"'She doesn't even go here,'" I said, quoting one of my favorite movies. Piper and I both cracked up, but Sonja looked on blandly.

"You don't like *Mean Girls*?"

"I've never seen it."

My mouth hung open.

"She's never seen anything," Piper supplied.

Sonja went about filling up a filtered pitcher with water as if we weren't talking about her.

"Tell her about your parents and stuff," Piper prodded.

Sonja bobbed her head back and forth, her voice flat as if she'd told the story a million times before. "My parents raised me and my brother kind of differently. My dad grew up in California in a strict household with a bunch of kids and not much money, and my mom is originally from Berlin, with her grandparents on the other side of the wall.

They spent a summer in Bolivia, administering medical supplies, and they fell in love." Her eyes landed far off on another decade. "They ended up getting married and moving to South America, living in a commune. They had me and my brother down there. We were one big happy, hippie family."

"What was it like living down there?" I asked.

She scrunched her nose up. "I don't remember all that well, but I liked being free. I remember running around in the middle of the day with no shoes. I remember hanging out in the village with my adopted *abuelas* while my parents worked at the hospital. When we moved to the States, all of a sudden we were in a different world. Darius and I had a tough time in school. We moved to Ohio, and all the kids thought we were weird. Our mother is this blonde woman with a funny accent. Our father's a black man from Oakland. And we spoke Spanish. In the middle of Ohio."

I wasn't sure whether it was okay to laugh, but she did.

"My parents kept us busy with activities and school. We had just started to fit in in middle school when we moved here because my dad was offered a job."

"That sounds rough," I said. I could imagine moving at that age. Horrible.

"It was, but like I said, we were busy all the time. If we weren't doing something in school, or violin practice, or running on the track team, we were volunteering. My parents wanted us to learn the value of giving back. I worked in an animal shelter."

I smiled, because Sonja was always sweet, but especially about animals. Just the other day she'd found a chipmunk on the side of the road with what seemed to be a broken leg that she'd tried to talk me into keeping.

I leaned my hip against the counter, not quite understanding how her history fit with who she was now. "So, how'd you end up boxing?"

She bit the corner of her lip as she put a pack of her no-butter, no-sodium, no-anything-good popcorn in the microwave. She hesitated a few seconds, seeming to measure her words. "I had a rough time in college and ended up in therapy. I started boxing as a way of working through anxiety and regaining focus."

I nodded. It was quite a way to work out anything.

"What do your parents do?"

"My mom now teaches at a nursing program and my dad is an ER doctor. My brother is completing his residency in pediatrics. I'm the only one not in the family business."

"Wow." I'd had no idea, and suddenly my view of Sonja shifted. I'd thought she was this literal superwoman, but she was a black sheep, like me. Like Piper. We all had this in common. In one way or another, we were the odd women out. "I'm impressed."

"They aren't." She let out a pitiful laugh. "I'm in a family of doctors, and partake in a sport that consistently gives me cuts and scars. The irony."

"At least they can sew you up."

"True. I mean, they don't like it, but they aren't like Blake's parents."

I turned around to Piper, who shook her head. "He hasn't spoken to them in months."

"Blake doesn't talk to his parents?" I asked, shocked that good-natured Blake would have an issue with anyone.

"Old money, old bullshit morals." She made air quotes around the word *morals*. "They don't like the Public, don't like me, don't like anything that's not up to their standards."

"People can be assholes," I said, "including family."

"But that's why we have friends, am I right?" Piper grinned, and rested her head on my shoulder, her hand on Sonja's head.

We stood like that, all connected, for a while until it got awkward.

"Okay." Piper clapped. "Who's brewing the pumpkin coffee? I'll cut up the roll. Somebody take a picture. I want to social media this. Hashtag basic bitch."

I threw my arm around her shoulders. "That may be the most millennial thing I've ever heard."

Piper playfully rolled her eyes and grabbed her phone from her pocket. "Just stand there and smile."

With the press of her finger, I became a #basicbitch. And I couldn't have been happier about it. We went full-on "basic" with leggings and fleece blankets and Pinterest boards. We talked about everything and anything for hours on end, and after finding out the struggles of these ladies and what they'd each had overcome to do what they loved, I was over the moon to be able to call them my friends and confidantes.

But I still didn't tell them about Connor.

I didn't tell anyone about him.

I WALKED through the halls at school the following week, a secret smile gracing my face when I passed his room. We worked out together in the mornings like buddies, teammates. We spent our afternoons coaching side by side, and then in the evenings parted ways with nothing more than a kiss.

Or two.

Or three.

It was all very clandestine, and I kind of liked it. The undercover glances, sly flirtations when no one was looking. The way his lips found mine in the darkness of a deserted school parking lot. As if we were starring in some classic black-and-white film.

But we weren't old Hollywood movie stars. We were football coaches, who had a big game coming up. And the few days leading up to the last regular game of the season did not go well. Nate fumbled all over in practice. Marcus pulled a hamstring. Scottie Butcher, who had improved over the season, losing some baby weight and gaining some speed, seemed to be reverting to his old ways.

I was nervous about the game, but I couldn't show it. I

could never let the team know I had any doubts about them winning, but from the way the week had gone, I wasn't sure we could pull this one out.

I hadn't spoken my fears out loud to anyone, including Connor, but with the rate he chomped through Dum Dums as the game progressed, I knew he was anxious too. This time, though, I didn't say anything about the crunching.

We'd gotten off to a rocky start, trailing by seven almost the whole game, unable to catch up until Jaylin pulled out a forty-yard run, our blockers—including Scottie—clearing the way for him. After the touchdown, I pulled Scottie aside and praised him for coming through. He beamed with pride and took his place on the sideline as we watched the kickoff and return.

Our defense took the field at the forty, and I clapped a few times, calling out to Spencer to keep his eyes open for thirty-three. He did, reading the pass perfectly, and intercepted.

With a few minutes left, we had enough time to take the lead. Connor and I, headsets off, motioned and yelled instructions out to the players. Nate led the team to the line from the huddle, and hit a slant to Marcus right in his numbers for ten yards. From there, Nate put us ahead with some rushing yards, and we were officially in the playoffs.

I breathed a sigh of relief. Coming out of the regular season with a winning record was a big deal. Making it to playoffs was even bigger. Going to state . . . that would be incredible.

As I watched the boys celebrate, I reminded myself to enjoy this moment. A couple of the boys gave me high fives, and I followed the players onto the field to shake hands with the other team. It had been a tough game, but we'd pulled it out, and Tony Schift, the other team's head coach, congratulated me. It felt good to be acknowledged by my opponent. He praised me for the team's work, for my work.

But my happy grin faded immediately when I turned toward the sideline, and witnessed Brett freaking Spencer chasing after one of the cheerleaders, flipping her skirt up. Like it was all a big joke.

"Spencer!"

He turned to me, his hair matted to his face from sweat, seeming somewhat surprised that I'd called him.

"Get over here."

He jogged over to me as the cheerleader clenched the bottom of her skirt in her fists. She wore one of those embarrassed, forced smiles that all girls learn when they're young. The smile that hides how uncomfortable they really are.

"What?"

"What?" I repeated. "Don't think me and a lot of other people didn't see what you were doin'."

He glanced over his shoulder before looking back at me. Once again asking, "What?"

I poked him in the chest. "I don't know who you think you are, but you need to respect those around you. Between your attitude and your actions, I don't think you do."

He didn't say anything, his eyes on all the players around

me, probably wanting to continue the celebrations with his friends.

"Do you know what you're doing is sexual harassment?"

His eyes went wide. "Huh? No."

"You are clearly crossing a line that girl doesn't want you to. First with the bra strap in science class, and now the skirt of the cheerleader. I don't even want to think about what you do when you're not in school."

He grunted and started to turn away from me, but I didn't let him. "You look at me."

His attention slowly drifted back to me, bored. "What?"

"If you want to stay on this team, you'll go over there right now and apologize to her for your behavior. You apologize sincerely, and I never want to see or hear you treating anyone like your personal play toy again."

He didn't move.

"You have five seconds to start walking."

He crossed his arms in challenge, and I about lost it. Gritting my teeth, I leaned in close. "Don't test me. You won't win."

He smiled, and that was it. I'd had it with him.

"You're off the team. When we get back to school, clear out your locker. You're done."

"You can't do that!"

"Yes, I can." I walked away from him.

He followed. "I didn't do anything wrong."

"You did. And you know it. We have standards on this team, on and off the field. You know that. You've acted like a jerk at practice, whispered things under your breath about other players. You've got a bad attitude. And your actions off the field are just plain disgusting. You're done here."

"You bitch!" He ran off to the other end of the field, where his father was chatting with other parents. I braced myself for the storm about to hit. Kicking Brett off the team was the right thing to do, and I was well aware of the waves it would cause throughout the team and among the parents. But the kid was a spoiled brat. He needed to learn some manners, and I happened to be tired of trying to teach them to him.

I watched as Brett and his father walked off a few feet from the group. Brett's jersey was dirty with grass stains and evidence of how well he'd played. I watched Mr. Spencer keep a blank face, until he lifted his head.

Our gazes met, and I saw the fury in his eyes even across the field—but surprisingly, he did not approach me. He patted his son on the shoulder, and they walked off together. I presumed I wouldn't be seeing any more of them tonight or in the future.

I was one of the last people on the field along with the attendants who were making their way about the grass, picking up the chains and any leftover equipment. I hightailed it out to the bus. Just as I was about to step on, I noticed Jack Spencer talking to Connor.

He pointed toward the field, his face red, and I guessed Connor was taking the brunt of his ire. Connor raised his hands, as if to calm a bull. Mr. Spencer shook his head before walking off toward Brett and his wife. They got into their car and drove off.

I could just imagine the conversation he'd had with Connor, claiming that it wasn't Brett's fault. It was mine.

Made me want to puke.

Connor met me at the bus. He took his hat off and ran his hand over his head and face. "What did you do?"

"Brett's off the team."

He tilted his head back, surprise coloring his face.

"It was long overdue."

"I'm not arguing," he said. "But his father is pissed."

"Obviously," I said. I turned around and stepped up into the bus, Connor following me into the first seat. "What did he say?"

"I couldn't really follow." He unbuttoned his coat. "Something about getting what's coming to you. And that I'd hear from him soon."

"*You'd* hear from him?" I clarified.

He nodded.

"What's that mean?"

"No idea." He rested his head back. "Probably thinks I had something to do with it too." When I didn't say anything, he turned to look at me. "You okay?"

His question made me doubt myself. "Would you have done it?"

He hesitated, and I didn't need him to verbalize his answer. He wouldn't have done it. He wouldn't have had to, because Brett wouldn't act like an asshole to him. He'd demonstrated as much on multiple occasions. But I was a woman, and it was clear that he didn't respect me.

"Whatever," I said, redoing my hair with one of the elastics from my wrist. "I don't want to talk about it."

He leaned in close, right in my ear. "I've got a bottle of red at home."

I smiled. The word *home* reverberated through my body like a bell. As much as I tried to keep this to myself, I wanted to scream it out. I wanted it to be real between us. I wanted to go home with Connor every night, fight over the open window, and wake up to his early-morning growly voice every day.

"Look at you being all romantic."

"Nah," he said, smirking. "You just tend to argue with me less when you've had a drink or two."

I punched him in the arm.

CHAPTER
24

Connor

I wouldn't describe myself as a morning person; I didn't particularly like waking up before the sun, but when you worked at a job that required you to be there for the first bell at seven forty-five, rolling over at five forty-five wasn't totally abnormal. Waking up next to Charlie *was*.

She'd won the fight about the window last night after we alternated getting up to open or shut it so many times that I gave up. I'd kicked the covers off of me a few hours ago, but she had the fluffy white comforter up above her chest. I dragged it down to her hip. The glow from the small digital clock barely illuminated her, hands folded up on her chest in that creepy vampire pose.

As I traced shapes into the skin at her waist with my finger, she slowly shifted, but her eyelids stayed closed. "Go back to sleep."

I inched closer, tangling my leg with hers.

She scooted her hip away from me. "At ease, soldier. It's too early for that."

I tried again, running the tip of my nose over her shoulder as I unfolded her hands. She made a noise of dissent but didn't stop me when I eased myself over her. "Open your eyes," I said, kissing her jaw. She didn't, and I lightly kissed each of her eyebrows. "Please."

They fluttered open, her brown eyes black in the darkness of the room. She blinked a few times, fully waking up.

"Good morning." I nudged her legs apart with my own.

"Why do you torture me?"

"Because you secretly love it."

She hmmed her sleepy agreement, and I kissed her. We shifted, rolling in a tangle of sheets until she was over me, her shape barely visible, but I knew it by heart with my hands. I didn't need my eyes to tell me how her hair hung over her shoulders. I didn't need to see the goose bumps on her skin when I lightly skimmed her sides, hip to breast. I was already well acquainted with the sounds she made when I kissed her neck and gripped her hair in my fist.

Hard and soft, that was Charlie. Strong yet delicate. Her body was made for mine, and we spent the morning mapping each other with our hands and mouths, bathing in the morning sky bleeding in the windows, blue, then purple, orange, and finally yellow.

I had gotten so used to keeping a wall up with every woman that I'd forgotten how nice it was to let it down.

Charlie hadn't knocked and asked politely to come in; she'd just walked inside like she owned the place. I'd been taken by surprise and had no time to even put up a fight.

Not that I wanted to. At least, not now.

I kissed her breastbone and laid my head on her chest, her heartbeat in my ear. A bird chirped outside. A car or two passed by.

"I don't want to get up," she said.

"Don't."

"I have to. We have films in two hours. And I need coffee."

She pushed off her elbow to get up, but I refused to move, keeping her against the mattress. She sighed, but went back to petting me. "Tell me about Alison."

I didn't want to interrupt this perfect moment and kept quiet.

"Silent treatment, huh?"

I thought maybe if I didn't move or breathe for a while, she'd let it slide.

"Come on, Connor, I think it's about time you told me."

But of course she wouldn't. Charlie Gibb, always on my case. "Why?" I asked, sitting up. "I don't want to talk about it."

She followed me as I threw on a pair of sweats and a T-shirt. "Why not?"

"Because I don't feel like it. We had a nice morning, why don't we get some coffee and hang out?"

She did that dragon-like growl as she put her own clothes on. "Yes, let's get coffee and hang out and *talk*."

I went down the hall to the kitchen, but she dodged in front of me so I couldn't open the cabinet for the coffee. "Talk to me. I want to know about Alison."

I hung my head, staring at my bare feet, at Charlie's toenails painted fire-engine red. I didn't want to talk about my past. I was okay with leaving that particular history alone. Couldn't we enjoy the present, have some coffee and another go-round on the couch? Besides, that story was humiliating—I didn't want to tell it to a tough, confident Charlie. I wasn't going to be the hurt puppy while she got to be the pit bull.

"You haven't told me about any of your past relationships," I said.

"Because I've never had any worth mentioning. You want to hear about Bobby Miller in first grade who told me he didn't like me anymore because I could run faster than him? Or Ryan Lipton, I think I told you about him. He took me out on a pity date after a dare at the end of senior year because everyone, *everyone* knew I hadn't been kissed. There was Eli, the *Star Trek* guy who didn't care that I played football or had big shoulders. We had some fumbling nights in the dark during college. Or maybe you want to hear about Ira? He broke up with me because I didn't know how to juggle my twelve-hour days at Tech with a guy who actually wanted to take me to nice restaurants. He said he wished I'd find another job. One that wasn't so strenuous for me. Because I couldn't handle it."

I stared at her. Charlie's poise shone like a sunbeam on

the field. I never questioned her self-confidence. She'd face down giants. She was David against Goliath. But hearing this now, with the tiny crack in her voice, I realized that she hurt too.

"What do you want me to say?" I asked.

"Anything!" She slapped her hand down on the countertop. "It's like pulling teeth with you."

Looking up to the ceiling, I took a deep breath before lowering my gaze to the yellow-and-white-checkered curtains that still hung on the windows. Alison had picked them out.

"Ali and I met in college in a public speaking class."

Charlie snorted. "You took a public speaking class?"

"You want the story or not? Christ." I glowered at her.

She rolled her eyes at me, but stayed quiet.

"The class was a required credit. We got paired up for a presentation." The memory of the day I'd met the little brunette at the library was seared into my brain. She'd looked up at me and smiled, saying, "I can tell you're the strong silent type. I like that kind." But I glossed over that part with Charlie.

"She was with me when I busted my knee. She wanted to be a writer and squirreled away notes in a journal she kept in her purse all the time. I used to tell her she didn't need to write any secrets down because she always said the first thing that came to her mind."

Charlie made a noise but didn't say anything.

"She was a little bit wild, she liked parties and going out.

She pushed me out of my comfort zone. Looking back, she probably had to push me a lot."

Charlie tilted her head. "You, stubborn? I can't believe it."

I ignored the comment. "I asked her to marry me just after graduation. I had my job lined up, but she didn't know what she was going to do. I bought this house, and she made it our home."

"That's why you have a china cabinet and cute little decorations everywhere?"

Here she was, asking me to cut myself open, while she made jokes and comments. "You wanted the goddamn story, and you keep interrupting me."

She stopped me from walking away. "I'm sorry. I'm sorry, Connor."

I set my attention on the corner of the ceiling and took a deep breath. I told myself it was like a Band-Aid. "She was acting all funny leading up the wedding. I assumed it was nerves. But after the rehearsal dinner, she left pretty quickly. I figured it was the whole groom-isn't-supposed-to-see-the-bride thing. But it was really her going home to clean out all her stuff. She left a note that said I was holding her back. She needed to explore the world. And that was it, I never saw her again."

I expected Charlie to have some kind of reaction, after all the begging to tell her about Alison. But she only gazed at me with a blank face.

"That's the end."

"Oh," she said.

"'Oh'? That's all you have to say? After all of that?" I moved my arm in a circle encompassing every single time she'd asked me about Alison. "All you say is 'oh'?"

"That sucks."

"You know what? Forget it." I waved my hands and stepped around her, heading back to the hall.

She grabbed me by the arm and swung me around to face her. "Don't act like that."

"Well, you bugged the shit out of me about it, and now you're acting like it's nothing."

"It isn't nothing. Obviously you were really hurt, are still really hurt. How many years later? You were kids, twenty-two, twenty-three years old?"

"So what? You're going to tell me to get over it. I am over it."

She motioned around the house with her hand. "Yeah, real over it. You live in a fucking shrine to her." When I shook my head, she pointed at a side table in the living room. "There are purple and pink flowers painted on that lamp. You're going to tell me you bought that?"

I stomped away from her. I didn't need her telling me about my house. I lived in it. Every day. "I don't need you to point out to me how pathetic I am."

She followed me into the bedroom. "I never said pathetic, but the way you're acting right now is childish."

I sat on the bed, my elbows on my knees as I cracked my knuckles.

"Alison was an important part of your life. Thank you for

telling me. But don't make me be the bad guy because you're still ashamed about it."

"I do—"

"Don't argue with me, McGuire. You've got the emotional maturity of moss. It's pretty easy to see you've never quite gotten over what happened, no matter how hard you ignore it."

In the past couple of weeks, I'd forgotten how much I could hate her, and right now I remembered.

She waited for me to say something, but I wouldn't.

"Great! Sit there like a statue. Perfect." She spun in a circle. I could feel her anger toward me like arrows that clanged against a metal shield. "You're infuriating, you know that? Everybody has a past. I don't know why you try to hide yours all the time. You're humiliated. I get it. I've been humiliated too. But you're not the only one in the entire world who's ever had their heart broken."

I kept my eyes on the dresser in front of me as she picked up her things and put her shoes on. She finally stood right in front of me, her voice low as she asked, "What are you afraid of?"

You, I wanted to say, but didn't. She walked out of the bedroom and through the house. The click of the front door shutting was her good-bye.

Just when I thought I was doing enough, I wasn't. She'd met my family, knew my friends, had learned more about me than anyone else ever had, but still she wanted more. She wanted me to, what, be some kind of open book? I'd told her all of it. There was nothing else. What you saw was what you got with me, yet she acted as if I'd lived a second life and had all these secrets.

The only secret I'd kept was that I felt inadequate. I was a poor substitute for my father after he died. I wasn't enough to keep Alison. And I evidently didn't have the qualifications to be head coach. After all this time of coming in second place, she'd cut right to the chase and wanted to know what I was afraid of?

I mean, wasn't it obvious?

I'd already lost out to her once for a job. I wasn't going to lose out to her again for my heart.

I lay in bed for a while staring at my ceiling until it was time for me to get ready for film. I barely made it on time, but that was okay. I sat in the back and left as soon as it was over. She caught my eye once or twice when she wanted me to chime in with notes, but that was it.

When I got home, an alert came on my phone that Piper's brewery opening was tonight at six. I didn't feel like going and pulled up Blake's number, figuring he'd be the one to tell since she was probably busy.

"Hey, man," he said, after one ring.

"Hey. I'm not gonna be able to make it tonight."

"You're shitting me, right?"

"No."

"Why?" Noise on his end faded as if he'd gone into a quieter room.

"Not feeling up to it."

"You're sick?" When I didn't answer, he scoffed, "You're not sick. Don't bail, man. This is really important to Piper and to me."

"I know, I just . . ."

"What?" He waited a few moments before saying, "Don't make me send Bear over there."

Bear was the most emotional of the three of us. He read psychology books and shit, he listened to podcasts about communication and feelings. He hadn't gone to college because of hockey, but he read a lot and didn't think twice about dropping knowledge on any topic. I was sure that if he came over, he'd bring some *feelings* stick or something and annoy me until I spilled my guts.

"It's Charlie."

"Charlie? You got a thing going with Charlie?"

I pushed my fingers into my eyes. "A little thing, yeah."

"You hesitated."

I didn't know if that was a statement about my sentence or my well-being.

"That means you're not sure."

Maybe it was both.

"Jump into the deep end for once," he said. "It's not so bad."

I liked to stay away from the pool entirely, and Blake knew that. He also knew what to say to make the connections in my brain.

"You and Charlie are a lot alike. I think that's why you butt heads so much."

I didn't disagree.

"Remember what you told me when Piper and I had our big fight? The opposite of love isn't hate, it's apathy. Alison was indifferent to you. No one who really cares about someone leaves a note and vanishes with all their stuff. But someone who cares will fight for you, fight against you, fight with you."

"Yeah," I finally said.

"He speaks! So, you're coming tonight, right?"

"Yeah, I'll be there."

"Good."

"Hey," I said before hanging up. "Don't tell Piper about this."

"No, I won't. Unless she sexes it out of me."

"Oh, Jesus."

He laughed on the other end. "I can't help that I'm a sex god, and she's wild for me."

"Okay. Good-bye."

I hung up and tossed my phone on the couch.

Charlie was wrong in one assessment of me: I *was* over Alison. After a while, I'd gotten tired of chasing a ghost. True, I hadn't changed my house at all, but it wasn't like I had any idea what to do to change it. By the time I forgave Alison, I didn't care much about the lemon wallpaper in the kitchen or the fancy pillows on the couch. They were just there, and I didn't want to bother with it.

I'd assumed eventually it would change, maybe be changed by another woman, but I spent so much time keeping myself locked up tight I didn't allow anyone to come to my home. Charlie was the first woman in my bed since Alison. And I wanted to keep her there.

BY THE time I got to Out of the Bottle, it was almost seven. The whole front of the building was glass, and I could see the nice-size crowd from the parking lot. Inside, huge tanks lined the right side, with a bar on the left, where I spotted Bear and Sonja serving pints. In the middle were picnic tables with different board games on each one. Everyone seemed to be enjoying themselves, and I could just make out Piper's red hair bouncing among the bodies. I found a place at the bar in front of Bear, and he greeted me with a cheesy grin.

"So, Charlie, huh?"

I groaned. "Son of a bitch."

Bear got me the beer I liked, the Gray-Haired Lady. Usually it came in a bottle with a dark label that had the name scrawled across in gray with just the very top of a head with curly gray hair all over it like it blew in the wind. But here all the beers were served in pint glasses that had the Out of the Bottle logo printed on them.

"I told him not to tell anyone."

"Correction," Blake said, coming up next to me. "You told me not to tell Piper."

"Well, I didn't think you'd tell everybody else."

"I didn't tell everybody else," he defended himself with three fingers up in a Boy Scout salute. "Only Bear."

"That is basically telling everyone else."

Bear shrugged.

"And stop trying to lawyer your way out of this."

"Whatever. I have more important things on my mind. Stay right here—I'm going to get Piper, and then I'm asking her."

Asking her, meaning *the question*.

"Here?" I said.

"Yeah, what better place? I've got it all worked out with Sonja. Just don't go anywhere."

He backed away from us, practically kipping, just as I found Charlie across from me at the other end of the bar. She wore a pretty blue top and tight-as-hell jeans. No fire-engine red lipstick though.

I stared at her, hoping she'd get the message and look over at me, but she didn't. Not even when Blake motioned us over to the middle of the bar. Sonja made sure everyone had a glass. Charlie's was only half-full, but she held it up, pretending she'd drink it.

She wouldn't.

"I just wanted to say a quick little something," Blake said.

I huffed. "Quick?"

"Yes, quick." He elbowed me. "But I wouldn't be making jokes about length of time, if I were you."

"Yeah, just length," Bear added, and I quietly told him to go to hell.

Blake stood between us like a teacher between students.

"First of all, I wanted to thank you all for being here to support Piper, but also for being great friends. You're all more than friends, you're family."

He held his glass aloft, and we did the same. I once again found Charlie, and as she brought her glass to her lips, her eyes met mine, unreadable. I watched her, ignoring the commotion of Piper finding an engagement ring in her pint. Her laughing and crying over Blake on his knee was distant from Charlie's small but sad smile. For such a happy moment for our friends, neither one of us seemed that way.

I was jealous of Blake and Piper. For sure. I wanted to have what they had. At one time, I'd had it in my fingertips, but it had fallen through my grasp. And I knew Charlie wanted the same thing. She'd hinted at it before.

But before I could talk to her, apologize about today, she hugged Piper, talking animatedly. I suspected she purposely stayed away from me for the next hour. Always putting distance or people in my way until finally she was gone. Without a word to me.

She'd told Sonja she was going home to sleep. She had a big week coming up with round one of playoffs.

I had a big week too.

The whole team did.

And I couldn't argue with that. I couldn't tell her to pay attention to me. To not focus on the team. So I let her go.

CHAPTER
25

Charlie

Peach cobbler was my favorite. Apple came in a close second.

There weren't many things Gram and I had in common, but her baking was one of them. I had always loved being with her in the kitchen. It was just about the only place we got along. She let loose in the kitchen, sang songs, danced. She never followed a recipe but knew by intuition how much butter to use.

At times when my stress was maxing out, I took a trip to the grocery store for fresh fruit. At the beginning of November, I wasn't going to find any peaches, and settled on a couple of Granny Smiths for a pie. Normally on Thursday nights I'd stay late in my office preparing for the game, but I couldn't tonight. I needed to get out and relax.

I needed to feel close to somebody. And baking always made me remember Gram.

I'd invited Sonja to join me, but she had plans to go to yoga with Bear. I'd almost decided to tag along to witness Bear hitting a triangle pose, but chose the smell of a freshly baked pie instead. Even though my love life had taken a turn for the worse, I was glad Sonja had whatever she had with Bear. Romantic or not, they had a special connection.

With the pressure of the game tomorrow and Connor completely blowing me off, I wanted to eat my feelings. I mindlessly scratched my fingernails on the counter as the crust browned in the oven. It was hard enough to think about whether or not we were prepared for the spread by the team from Eden Prairie, but to have Connor giving me the silent treatment made everything worse.

Other than speaking to me when absolutely necessary, he'd pretty much treated me like a ghost. He ignored me in the halls and stood on the opposite side of the room during lunch duty. I'd like to say I was totally unaffected by it, but I wasn't.

Connor had been my frenemy and then, for lack of a better word, he'd become my lover. And now he acted as if he was nothing. Yet even as I contemplated what he could possibly be thinking, I smiled at the fact that he'd hate the word *lover*.

But there was no other way to describe him. I'd grown from hating him to loving him. He challenged me and lifted me up. He had ways to make me angry while being desperate to kiss him. I felt things for him that I never had for anyone else. And now that he wasn't speaking to me, I wasn't sure what to do.

The pie smelled done, delicious and sweet, and I carefully pulled it out of the oven. With a fork in my hand, I was ready to drive right in—screw the plate—but I knew I'd burn my mouth, so I waited.

If only I were that patient when it came to Connor. Instead of following my instincts, I'd followed my heart. In the heat of the moment weeks ago, I'd kissed him, and I hadn't been able to stop since. But look where it'd gotten me.

Staring longingly at the pie, I wondered how long it'd be before I could shove it down my gullet. I grabbed the pint of vanilla ice cream from the freezer and dished some into a bowl.

It seemed as if I wasn't getting any closer to Connor, not on an emotional level. He refused to let me in. Getting him to answer any questions was like pushing a weighted sled down the field. And I couldn't continue to do all the hard work. I needed something in return. But he didn't feel the same. After we'd got into it on Saturday, I thought he'd come after me. I thought he'd call, text, write me a note, anything to show me he had a heart deep down behind that stone face and stoic stance. But he hadn't.

And now I had a team to coach tomorrow with an offensive coordinator who wasn't speaking to me.

I didn't want to wait any longer and scooped out a slice of pie, laying it next to the ice cream in the bowl. If I was going to have something that would hurt me, I wasn't going to go in halfway. I went full-tilt.

Gram's apple pie à la mode made a delicious dinner. And bedtime snack. Sad to say, by the time I left for school the next morning, the pie dish was empty save for a few crumbs. But this time, Gram's baked goods didn't make me feel any better.

My nerves got the best of me all day. Especially when I dropped some papers just outside of my fourth-period health class.

"I got it."

Connor.

The most words he'd spoken to me outside of practice. He sped up a couple of paces to bend down and pick up the copies of quizzes on the hazards of tobacco and alcohol. He looked them over before handing them to me. "Fun stuff."

Those two words hit me right between my ribs. I'd missed his voice.

Romantic adult relationships should come with a warning—nobody talked about the hazards of those the way they did about smoking. What to do when you wanted to kick your coworker/friend-with-benefits/lover in the shin? Or how to keep from cursing them out? Or begging them to stay?

"I hope you had a good week."

"Yeah, you wouldn't know," I said, trying to keep the anger in my tone, but I couldn't hold it. Not when his tie hung slightly off-center. I reached out to adjust it, but dropped my hand before it made contact.

He winced slightly and fixed the dark-blue tie so it lay flat against the pale-blue shirt that matched his eyes. "I was trying to give you space."

The quizzes crinkled in my hands. The knowledge that the period had started one minute ago didn't stop me from raising my voice. "I don't want space."

His attention drifted to the inside of the classroom, visible through the window of the closed door, then back to me. Guess he didn't care about my students chatting in the background either.

"I'm sorry," he said, the last syllable lilting up in a question.

"Are you sure about that?"

He nodded.

"What are you sorry for?"

"For . . . giving you space."

Again I heard the question mark at the end. I waved him away with my quizzes. "I have to get to my class. And you have to get better at this," I said, gesturing between him and me. "I'm tired of this seesaw. You either want to be with me or you don't. I have a lot at stake here, and I'm not willing to give it up for someone who doesn't care about me the way I care about him."

"Hey, wait a minute," he said, taking hold of my elbow when I tried to turn away from him. "I have put myself out there. I've *tried*. You're the one who didn't want to tell anyone. You're the one who's been making the rules for this."

He stared at me, unmoving, waiting for my reply, but I couldn't argue. He was right, and I didn't want to admit that

I was partially responsible for the difficult nature of our relationship. I jerked the door open behind me; the echoing slam
scared the students into silence, and twenty-eight pairs of
eyes shot up to me.

"Sorry I'm late. Get your pens out. Y'all got a quiz to take."

"Miss, can I—"

I didn't even look up, knowing it was Avi asking to go to
the bathroom. "No. Sit down."

"But, Miss—"

"No." I finally looked at him and pointed to his desk. "Sit."

"You're in a bad mood today."

I showed my teeth in a forced smile, and Avi scampered
back to his seat.

I spent the rest of the day attempting to get in a good
headspace and prepare for the game, steeling my nerves. But
as the team waited in the locker room for the game to start,
it was uncharacteristically quiet. Knees bounced and knuckles cracked as I stood in front of them.

"I know y'all are nervous," I said. "But there is no reason
to be. Look how far you've come this season. Look at what
you accomplished."

Most of the players kept their heads down.

"Nate's stepped up as QB, turned our passing game
around." Nate smiled. "And Marcus has a team record for
passes received." I slapped Marcus's shoulder pad, and a couple of the players clapped. "And Joel, where's Joel?" Joel
raised his hand in the corner. I walked over to him, yanking
him up. "And Joel's put on eight pounds of solid muscle.

Show off those biceps." Most of the team hooted and hollered as he raised his scrawny arms in a strongman pose.

"We've got Noah Tremble, who's moved up from JV to help us out big-time on the line. J. B. Donnerson, who's scrambled to recover a whopping four fumbles on defense this season. And Jaylin, superstar Jaylin, leads us with highest average points per game and set a new school record for yards run." I smiled at him. "He's recently been offered a full ride to Humboldt State."

Jaylin's face turned red, but the entire team stood up cheering.

I raised my voice so they'd hear me above the noise. "I asked you to work hard, and you did. I asked you to be better, and you are. We made it to the playoffs for the first time in years. You've already got a winning record. We showed them all what underdogs could do. We're the phoenix who rises up. Go out there and play with no fear. Leave it on the field, that's all you can do."

The volume of the boys yelling drowned out my clapping. I nodded at Jaylin to take over. All of their hands went to the middle where he stood.

"Douglass on three. One, two three."

"Douglass!"

Chills raced up my spine as the team ran out of the doors toward the field. Dave patted my back as he jogged past me. Everyone was worked up, but I took my time retying the laces on my lucky sneakers and zipping up my coat. I couldn't let my emotions get the best of me. I needed to stay composed.

"You all right?" I asked Sam Long, whom I caught up to as he walked around the side of the building. I guessed he had thrown up back there. Sam was a great tailback, but for some reason couldn't keep it together before he got on the field. Once he was there though, he was home.

Sam wiped his mouth with the back of his hand and put his helmet on. "I'm good, Coach."

I slapped his helmet once. "Go get 'em."

He ran out in front of me as we reached the gate in the chain-link fence. The Otters band began to play the fight song as the cheerleaders lined up, creating a tunnel for the players to run through. Connor stood beside me as we watched the players bounce up and down, hyping themselves up, and then run down the field, breaking the rows of blue and yellow streamers the cheerleaders held.

"Ready?" Connor asked.

"Always."

Without looking, we bumped the sides of our fists and took our places on the sideline.

I put on my headset, testing the sound with Ken up in the booth before giving a nod to the captains as they took the field. Jaylin, Sam, and Robby Eck shook hands with the other captains and called the coin toss. We lost, and Eden Prairie decided to receive. Our special teams lined up, and Joel started us off with the great kick down the field.

We held them off at 0–0 through halftime until they finally broke through with a long pass to score in the third quarter. Our defense had trouble getting a read of the field, and their spread started overtaking us. The quarterback had quite an arm.

I had my headset off most of the game, ignoring Ken's calm voice up in the booth. Instead I screamed directions to the players, not acting at all like the composed coach I was supposed to be. With the end of the fourth quarter approaching, we were still behind by one touchdown. I called a time-out, and before I even got any words out to the players, Connor was next to me.

"Charlie, don't do it."

"Don't do what?"

"You always go for the Hail Mary. Play it smart. We have plenty of time to try to get the ball back."

"I'm not punting. If they score again, there'll be no time to overcome fourteen points." He shook his head at me as I said, "We're going for it. Call the play." When he did nothing but frown at me, I turned my back to him to face Marcus. "We're going deep. Waggle right. Got it?"

Marcus nodded, and I made a point of looking at the linemen. "Clark needs time to get up the field—make that happen." Then I held on to Nate's jersey. "And you need to get that ball to him. Hands in, let's go."

They all chanted and broke up to head back to the field, but Connor called Nate over. He said something to him with a small motion, giving advice. I assumed it was something about making sure he got the ball over the head of the safety. And I was thankful he wasn't giving up.

I closed my eyes as the ref's whistle blew and felt Connor's presence next to me. I opened my eyes and held my breath as Krajewski snapped the ball to Nate. Connor held the microphone of his headset in his hand, his knuckles white, as he threw another lollipop stick on the ground. I said a silent prayer when Marcus took off and the ball lifted into the air. It sailed into the end zone, where Marcus jumped up over the head of the safety, his fingertips grazing the ball in a slight bobble before catching it, and dropped his feet back down into the grass.

Just outside of the lines.

Out of bounds.

No touchdown. The audible letdown gasp of the crowd echoed in my bones.

I threw my headset to the ground. I'd just lost the game for us.

CHAPTER
26

Charlie

I didn't have it in me to give a rousing speech after the game. We'd made it to the first round of the playoffs and lost. I ended up telling them it was okay to be disappointed in the outcome of the game, but they had no reason to be disappointed in themselves. They'd played well all season, and for that, they should be proud.

Me, on the other hand—I wanted to lock myself away. I shook the hands of all the assistant coaches, and thanked them for their dedication, but turned down their offer of one last postgame beer at the Public. I was in no mood to go out.

Two knocks sounded swiftly on the door before Connor came in and closed it behind him. "Hey."

I didn't respond.

"Can we talk?"

"I'm busy."

"I can wait."

I ignored him.

"Just for a few minutes . . . or I can give you a ride home."

I flicked my pen on the desk. "I don't feel real chatty right about now."

"When are you going to feel like talking?"

I leaned back in my chair and folded my arms before turning to look at him as casually as possible. "I suppose I should be on your schedule. Like always. But the hell with that. I don't feel like talking, especially to you, and I don't know when I will want to again."

Connor's eyebrows raised. "What's that supposed to mean, *especially to me?*"

The frustration and regret hit me all at once. "It means I blew it. You told me not to pass, but I did. I should've played it safe and punted."

"That's not why I'm here." He hung his head. "I'm upset too."

"You're here to rub salt in the wound then?"

"No, I just wanted to check on you. Make sure you're okay."

"I thought after all this time together you'd get it." I shook my head. "I don't need to be coddled or soothed. You want to fix me because I'm a girl. But I'm also a coach, who just lost a big game. I want to sulk and curse in my tiny pea-size office, and I don't need you to do that." I stood up and motioned him toward the door.

Connor didn't move. "Why are you pushing me away right now?"

"Me push you away? All *you've* done is push *me* away." The fact that he wanted to have this discussion right now had me livid. My blood pulsed in my ears and my body went so hot I felt a tingle of sweat along my spine. "All week you've ignored me, and now you suddenly want me to talk. Crawl into the cab of your truck. No thanks. I've got my own car. I don't need a ride. Or a chat. Or whatever else it is you want to do."

I shoved past him, pulling my coat and hat on as I walked out of the building, ignoring Connor calling after me. I held it together until I got home. Sonja was there in the living room, relaxing. Her cat jumped off her lap at the sight of me and sauntered into the kitchen.

"Hi," she said with a smile. "How'd it go? I'm sorry I couldn't come, I would—"

"We lost."

She sat up. "You lost?"

My vision blurred with tears as I nodded, and she tugged me by the hand to sit down next to her. "Eden Prairie was good," I said, wiping my cheek. "Really good. And we held them off for a while. Until the end."

She rubbed my back.

"I wanted to win. Bad. I wanted to win for the team, but for me too."

"I know."

"I wanted to prove I could do it."

"You can do it. You did do it. You turned that team around."

I sniffled, wiping at my nose with the sleeve of my shirt. "And then Connor."

"What about him?"

"Ugh, everything." I groaned. "Can I tell you somethin'?"

"Of course."

I breathed deeply and straightened my spine, readying myself to say the words out loud. "We've been sleepin' together."

"I know."

I jerked my head back. "You know?"

"Yeah." She laughed. "Are you surprised? Was it a secret? You didn't hide it well."

I pressed my palm to my forehead. "Who else knows?"

She raised one shoulder. "I don't know, but maybe everyone? Piper, for sure. And if I know the boys like I think I do, Blake and Bear have talked about it with Connor already."

Falling back onto the cushions, I didn't know whether to be embarrassed or happy that Connor would have talked about me with his best friends.

"And unless they're totally obtuse, the other coaches must assume something is going on. I mean, you two set off fireworks together." She handed me a box of tissues.

"I hate him," I said, hugging a pillow into my chest. "But I love him."

I couldn't believe that I'd admitted that. Even more, I couldn't believe that I loved him. I loved Connor, and everything was so screwed up that I didn't know how to fix it.

Sonja's face lit up in a smile. "You love Connor?"

I waved my head side to side. "A little bit, yeah."

She clapped and leaned over to grab her phone, but I stopped her. "What are you doing?"

"Texting Piper. You think we're going to talk about this *without* her?" She grinned as her fingers sped over the keyboard. For someone who had a boring social life, she was an excellent texter. "She says she'll be over in twenty." I stood up, intent on showering, when Sonja added, "She also says, quote, How dare she not prepare me? The place with the good cupcakes is closed. I hope she knows I can't get carrot cake cupcakes at the grocery store. End quote."

I laughed. I didn't know about the place with the good cupcakes, but I was glad to have a friend who did.

Just as I finished my shower, I heard Piper downstairs. I slipped into sweats and a pair of reinforced Nike socks my dad had sent me for my birthday. Always practical.

"I thought you said twenty minutes. Did you teleport here?"

Piper whirled around. "You weasel."

"I'm not a weasel." I pressed my hand to my heart.

"I have a lead foot and I utilize talk-to-text. My keys were already in my hand by the time Sonja finished telling me about you. Now, get your snacks and fill me in already. I can't believe you started without me."

Piper waved her hand over the smorgasbord of sweets on the counter: chocolate chip cookies, sugar-free iced cookies for Sonja, cupcakes with fluffy white icing and plastic turkeys on top, and marble cheesecake. I grabbed a plate and took one of everything before sprawling on the sofa. The girls followed, Sonja on the other end of the sofa, legs stretched out to an ottoman, while Piper wrapped herself up in a blanket on the floor, looking at me like a child on Christmas morning. "Tell us everything."

I started from the beginning, not skimming over anything as if they didn't already know most it. No detail was spared. Including our romps in his truck and bed. I didn't think I'd enjoy hours of girl talk, but staying up until after two in the morning was cathartic. When Sonja finally asked, "What's your endgame? What do you want out of this," I held my hand over my mouth as I yawned.

"I want to be with Connor. I want him to want to be with me."

Piper nodded. "I think he does."

"Doesn't act like it."

"He might just need some time," she said.

Maybe she was right, but I'd waited my whole life for men. I'd soothed and petted and cajoled. I hadn't spent my days with collegiate male football coaches and not learned to have some patience. But I'd come to the point in my life when I wanted answers now. I wasn't going to wait on or wait for men anymore. "I'm not going to twiddle my thumbs while he figures out what he wants. I'm done with that. I know that sounds kind of bitchy."

"There's nothing wrong with asking for what you want.

If more women did that, we wouldn't have to be afraid of sounding bitchy—whatever that even means."

Piper high-fived Sonja. "Perfect advice. As usual."

Sonja lifted one shoulder toward her ear with a shy smile that made me wonder what she asked for.

"Okay, kiddies, I've got to get home." Piper rose and dropped the blanket on the floor.

"Hey, pick up after yourself. You don't live here anymore. Mess up your own house."

Piper stuck her tongue out at Sonja as she folded up the cream fleece blanket and put it on the sofa. "Blake isn't so sassy when I make a mess."

"That's because of the sex."

"True."

We all laughed and hugged, and I went to bed knowing that even if Connor and I didn't work out, I still had my friends to back me up.

Except I didn't like them very much when I got a call at eight later that morning. Philander wanted me to meet him at the school in an hour. I thought it was odd, but in my sleep-deprived state I agreed and jumped out of bed to get dressed. I thought he might want to congratulate me on the season, but a bad feeling formed in my belly.

It only got worse when I got to the school. Normally on a Saturday the school was empty, but there were a handful of cars in the spots closest to the front door, including Connor's truck. Using my key fob, I went inside and jogged down the hall toward the main office, sensing that I'd missed out on something.

I opened up the thick wooden door to the principal's private office to find that I *had* missed something. Philander, Jim, Connor, and Jack Spencer were all there. And I was late to the party.

"Good morning," I said, the hair on the back of my neck standing on end.

"Charlie, hello. Would you like to have a seat?"

Connor was already seated in one of the two chairs opposite Philander's desk, eyes on the floor. I glanced at Jim in the corner, for once not smiling at me. My stomach, which had been in knots, bottomed out. Easing into the empty chair next to Connor, I caught Mr. Spencer's gaze as he leaned against the wall to my right, and he smirked. I hated him. He had no reason to be in this office, acting as if he was on top of the world.

I looked to Philander, who sat back in his chair, totally relaxed, displaying who had the power here. Nothing about this scenario reassured me.

"What's goin' on?"

"I'm going to cut to the chase. We called you in today because we're going to make some changes." Out of the corner of my eye, I noticed Connor move, but I ignored him, my focus solely on Philander. "You are not going to be coaching the football team next year."

"What?" The one-word question came out of my mouth a whisper, but in my mind I screamed.

"We gave it a try, but it didn't work out."

"What do you mean?"

Spencer laughed, and I flipped around to him. "What did you do?"

"*I* didn't do anything other than point out the obvious. *You* couldn't finish out the season."

"This is absurd!" I stood up, my lungs heaving, my palms sweaty, tunnel vision closing in. "You hired me to coach, and you're going to get rid of me after one season?"

Philander stood, his height easily taking over mine. "Yes."

"And you're goin' to tell me it has nothing to do with me bein' a woman."

He shook his head. "It has nothing to do with you being a woman."

"Then explain to me how you're firing me when I led this team to a winning season after a decade of losing?"

"You don't know what you're doing," Spencer cut in, and my nails bit into my palms to keep me from cursing him out.

Philander held his hand up to that fucker as he said, "You did well with the team, but not good enough. We need someone who will be able to bring a championship here. You did bring some good notoriety to the school—"

"So this really was just a publicity stunt?"

He ignored the question. "After weighing the pros and cons, we've decided Connor is better suited to lead the team."

I stared at the man next to me, the traitor with his head still down, not acknowledging any of this. "You son of a bitch."

"Watch your language, please, Miss Gibb," Philander said, and it took everything in me to not flip out and throw some shit around.

"Charlie," Jim said, reaching out toward me, but I lurched away. "Listen—"

"No." I pointed my finger at him. "I thought you had my back. I thought you supported me."

"I do," he said.

I shook my head and turned toward the door.

"You're welcome to stay on the coaching staff, if Connor allows it," Philander offered pleasantly, as if he hadn't just ripped everything away from me. "And your teaching position remains the same, of course."

I bowed. "Oh, thank you for the generosity. But sorry not sorry when I say fuck you."

I slammed the door, viciously wiping at the tears that spilled down my cheeks.

"Charlie, wait up, please."

I didn't stop at Jim's voice, but with my blurred vision, I couldn't run as fast as I wanted to, and he caught up to me just as I reached my car.

"Please, give me a chance to explain."

"I don't want to hear it, Jim. I know it's bullshit."

"It is," he agreed, holding on to my arm. "Total bullshit. You have to know that I fought them on this. Hard. Spencer has been on me about getting rid of you for a while, but I wasn't going to give in. After yesterday, he went to Philander and threatened to pull all of his booster money, and that's when he called me. Charlie, I swear, this wasn't my choice. I was outnumbered."

I shook my head. I couldn't listen anymore. I couldn't form any words through my shattering sobs. I got into the driver's seat just as Connor appeared a few yards away. He ran toward the car, but I sped away, silencing the protests behind me with the hum of the engine.

I didn't care about any of it anymore.

Connor had gotten what he wanted. They'd all gotten what they wanted.

They'd broken me. They'd won.

CHAPTER
27

Connor

I tried calling her all day Saturday and Sunday, but Charlie refused to answer, evidently electing to turn her phone off because my calls went directly to voicemail sometime in the afternoon. And I'd left so many *Please call me, please* messages that her mailbox was full. Monday she took the day off, not giving me any chance to see her. I wanted to speak to her, to tell her my side. I was sure she wouldn't listen or care, but I wanted to at least try.

First, though, I needed a plan. I had to get my head on straight. Everything had happened so fast this weekend; I wasn't quite sure how I felt about any of it. After school, I drove to Mom's house and knocked once before using my key to open the front door. She and Sean were in the kitchen paging through a cookbook.

Mom's head popped up. "Hey, what are you doing here?"

"Nono, are you staying for dinner?"

I scratched the back of my head. "No, I'm not staying for dinner."

He pouted slightly, but my mom came over to my side, slipping her arm over my shoulders. "You okay?"

I shook my head, pushing my hands into my pants pockets.

"What is it, Monkey?"

I shrugged away from her and sat down at the kitchen table. I rubbed at my forehead as she went back to Sean at the counter. They went about deciding what to make for dinner while I found my words.

"I'm the new head coach of the Otters."

Her face lit up. "Oh, honey that's great. That's—" She stopped, and walked around the island to me. "What does that mean?"

"They called me into school Saturday morning and told me I was going to be the head coach. Then Charlie came in, and they told her she wasn't going to be . . . and then she told us all to . . . eff off."

With one hand on her hip, she huffed. "I would've too." She soothed her hand down my cheek. "You're my son, and I love you, and I think you are an excellent coach and could definitely lead that team—but you do realize what happened, right? The good old boys' club . . ."

I nodded.

Sean had taken interest in the conversation and sat down opposite me. "What's wrong, Nono?"

I tried to find the root of the issue. "Charlie and I are fighting."

"Oh." He nodded somberly. "You're not friends anymore?"

Even in my mixed-up state, I smiled when I remembered how he'd pointed out that he didn't kiss his friends like I kissed Charlie. "I don't think so."

Mom sat down with a sigh. "What did you say? How do you feel?"

"I didn't say anything."

"Connor," she chided.

"I know." I put my hands on my head, elbows on the table. "I . . . didn't know what to say to them. Or to her."

"You should've told them it's not right. She did a great job with the boys. There is no good reason for her not to continue as the head coach."

Sean raised his hand in the air, catching on. "Charlie isn't the coach anymore?"

"No, she's not," I said. "I am."

Sean's eyes toggled all around as he processed the information. He fixed his glasses, clearly not sure how to feel, going from a smile to a frown. "Can't you share? One day you're in charge and the next day she's in charge?"

"I wish." I blew out a big breath, then looked at my mom. "I think I love her."

"I know. I've been your mother for thirty-one years. From the first time I saw you two together, I knew you loved her."

I dropped my head to my arms on the table. After all

this time, why hadn't I figured it out? Love and hate were two sides of the same coin. I should've known every time I felt fire inside, it wasn't from rage. It seemed obvious now.

Now that I was the head coach.

I'd finally gotten the job. *Her* job. But I'd wanted it so badly, and after all this time, was I supposed to give it up for her? I didn't know how to begin to make the situation right, or if I even could.

"I don't know what to do."

Mom rubbed her hand over my back, and after a minute I sat back up as she said, "It's up to you, but you know what's right. If Charlie were a different person, a man—or if she were you, and they decided to get rid of you, or anyone else, after one season with a good record after all this time—what would you do?"

"I'd tell Mr. Spencer to mind his own damn business, and I'd tell the principal he had no idea what he was doing."

She patted my hand. "I think you should start there."

I nodded, and got up to hug and kiss her cheek.

"I love you, Monkey," she said. "You're a good man. You make your father proud."

"Love you too." I called out good-bye to Sean before heading home.

With the realization that I loved Charlie, the situation only got more complicated, but after talking with my mother, I felt a tiny bit better. No matter how any of this turned out, Charlie would hear how I felt about her, and the administration would get an earful from me.

Not five minutes after I'd gotten home and taken my shoes off, a barrage of knocks sounded on my door. I opened to up to Piper, Sonja, Blake, and Bear.

"Hey, dick," Piper said, forcing me back from the door as she walked in.

Blake followed her. "Be nice, Sunshine."

"What's going on?" I asked.

Piper jerked her finger out the door. "You're lucky I didn't key your big, stupid truck."

I didn't get any words out before Sonja backed me up against the wall, her petite height making no difference when she pressed her forearm into my chest.

"Sone." Bear pulled Sonja away from me, but the look in her eyes actually made me a little nervous that she'd really go after me if she could.

"Charlie told us what happened. She came home Saturday morning hysterical." She practically spat the words at me. "I thought you were a good guy, but you just sat there. After everything between you two, you just sat there."

Bear grabbed Sonja's hand and yanked her to his side.

"It wasn't my fault," I said, and immediately knew those were the wrong words.

Blake stopped Piper before she could say anything, ever the peacekeeper. "All right. We came here to get the whole story, let's hear it." He turned to me. "Charlie said she was fired. The girls were with her all yesterday."

I looked at Sonja and Piper. "I had nothing to do with what happened. I swear." Sitting down, I ran my hands over my head a few times. "I didn't know what Philander was going to do. I got to the school only a few minutes before Charlie. I should've guessed Spencer had something to do with it because he's been on her case all season, but I truly never believed they'd fire her. I didn't ask for or want the job."

The girls seemed to soften a bit toward me.

"You wanted that position. You always have," Piper pointed out.

"Yes, I did. But not at Charlie's expense . . . not anymore."

"What's changed?" Sonja asked.

"I love her."

"You love her?" Sonja and Piper said at the same time.

I nodded, and Piper knelt in front of me, holding my hands. "I say this with all the love and compassion I have, but you are so fucking dumb. You love her, and you didn't say anything when they fired her?"

"Technically," I said, pulling away from her, "they didn't fire her. They said she could remain on staff. And she still has her teaching position."

"Technically"—Sonja cracked her knuckles—"she should've kicked you in the balls." She plopped down on the sofa next to me. "What are you going to do?"

"What I should've done Saturday morning. I'm going to talk to them tomorrow."

"Great," Blake said as the girls stared at me, unsatisfied.

I understood that I should've done something before, but I'd been taken by surprise. Yes, it made me the number one asshole among a room full of them, but I was going to try to make it right. I hoped.

"How is she?" I asked no one in particular.

"Upset," Sonja said.

"I believe the words she used in reference to you were 'I wouldn't piss on him if he were on fire.' But, of course, in an accent," Piper said.

Bear laughed. "Got a real way with words."

"Like this one," Blake said, jerking his thumb in my direction.

"You think she'll forgive me?"

Sonja and Piper exchanged a look before casting sad eyes at me.

"I don't know," Sonja said after a while.

I hung my head. I hadn't expected an ecstatic yes, but I also hadn't thought they'd seem totally uncertain either, like it was a long shot. A very, very long shot.

They all sat with me a little longer, not managing to make me feel any less pathetic, as if they expected I was going to jump off a cliff at any moment.

I wasn't. I wasn't nearly that dramatic.

But I put on a good show the next morning.

I strode into the main office on a mission before school started. I didn't even look at Lucille, Mr. Philander's personal secretary. She tried to stop me, but I opened his door with enough force that it crashed into the wall. He jumped in his chair and slammed his laptop closed, his normally easy disposition thrown off.

"Connor, what are you doing here?"

"I need to talk to you."

"I'm busy right now." He intentionally moved his elbow over some papers, but I didn't care what he was working on. I had more important things on my mind.

"I'm not taking the head coach position. Charlie should have it."

He skimmed his hand over what was left of his hair, then over his suit jacket. "Connor, listen, you know—"

"No, you listen. She deserves that title and you know it. Whatever reason you're doing this, whatever Spencer is doing or not doing, is bullshit. He doesn't run this school, you do, and you can make this right."

He folded his fingers together. "The decision has been made."

"Your decision is wrong." I leaned over his desk and slapped my hand on it. "Dick lost season after season, and no one said a thing. You all let the ship sink." I stood up straight and gestured to the open door as if Charlie were there. "Gibb came in, and in one season turned the team around, got us to the playoffs. Yeah, we lost, but with the best record in years. *Years*. But you want to get rid of her? Because she doesn't know what she's doing? Cut me a break." I stopped him when he tried to cut in. "You want to get rid of her because she's a woman, and she's doing better than anyone else could do, and you don't like it. But I have news for you—if she goes, *I* go."

He sat back in his chair and folded his arms, calling my bluff. "You wouldn't leave."

"I would," I said without blinking. "I won't stay at a school that doesn't do what's best for its students or staff, not to mention how sexist this all is. Charlie is what's best for the team, students, and school."

"You're basing your decision on a woman?" He huffed out a low laugh.

"No. I'm basing it on your actions and doing what I think is right."

He stood up, but his attention skidded to the door. I turned instinctively. Charlie *was* there.

Her hair was down around her slumped shoulders. I wanted to go to her, but the fire in her eyes told me not to.

"Nice of you gentlemen to have this discussion without me." With three steps farther into the room, she dropped a piece of paper on Philander's desk. "I wanted to let you know that I'm finishing out the semester, and then I'm formally resigning."

Philander didn't say a word as he picked up the paper, which I assumed was a letter of resignation. She turned on her heel, barely sparing me a glance.

I followed her out. I could deal with Philander later.

"Charlie, wait."

She didn't listen to me, continuing down the hall as students filtered in. I slipped behind her and pulled her off to the side. She stopped and reluctantly faced me.

"Can you look at me, please?"

Up close, I noticed her bloodshot eyes. I reached out to touch her cheek, but she reeled away from me. "Don't."

"I'm sorry."

She took a quick glimpse over her shoulder before turning back to me, and lowered her voice to a whisper so the students couldn't hear. "Why did you go in there this morning?"

"I'm trying to make things right."

"I don't need a white knight."

The argument I had formed on my tongue died at her words. "I thought—"

"You thought I'd want you to miraculously save my job so you could be the hero? I'm not some maiden stuck in a tower."

"I know that." She was one of the strongest people I knew. "I wanted to help."

"You making a scene is not helping. I don't need to be made to look any weaker than they already think I am. You're only making it worse for me."

"I'm sorry. I didn't realize—"

"And you threatening to leave is crazy. You will never leave here, you love it too much."

"But I will." I put my hand on the wall next to me as if I were holding the place up from falling down around us.

"No, you won't. You're not a quitter. It's not in your blood."

"You're not a quitter either."

She used one of her hair ties to put her hair up. "I'm not, but I know when an environment is good for me, and this one isn't."

"What are you going to do?"

"I'm not sure yet." Her gaze landed somewhere over my shoulder. "I'll figure it out though."

I cleared my throat. "And what about us?"

"Us? We had a good run, I guess." She patted me on the shoulder like she would a teammate.

She was hurt, I got that, but her apathy cut deep. "Don't say that."

"Oh, now you're upset? Now you want a redo?"

I crowded her space, forcing her to take me seriously, look me in the eyes. "I'm sorry that everything went down like this, but I'll do what I have to in order to be with you."

She blinked away from me. "Maybe in a different time or a different place. Maybe if we were different people. . . ."

I caught her hand as she started to walk away, but she shook her head, refusing to turn back to me. "Charlie, please, don't leave."

"Good-bye, McGuire."

CHAPTER
28

Charlie

hree weeks had gone by of me living a relatively quiet existence. I kept to myself at school, half embarrassed and half enraged. The whole school had heard what had happened, and the players asked questions. But I didn't have it in me to explain the unexplainable.

I spent my time counting down the days and avoiding Connor. Sonja and Piper tried to keep me in good spirits, but with no plan of where I was going or what I was doing next, I put up a wall. They were hurt by my actions, always turning them down when they offered to take me out, but I didn't want to become any more attached to them than I already was. Besides, they were friends with Connor. I wasn't about to ask them to pick sides, so I gave up.

We had a few days off for Thanksgiving, but the only thing I had to be thankful for was the reprieve away. I'd bought my ticket home to Georgia, cringing at the money I spent for the late booking and direct flight. I was mere weeks away from not having a job and already worried about my checking account. I needed a few days to regroup and come up with a plan.

I got into Atlanta on Wednesday and picked up my rental car. My dad had halfheartedly asked if I wanted him to pick me up from the airport, but I knew he was busy with the team. They had a big game coming up on Saturday, Tech versus State—rival Georgia teams—and I was sure he wanted all the time possible with his staff and players.

I stopped by the market to pick up some flowers before driving to the cemetery. My mother was buried in a family plot in Savannah, where she grew up. I didn't get around to seeing her very much, but I always made time to visit Gram. She had a little spot under a tree next to First Baptist Church, along with her husband, my dad's dad. I sat down and placed the white daisies at her gravestone.

"Hey, Gram."

Birds chirping was the only response. The only one I ever got.

"Nice day out today." With the sun at its highest, I wore sunglasses and an old zip-up over my T-shirt. "I came home for Thanksgiving. It's tomorrow."

Raised in church like the good southern girl I was, I believed I'd meet my grandmother again, but until that time, I wasn't sure what she was doing or if she even knew what day it was. I liked to fill her in.

"I . . ." I swallowed. "I feel awful, Gram. I was doing good up there in Minnesota. I made friends and had a job I was good at. But I tried to hold on to it all too tight."

I looked around at the rows of headstones, the trees losing their leaves, the blue sky, as my heart filled with heaviness. My eyes watered, and I dabbed at my nose with my sleeve. "I wish you were here. That you'd talk to me. I don't know what to do. We argued a lot, but you always had something smart to say. I'm sure you'd have some good words of advice right now . . . and I could use some. I really need 'em."

Tears ran down my face, and I pushed my sunglasses up to wipe at them. "I'm lost, Gram."

A cool wind blew my hair in my face, and I tucked it behind my ear. Curling my knees up, I hugged them to my chest. "I met a boy, he's kind of a jerk. But sweet too. He's a stand-up guy, you'd like him. I think. Actually, I don't know." I laughed to myself, wiping the last of my tears away. "He reminds me a little bit of Daddy . . . maybe you would like him. He's handsome too. Tall, with blue eyes." I focused on the orange mums someone had left at a grave a few over. "It didn't work out between us though. I should've known it wouldn't. It never does. But I really loved him . . . still love him."

I wasn't sure if I believed in soul mates, but living with my father had convinced me that losing my mother was like losing half of his soul. And for the first time maybe ever, I had empathy for him. Because even with all the arguing, being with Connor felt like being home. I was myself. Comfortable and cozy.

I sat with my grandmother for a little while longer, listening to the soft sounds of nature, soaking up as much sun as possible before rubbing the headstone. "Thanks for listening."

I arrived home just as the sun set, lighting up the hardwood floor of the living room through the big bay window. I tossed myself on the brown couch that was probably as old as I was and kicked off my shoes. My dad's house was small compared to what some other college coaches' houses looked like, but after Mama died, he'd sold the big house with the garden and pool to move here, a craftsman home with a tire swing in the back. I'd heard him say once when I was little that he couldn't live with the memories of her haunting him.

Sometimes I wondered if I haunted him.

I'd grown up in this house with Gram and Daddy, his father having died a few years before. And as I gazed at an old photo of the three of us, I realized my father was alone too. We only had each other left.

For all the time I'd spent resenting his quiet reserve, his sometimes absentmindedness when it came to being a parent, I finally understood how much of a struggle it must have been. He'd been younger than me when Mama died, and just out of college when his daddy died. He had all of that before he was even really a man. And he'd had to figure it out on his own.

I made myself at home in this house that I hadn't lived

in for years, though nothing much had changed. The refrigerator was still filled with sweet tea and cold cuts. The light in the kitchen had been left on, a surefire trait of my dad's. I put my suitcase up in my old room, empty of anything except for a bed and one lone *NSYNC poster on the back of the door. After changing into sweats, I made a sandwich and turned on the television in the family room just a few minutes before Daddy walked in through the garage.

"You here, Charlotte?"

"In here," I called, waving a potato chip.

He dropped his bag with a clunk in the hall and came to sit down next to me. He flipped off his shoes and put his arm up on the back of the sofa. "How was the trip?"

"A little turbulent, but okay."

He nodded. "Got yourself somethin' to eat?"

I held my plate up.

"Good. What's this?" he asked, pointing to the TV.

"Hallmark movie."

"Since when do you watch this?"

"My friend Piper got me hooked."

We watched a fire start in the bakery, ruining the pies for the woman trying to win the annual pumpkin pie contest. But luckily the handsome hero was close enough to help her out.

"*You* like this stuff?"

"Yeah. It's nice to see happy endings. There's nothin' wrong with that."

Daddy rubbed his forehead and then met my eyes before giving in with a small nod. He patted my knee. "You're right."

I had filled my dad in about what had happened with the team, but skimmed over most of the other stuff. I hadn't told him everything about Connor or my life in Minneapolis.

But I thought it was about time we talked. Really talked. "Did I ever tell you about the offensive coordinator there?"

He tapped his foot. "Uh, yeah. I think."

"His name's Connor. He played for a D-Two school, he's a good coach." He nodded along as I said, "He didn't like me in the beginning, but then we started gettin' along. . . ."

Dad hmmed, his attention on a shampoo commercial. Seconds later he turned to me, comprehension lighting his brown eyes.

"You and this Connor guy are together?"

I shook my head. "He was offered head coach."

"Guess that's the end of that then." He sucked air in through his teeth.

I pulled my ponytail out and redid it. "I like him a lot though. I think I love him."

"You think?" He swiveled his head back and forth in thought. I couldn't remember the last time I'd talked about a boy with him, and I bet he couldn't either. "There is no thinkin' when it comes to love. You either do or you don't."

I dropped my head back. He got right to the point, like a coach, but the subject matter wasn't anything that I was accustomed to. "I love him."

"Did you tell him?"

"No."

"Why not?"

"Because I'm leavin'."

He hmmed, doing the head turning again. "And you want to leave because you aren't coachin' there, right?" When I nodded, he moved his arm to hold my hand. I don't think he'd done that since I was a little girl. "You know, I, uh, I don't think I did this dad thing real well."

I thought he'd done fine, especially after I'd done some soul-searching today. And I told him so.

He disagreed. "I never told you that you're so much more than a football player. I never knew how." He cleared his throat, casting his eyes away from me as if he couldn't look at me when he said, "I didn't talk about your mother enough, or how much I loved her." He rubbed at his chin. "Sometimes you remind me so much of her. She didn't like to be told no either." He wiped at his eyes as my own clouded with tears, and he cleared his throat. "I'm sorry for keepin' you away from the memory of her. It was hard for me to share it . . . her. You deserved better."

I accepted his hug and apology, and kept my head on my dad's shoulder even as he laughed to himself.

"I was late to the hospital when your mother had you because of practice. By the time I found out she was in labor, you were already halfway out. You weren't waitin' for anyone."

I'd never heard this story, and I smiled at how his voice filled with emotion.

"You were, still are, so headstrong. You did what you wanted to do. When you were a toddler, it was infuriating, but as an adult, it's admirable. You make a goal, and you go after it." He faced me, looking at me as if I were a little girl again. "I only ever wanted you to be happy."

"I know, Daddy. I was happy."

He tapped my chin. "I want you to be happy all the time. I know coaching makes you happy, but what else? I know you're more than a girl with dirt on her knees and a ball in her hands. I always knew that, but never told you. You're smart and courageous, and a damn good motivational speaker. If you wanted, you could write books or go around and give speeches. You can do anything you want to, and should. If you love Connor—and I'm sure you do, otherwise you wouldn't have told me—then you should be with him. Don't run away because of the team. Stay and do something else. Or stay and coach at another school. There is more than one way to skin a cat."

It seemed so simple when he put it like that.

"Do whatever you want to do, except run away. That's not for my brave, stubborn daughter. She doesn't run. She fights."

My heart sped up at his succinct description of me. I wasn't a coward, and I wouldn't let some misogynistic men chase me away. "I'm going to stay in Minneapolis."

"Good." He nodded.

"And I'm going to see what other positions are available."

"I love you, Charlie-Larlie. I'm so proud of you."

He hugged me, and I squeezed him tight around the neck. "I'm proud of you too, Daddy. Love you."

He kissed my cheek, then released me. "Glad you're home. Want to come to practice with me tomorrow? We got this freshman kicker I want you to look at."

"Okay. Dinner later tomorrow?"

"Absolutely. Got the turkey defrostin' now."

There would need to be more heart-to-hearts, but this was a good start. After the good conversation, I felt a weight off my shoulders. I still didn't know what exactly I was going to do, but I felt much better hearing my father tell me I had other options than football.

THE NEXT morning, I was greeted with big hugs and even bigger smiles at the college. Some of the older players ribbed me for leaving, but most told me how much they missed me. The other coaches were just as effusive with their praise, and for a few moments I questioned why I'd left. I'd made good money there, but I had no chance of moving up—and I was reminded of that when I met the new male coaches. They had less experience than I did, but had higher titles than me while I was there.

It was a slap in the face. I'd gotten used to the sting. Didn't mean I liked it though.

Mediocre men were celebrated. Highly skilled women were doubted.

That aside, I had a good time. The practice was always short on Thanksgiving, a small reprieve for the players on the holiday. It was nice to be back, but also kind of made me miss the Douglass team. I felt like I had a special bond with those kids, working our way up from the bottom together. Thinking about leaving them did make me sad.

After practice, Dad and I took the long way home, weaving through yellow trees outside the city. We talked more, this time about the Otters. I told him about Brett Spencer and his dad, and how he had certainly had a big hand in getting rid of me. Football parents were everywhere, but I'd never thought one would be my downfall.

At the house, we changed into our comfy turkey-eating clothes and got to work on dinner. I made the mashed potatoes and green beans while Dad got the fryer ready. It was tradition, one that I thought made our unconventional father-daughter relationship one step closer to normal, me watching him outside, drinking a beer and frying a turkey.

Just as I set the table, the doorbell rang. Dad was washing his hands. "Who's that?"

"I don't live here anymore. I don't know."

"I got oil all over my hands, can you grab it?"

I put the plates down on the table before going to the door, but couldn't see anything out of the peephole with the obnoxious wreath the house cleaner had hung.

I opened the door a few inches, and my eyebrows shot up in shock. "What the hell are *you* doing here?"

"Is that how you greet everyone at your door?" Connor held a straight face, but his question was laced with humor.

I shut the door on him, half in reflexive anger, half in utter disbelief that he was here.

He knocked on the door three times, and I got my bearings before I opened it again.

He tilted his head. "Is *that* how you greet everyone at your door?"

All kinds of emotions rushed through me as all my words left me. What a terrible time to be speechless.

He took his hat off and ran his hand over his head. "Can I come in?"

I mechanically opened the door wider for him, and he stepped inside my childhood home, suddenly seeming much smaller than it ever used to feel. I took a deep breath, inhaling his familiar scent, and looked into his eyes. In the time I'd spent purposely dodging him, I'd forgotten how much I enjoyed looking at him. His sharp features, soft blue eyes. The nonsmile smile. I hated his stupid face and couldn't believe that it'd taken me so long to figure out that I loved him.

"When I heard you went home, I decided I had to come after you." He grabbed my hand. "You can't move back here without hearing me out."

I pulled my fingers out of his grasp, his sudden appearance with wrong information catching me off guard. "Who told you I'm moving back here? I'm not."

"You're not? I just figured—"

"You figured wrong."

"Charlotte, who is it?"

For the first time since I'd answered the door, Connor's eyes lifted from mine to where I knew my father stood in the kitchen. I turned around as he wiped his hands on a dish towel.

"Daddy, this is Connor McGuire. Connor, this is my dad."

He pointed at Connor. "The OC?"

Connor held his hand out to my dad. "Nice to meet you, Mr. Gibb. Big fan."

My father looked him up and down, sizing him up as he would one of his players, then shook his hand. "Nice to meet you too." With one last look, he patted Connor on the arm. "I'll be outside. Let's eat before the food gets cold."

When he was out of earshot, Connor looked back to me. "He seems nice."

"He is."

His gaze bounced all over my face, to my hair, down to my feet, everywhere, as if checking to see that I was whole. I did the same to him.

"I can't believe you're here," I said after a while.

"You surprised?"

Of course I was surprised. The last time we'd spoken was more than a week ago. For all the times after our arguments I had wished he'd come after me and he didn't, I'd gotten mad. But this time I'd been glad he'd stayed away, because I'd needed time to work through the uncertainty and heartbreak. I'd been fixated on my career goals for so long that when they intertwined with my personal life, I couldn't see a way out. I'd needed time to be by myself and cry, think about what I wanted, and learn that I truly missed him. And I couldn't have been happier that he'd finally come after me.

He reached for me again, and this time I didn't pull away or deny his fingers lacing with mine.

"I got scared when I thought you'd packed up and moved back here." The fear in his voice was real.

"You did?"

"Yeah." His thumb caressed the back of my hand. "I didn't try hard enough before. But I need you to hear me out." His words came out in one big uncharacteristic rush. "I thought that I was supposed to fix things for you, but what I realized was I had to move out of the way. You don't need me or anyone else to fix things. You can do that yourself. You need to know I'll be there to help you, stand with you, be your backup or whatever, though."

"But . . . you took my job." I stepped away from him to sit in the living room, my head and my heart warring with each other. I'd been fired. He was part of the most humiliating moment in my life. How could I ignore that?

"Not on purpose," he said, hesitantly moving toward me. "I'm so sorry that I didn't have the guts to do anything that day. What they did and said and how they acted was terrible, and I cannot tell you how horrible I felt. They caught me off guard, and I know that's not an excuse, but I couldn't understand why they were doing it."

He knelt in front of me. "You deserve to be the head coach of the Otters. They know, the kids know it, you know, and I know it. If I could go back in time, I'd do it all differently."

I laughed sadly. "Me too."

"I won't take the job."

I eyed him. "Yes, you will. You have to."

He shook his head. "You're more important to me than a job."

I gave him a small smile. Better late than never. "And you came here on Thanksgiving to tell me that?"

He nodded, one of his hands finding its way to my neck. "I had to come tell you in person that whatever you want to do, I'm down. I want you to be my girlfriend again, and I'll do whatever it takes to make that happen. You want to move back here? Okay, the weather seems fine. I'll look for a job here. If you want to move somewhere else and coach, I'll move there too."

"Girlfriend? I was never your girlfriend."

"Like hell you weren't. It may not have been official, but you were my girlfriend in every way that mattered. Charlie, you're the only woman I've let into my life since Alison. You're the only one who's ever been worth it."

"Really?"

He laughed like it was a dumb question. "Yes. I love you."

"You love me?"

He rolled his eyes. "Yeah."

"Say it again."

"Such a pain in my ass all the time." With the big smile on his face, his words had no bite to them. "How could I not love you?"

"Feeling's mutual," I said as he moved onto the couch next to me.

"I want to be wherever you are," he said, and I felt completely weightless. We could've soared high into the sky, drifting into the universe, but if he was with me it wouldn't matter. Wherever we were, we'd be together.

"That's good," I said, wrapping my arms about his neck, "because I'll be going back home to Minneapolis. It may have taken me a while to figure it out, but I'm more than a football coach. They can't get rid of me that easily. I've got some ideas of other things I might want to do, but I'm not going to run away because it's hard. That's not who I am."

He smiled a true smile. I didn't think I'd ever earned that many smiles in the whole time I'd known him.

"No, it's not. You're a fighter."

I tucked my arm around him. "You like the way I fight."

"No. I love the way you fight. Say the words, Gibb."

"I love you, Connor," I whispered.

He closed the gap between us, stealing my breath with a kiss. It seemed like ages since we'd touched like this. A million more ages passed before we finally parted.

"I can't believe you're really here." Leading him through the kitchen, I grabbed another plate. I imagined his whole family gathering together today. "What did your mom say? What did Sean say?"

"I texted them. I said I was going to find you and that I'd call them later."

"*We* can call them later," I said, and waved to my dad through the window.

We all sat down at the dining room table to enjoy dinner. Dad and Connor got along great, pretty similar in their personalities. And I just about burst with happiness. We spent the evening watching football and topping off our already full bellies with pie. So as not to scandalize my father, Connor volunteered to sleep on the couch, even though I was pretty sure Dad wouldn't have cared. He spent all of Friday getting ready for the game on Saturday, leaving Connor and me to spend the day relaxing by ourselves. We FaceTimed Sean and even braved Target on Black Friday, risking life and limb. But I ended up getting Christmas gifts for Sonja and Piper, making the escapade worth it. I experienced life as Charlie and Connor, and I liked it. A lot. Much more fun than life as just Charlie.

Saturday we snagged seats on the forty-yard line for the Tech-State game, and for the first time I introduced him as my boyfriend to the acquaintances I ran into. The title felt good, and Connor smiled each and every time, noticeably proud to be labeled that way. Funny how we'd spent so long avoiding labels and going public with any kind of affection, when it all came easy now. Looking back, it seemed like a waste of time pretending we hadn't loved each other from the beginning.

But I wasn't much for Monday morning quarterbacking, so I focused on our future together, which immediately included making it to the airport on time for the flight back. I sped down the highway as my phone buzzed for the third time. "Can you get that?"

He dug in my bag for my phone. "What's your code?"

"One one one one."

He made his growly annoyed sound. "That's the first thing someone would try. You might as well not even have a code on here."

"It's easy to remember."

"You have trouble remembering four-digit codes?"

"Just put the number in!"

He did. "Jim's been calling. Do you want to listen to the voicemail he left?"

I nodded and flicked on the turn signal to exit the highway as Connor put the speaker on and Jim's voice filled the space between us.

"Charlie? Where are you? Why aren't you answering? I have some news. Call me as soon as you get this."

We looked at each other, the urgency in Jim's voice disturbing both of us. Connor redialed and kept the phone on speaker as we got closer to the airport. I watched for the signs to drop off the car.

Jim picked up. "Charlie, hey, finally."

"Hi, Jim, I have you on speakerphone. I'm on my way back to Minneapolis. Connor is with me."

"Connor?"

"Hey, Jim," Connor said, and a few moments passed before Jim made the connection.

"I should've known, huh? Well, that's good you're together, because this will affect both of you."

I turned left into the rental car parking lot. "What is it? You're making me nervous."

"Philander is on administrative leave until further notice and an investigation is completed. He's been caught fixing state test scores. He won't be returning to the world of education anytime soon."

I parked the car just as Connor and I both exclaimed four-letter words.

"I always knew there was something off about that guy," I said.

Connor nodded. "Should've caught on how he locked himself in his office all the time."

"What happens now?" I asked.

"Pending school board approval, I've been asked to be the new principal."

Connor pumped his fist up and down. "Good for you, Jim."

"And I want you, Charlie, to be the new AD."

"You want me to be the athletic director?"

Connor lightly punched my arm, grinning.

"Yes. I think you'd be perfect. You have great experience with sports, and I think as a woman you would be a tremendous influence on all of our student athletes and our boosters."

I'd never thought of being an athletic director, but not only did it make sense, it was perfect timing.

"I think it's a great idea," Connor said.

"The head coach of the Otters is still open to you, Connor," Jim noted.

I leaned in close to Connor. "I'd still be your boss."

"Your favorite position," he whispered with a sinful smirk.

"I'll still have a say in what goes on with the football team," I said, only a slight warning.

He raised a challenging eyebrow. "Wouldn't have it any other way."

"Whaddya say?" Jim asked, snapping me upright as if I'd been caught doing something wrong, and Connor muffled his laugh.

"I accept. Thanks, Jim."

"Wonderful. I know this is all really sudden, but I think this is all for the best. You'll do a great job."

"So will you."

"Thank you. And I'll see you two when you get back. We'll have some details to discuss, but I wanted to get to you right away."

We said good-bye and got out of the car. I ran around to Connor's side, jumping into his arms, wrapping my legs around him.

"Who'd have thought when you almost ran me over that day we'd be where we are now?"

He kissed a spot under my jaw. "It was your ass in those pants that made me stop. Saved your life."

I slid down his body and turned his hat to the side, getting a better look at his face. "What?"

"You had on the black legging things that come to your knees and hug your butt. I'd noticed you walking inside as I got in line at the drive-thru. I didn't think your careless ass would jump out in front of my truck—"

"I did not jump in front of your truck. You were speeding in a parking lot. That's, like, rule number one in driver's ed."

He quirked his mouth down in disagreement. "I'd think the number one rule in driver's ed is the right pedal is gas and left is brake."

I dug my fingernail into his chest. "Oh, so you do know the difference."

"Saved your life."

"Or almost took it."

He smirked. "Same difference."

I nudged him forward as he threw our bags over his shoulder and took my hand. I was stupidly happy—fighting with Connor was better than loving anyone else, and I looked forward to a lifetime of arguments with him. And bless his heart, I'd let him win—sometimes.

EPILOGUE

Charlie

Are you crying?"

I dabbed at the corners of my eyes. "No."

"You are."

"I'm not." I grabbed a tissue, avoiding Connor's elbow in my side as the national anthem began to play on the television. "It's my allergies."

"You don't have allergies."

I wiped the tears that flowed freely, then balled up the tissue and threw it at Connor. "One of my best friends just won a gold medal. I'm emotional, okay?"

He tossed his arm around my shoulders and tugged me into his side to kiss my temple. We sat on the brand-new recliner couch, the final purchase in our effort to redecorate his house. The moment we'd arrived at his doorstep last fall, he'd told me he'd painted his bedroom, the first step in letting go of his fears from his past. Since then, I'd helped in picking out colors, rugs, and furniture, building what would eventually become *our* house. The perfect place to watch one of my best friends reach her dream.

Sonja was on the other side of the world and fourteen hours ahead in Asia, so even though we had found out she'd won the medal in the flyweight, we hadn't gotten to actually see it until now.

And it was beautiful.

She was beautiful, standing tall even in her petite red, white, and blue warm-ups, holding flowers with that medal around her neck. She'd done it. She was an Olympic gold medalist, and I sat in awe watching her bright smile on the screen.

"It is amazing," Connor said, admiration in his voice.

"Makes me rethink all of my accomplishments."

He sniffed out a breath next to me. "You're kidding?"

I kept my eyes on the television screen as I shook my head.

"Charlie Gibb, first female high school football coach in Minneapolis, first female athletic director in the district, and first-rate pain in my ass doesn't think she has accomplishments?" He pushed me so I fell over to the other end of the couch, and I finally turned to look at him.

"I didn't say I didn't have accomplishments . . . but, ya know, how do you compete with an Olympic medal?"

"You don't." I scowled at his feigned indifference before he broke out into a stupid grin. "You say, 'I'm proud of my friend, and I'm proud of myself.' "

He stared at me, eyebrows raised, waiting.

I gave in, knowing he'd wait forever. "I'm proud of my friend, and I'm proud of myself."

"I'm proud of you too," he said, pulling me to him once again. I stretched across his lap, my legs over his, his arms around my middle. His lips found my neck when he spoke. "Boss lady."

It had been his nickname for me ever since I'd taken over the athletic director position nearly seven months ago. He thought it was cute; I thought it was condescending, but I'm sure that was part of the reason why he insisted on it.

The bastard.

I kissed him, his lips still tasting like the beer he'd finished a few minutes ago. "Do you ever feel like our friends are racing ahead of us?"

"What do you mean?"

I blinked over to the TV where Sonja waved at the crowd. "Piper and Blake are getting married next month, Sonja's off being amazing. . . ."

He narrowed his brows at me. "Life isn't a race, but if you're alluding to the fact that we've been together for eight months—"

"Technically, ten and a half, if you go from the first time we kissed," I corrected.

He let out a long-suffering sigh. "Technically . . . I want you to move in here with me, but you won't. That's your fault."

"My fault?" I snorted out a laugh. "How is it my fault?"

He lightly snapped the hair tie on my wrist. "Your no

ring, no sharing a bed rule. But you do get how backward that is, right?"

"No." I sat up, putting on my most innocent tone. "I'm the good Christian woman my grandma raised me to be."

He clapped his hands twice as he laughed. "When you called out for Jesus three times last night, that was just you praying?"

My cheeks heated and I smacked his arm. "You heathen."

"You love me."

"Not really."

"You ready to call on God again?" He stood up with me in his arms, and I wrapped my legs around his waist, laughing, but I froze when I caught the picture on the television.

"Holy shit."

"What?" Connor followed my eyeline and immediately lowered me to the floor. "Holy shit."

We both watched as the commentators talked to each other in the middle of the screen, with Sonja and Bear kissing in the corner. They were in the stands, as if she'd climbed up there after the medal ceremony. But I didn't know for sure because we had been arguing through it.

Of course.

I shouldered Connor. "Our friends are making out and you made me miss what happened."

He held his hand out to the screen. "We're watching it."

"I meant beforehand. We don't—" My phone buzzed on the coffee table, and I picked it up, reading Piper's text out loud: "'Did you just see that?'"

I typed back Yep.

HOLY SHIT.

I know.

I can't believe she didn't tell us. That happened yesterday her time.

"Finally," Connor said, and I glanced up at him in a silent question. He shrugged at me. "They've been in love with each other for forever. It was bound to happen."

I nodded. "I guess so."

Just as I began to type another message to Piper, Connor grabbed my phone out of my hand.

"Hey!"

He held it out of my grasp. "You can talk to her all day to-morrow. I want to go to bed. Maybe do some more praying."

I couldn't keep a straight face. "Is that your version of sweet talk?"

"You should know by now I'm not a big talker," he said, working on lifting up the bottom of my shirt. I didn't fight him and raised my arms, the flimsy old T-shirt slipping easily over my head. He kissed my throat and collarbone, and my legs wobbled as I melted under his hands. As always.

He caught me around the waist, holding me up as he leaned his head away from mine, his gaze raking slowly over me. Even in my cutoff sweats and used-to-be-white bra, I felt sexy. But after everything we'd gone through, I knew I'd always feel this way with him, no matter what.

I was wanted, desired, loved.

He kissed me sweetly on the lips before pulling me close. He wrapped his arms around my middle, forcing my arms around his neck, our hearts beating against one another, in time with each other.

With his mouth against my ear, he said, "Just so you know, I haven't ignored your not-so-subtle hints. I've just been enjoying seeing you turn yourself inside out to make it look like you aren't desperate to be my wife."

I backed away from him with a gasp, anger bursting through my fingertips as I squeezed his biceps. "I am *not* desperate."

But I dropped my eyes to the floor, my first and immediate response quickly leaving me, replaced by embarrassment. Truth be told, I was kind of desperate. He was it for me. I already practically lived here, waking up next to Connor and his open windows and spending our evenings arguing over the right way to fold the towels at least four nights every week. I didn't need a ring or a piece of paper; I only wanted to be with him in every way I could.

A wicked smile crawled across his face as he held his thumb and index finger together. "Just a little bit. But don't worry, I'll whisk you away one of these days and make an honest woman out of you."

"Oh yeah? And until this mysterious day comes?"

He tossed me over his shoulder like a sack of potatoes. "We pray."

I squealed out in laughter. "I hate you, McGuire."

He lightly smacked my butt. "Love, hate, it's all the same, Gibb."